---- ★ ----

Something whizzed past my ear. Johnny pushed me to the ground and I gasped out, "What the hell was that? A bee? In winter? Talk about your survivors!"

"Shhh. Abby, keep down. That was no bee. That was a bullet."

I'd never felt this kind of terror in my life. Of course I'd never had a bullet fly by my face either. I suddenly, and quite irrelevantly, recalled my conversation with Shay about casting bullets and auditions. "You never hear the one that gets you." Well, that was a good sign, then. I had *very* clearly heard that bullet zip by. Guess that meant I wouldn't die of gunshot wounds. Not yet.

I was also remembering my vision. Central Park. Snow. Gregory Noble. Bullets.

"Johnny? What's going on? Is it cops chasing a mugger or something?"

"No. They wouldn't shoot with innocent bystanders close by, and they don't normally take aim at muggers anyway. Abby. Stay down."

I did. I knew the idea of cops shooting at muggers was dumb. But I liked it better as a possible scenario to the reality that someone was intentionally shooting at Johnny and me.

---- ★ ----

SWEET DREAMS

FLO FITZPATRICK

W⊕RLDWIDE®

TORONTO • NEW YORK • LONDON
AMSTERDAM • PARIS • SYDNEY • HAMBURG
STOCKHOLM • ATHENS • TOKYO • MILAN
MADRID • WARSAW • BUDAPEST • AUCKLAND

Recycling programs
for this product may
not exist in your area.

SWEET DREAMS

A Worldwide Mystery/July 2010

First published by Hilliard & Harris

ISBN-13: 978-0-373-26717-0

Printed in U.S.A.

Thanks to Mom, for the late nights watching
Gene Kelly and Fred Astaire movies on the tube
while sharing a batch of freshly made fudge.
And to Pop, whose love of the law instilled
in me a strong sense of justice and fair play.

ONE

THE SHORT BLONDE was wearing a red G-string, red pasties, one red six-inch platform shoe and nothing else. A cigarette dangled from her right hand. Standing slap in the middle of the living room, she was eyeing herself less than critically in a full-length mirror, ignoring the nicotine ashes gently floating towards the hardwood floors. A radio blared at full volume in the corner of the room.

I half faced Shay, who was standing awestruck in the doorway beside me, then muttered *almost* inaudibly, "I'm going to kill you. Then I'm going back to the convent on 14th Street. Or perhaps to O'Malley's for a serious drinking spree."

Shay punched my arm, steered me into the living room, all the while waving at the girl to get her attention.

"Yo! Cherry! This is Abby Fouchet. Uh. Abby, this is Cherry Ripe."

A dyed head of hair turned from its narcissistic inspection. A sharp nose sniffed at me.

"Abby? You serious? What the hell kinda name is that? Sounds like a dog from the pound. Ya should dye your hair, ya know. Brown ain't in this year."

I realized I was clenching my fists and wondered if I could betray twenty-one years of indoctrinating Southern courtesy by punching out my new roommate. Shay poked me in my side and hissed, "Say something."

I spoke with (admittedly) icy politeness.

"Hi, uh, Cherry? First of all, my hair is closer to chestnut. Not brown. And it doesn't take kindly to chemicals. Secondly,

Abby's a family name. Goes back about three generations. I'm not changing it. But, tell me, how did *you* come by the name of Cherry Ripe?"

The minute the words came out of my mouth I knew they were wrong. I was right.

The brunette glared at me with blatant dislike. "Oooh, ain't we miss *chi-chi* classy? I *came* by this name 'cause I picked it for my profession."

"Which is?"

"Same's you guys. I'm a dancer."

I was overcome by a sudden coughing fit. Shay poked me again. My ribs were beginning to hurt and I felt bruises forming.

"Oh, that's…nice. Um. Are you in a show now?"

Cherry gave me a look that indicated she perceived my intelligence was on the order of the one platform shoe still on her foot.

"I work at The Squirrel Shot Gentlemen's Club on 8th Avenue."

"Oh, that's ni…Shay? Didn't we leave the taxi waiting downstairs? Let's go pay the man."

I grabbed Shay's arm and began to forcibly pull her into the hall. Whatever techno-pop dance hit that had been playing mercifully ended. Cherry grabbed the radio as if she feared I'd steal it, turned it off and walked in front of me before making an important announcement.

"I'm taking a bath now."

She leaned down over the edge of the sofa to pick up a second cigarette reclining in the Lenox saucer currently serving as an ashtray. Then she stalked into the bathroom still wearing her barely there costume.

I stared at Shay, waiting until I was sure Cherry was out of earshot. "She smokes in the bathroom."

Shay seemed to be intently focused on a spot on the ceiling. "Well, yes. But don't let it drive you crazy. Just make sure you look in the drain before you fill the tub. Look, let's get something to eat, then hit the locksmith's for your keys."

"Shay, I don't know if I can even stay one afternoon here. And I know I don't really want to be here when Miss Ripe emerges from the potty."

"It'll be okay. I promise. Cherry's never home. She's either working or staying at someone else's place, if you get my drift. And we really do need help with the rent. And your suitcases are already here. And you have no place else to go."

I stared at those suitcases. She was right.

I arrived in New York nearly three months ago after obtaining my Actor's Equity Card doing half of the summer season with Houston's *Theatre Under the Stars*. The last two shows had been *The Fantasticks* and *1776*. There are no chorus dancers in either, so I'd packed five suitcases full of dance clothes, dance shoes, headshots, résumés, T-shirts, jeans, jackets and boots. I'd put all my savings into a cashier's check, kept out about $400 in cash, found a one-way ticket to La Guardia at a decent price over the Internet, then waved goodbye to Minette and Paul, my tearful parents.

The first month hadn't been too bad. I'd been taking classes, finding my way around New York, and going to the Gene Kelly festival at a revival theatre in the East Village for entertainment. I'd wandered around the city getting my bearings and playing tourist at the free attractions. I'd visited the Statue of Liberty three times (low-cost for the ferry ride. I hadn't gone in. Too expensive to actually peer out of the lady's lamp.) I'd spent hours gazing at paintings in the Metropolitan Museum and dinosaur bones at the Museum of Natural History. I'd gone to three different Broadway shows, paying "rush" ticket prices and skipping dinner for the next week.

I'd done all these things by myself. I hadn't been able to take more than one dance class a day due to monetary constraints and couldn't go out to eat with anyone I met in class for the same reason. I'd chatted with a couple of other dancers for a few minutes at the two auditions I'd braved. Most of the girls both in class and auditions had ignored me (that competition thing).

Mother Minette didn't help matters. Daily phone calls kept my emotions somewhere between angry and homesick. But then, Minette hadn't wanted me to come to New York in the first place. She'd made her feelings plain since the day I'd told her I wanted to drop out of college and head to Manhattan, two years ago.

"Abby, this desire to go to New York is sheer nonsense. You haven't even finished college yet. If you don't like the University of Texas, transfer somewhere else for your last two years. New York is big and dirty and crime-ridden. You don't know a soul there. You'd be miserable."

"But, Minette…"

"I'm not finished. It's nearly impossible to have a career as a performer. You'll end up like millions of hopeful dancers from all over the country working at Macy's behind a cosmetics counter or typing for some insurance company."

"I doubt that, Minette. Since I type about twelve words per hour, I don't think I'd get hired."

"Abby. Don't be impertinent. That's not the point. If you don't have the backup of a degree you can't even teach. And you'll never find anyone suitable to marry."

"You've got to be kidding! I am nineteen years old. I'm not terribly concerned about being Mrs. Somebody-in-Politics right now. And where is it written that people in Manhattan don't find spouses and get married? I mean, really, how did the city get so crowded if those people aren't reproducing? It's not just all immigrants."

I'd gotten upset and consequently found myself not making a lot of sense. Paul, my dad, gently intervened, but still sided with Minette in an effort to keep the peace. We were both well aware of the fact that Minette was not pleasant when her ideas were opposed.

He smiled at me and spoke in a low volume as he tried to make a compromise that would be palatable to both daughter and mother.

"Abby. We just want you to be a bit more realistic. Wait until you graduate from college. Then we'll see how you feel. If you still want to go to New York, then that's fine."

I went back to University of Texas and graduated two years later. Minette was, if not happy, at least a bit mollified.

Once I was *in* New York, I had the stupid idea that my mother might let up a bit. I was wrong.

She called daily on the public phone at the women's residence to inform me that this or that studio in my hometown was desperately trying to hire dance teachers. Then she'd throw in little bits about lawyers, doctors, mayor's assistants and oil barons who were "just dying to meet you, Abby." I'd hang up and give the phone to the next person in line. Usually that was another dancer or actress or artist who was as miserable as I was at St. Katherine's Women's Residence.

Life changed when I auditioned for, and got cast in, an Off-Off-Broadway original musical mystery entitled *Numbers Up*. I loved being busy and I was getting to know my fellow cast members, but the hours I was in rehearsal were causing major conflicts with the hours of operation at St. Katherine's. Conflict, hell. It couldn't even be termed a police action. All-out war was a more accurate description.

St. Katherine's Women's Residence. Nuns everywhere checking the whereabouts of their female boarders. Nuns checking to see if the beds were made. Nuns allowing ten minutes on the public phone. Nuns establishing curfews a nine-year-old would scoff at.

I'd finish rehearsal, trot to the closest subway station, wait on the platform with the drunks for fifteen minutes, then run down the street to pound on the door of the residence and enter through the back doors less than twenty minutes after the darn curfew expired at 11:30 p.m. I fought constantly with Sister Agnes about letting me in after hours. I kept trying to explain that I wasn't engaged in anything immoral or illegal and that I needed the job to pay the rent so the nuns could keep the place open and continue to harass others in my position.

I met Shay Martin one afternoon at dance class. We'd both been less than enamored by a has-been movie star who was pushing around everyone in class (literally). We eventually found ourselves crammed into a corner near the dressing room.

"Bitch!"

Shay's husky voice spat out the word. She looked at my startled face. "Sorry. Not you. The movie queen there. She truly pisses me off. Comes in here about once a month and makes life miserable for everyone. She can't dance. She can't sing. She can't act."

I grinned. "A triple threat."

Shay grinned. "Did you just happen to see *Singing in the Rain* last week at the revival in the Village?"

"I did—ten times. I went through an entire bag of bagels and six cups of coffee. I only left the theatre for the bathroom, which admittedly became frequent after those six cups."

Shay extended her hand to me.

"Glad to meet another Gene Kelly fan. Shay Martin."

"Abby Fouchet."

"Where are you from, Abby Fouchet? I detect a hint of South."

"El Paso, Texas, ma'am. That's far *West* Texas. Just be glad it's not far *East* Texas. Those folks sound like they got oatmeal in their mouth twenty-four hours a day."

Shay had been diving into her bag but looked up at this last remark. "Speaking of oatmeal, I'm hungry. Wanna grab a bite after class?"

"I do, but I'm broke until Friday. I think I have about five dollars."

"Abby, my new friend, my naïve little Texas bumpkin. Have you not discovered the joys of the bar buffet? I see by your expression that you have not. What do they teach you in Texas? Never mind. It's quite simple. We trot over to O'Malley's Ale House. We order a glass of wine, or a beer. Cost? Minimal. We place our drinks down, and head for the sumptuous feast spread out on buffet tables in the middle of the bar. We stuff ourselves. With any luck, a few nice gentlemen seated at the bar will appreciate the foxiness of two dancers such as us, and send another drink or two to the table. *Voila!* A ten course dinner for the price of a glass of wine. That's wine, mind you. No hard liquor. Too expensive."

I was thoroughly entranced. I'd spent far too much time in the dance studio and not enough in the real world.

"Are you sure this is legal?"

Shay struggled to contain her laughter.

"God, you are an innocent. Yes. It's clearly written into the dancers' code of ethics under great ways to get a meal. The bar owners love it because they know the regulars could care less about eating. Those guys want babes in the bar. The regulars want to buy drinks for the babes in the bar. The babes want to eat. Just don't leave with any of these clowns. They're all married or on parole, and they're all nuts."

I had a good feeling about Shay, like I'd known her at least six lifetimes. We finished class, threw jeans over our leotards, and headed for the bar. Three hours and six drinks later—Shay was right about the gentlemen eagerly waiting to pay—we'd become friends forever. Shay was from Wisconsin, had dropped out of college primarily to spite her father (Chairman of the English Department at a large university) and headed for New York to try her luck as a dancer. At auditions she was told she was wonderful, but quite honestly, too heavy, so she was shifting her focus towards becoming a choreographer and perhaps a director. She was bright, funny and as passionate about dance as I was.

I told her about Mother Minette, the Southern Belle parent with an attitude, not being thrilled that I was trying to be a Broadway dancer (especially since Broadway was located in that land of iniquity called Manhattan). Mother Minette, who consequently called on a weekly, often daily, basis with new reasons for her darling daughter to chuck it all and come back home.

Shay shook her head and said it all in one word, "Parents."

For the next two weeks, Shay and I met each day at class. I finally had a friend who loved touring the city with me whenever she wasn't working and I wasn't rehearsing. But I was continuously griping about my living arrangements.

"Damn that woman!"

"What woman?"

"Sister Agnes and her curfew."

"Whoa! Sounds like a wonderful name for a rock band."

"Shay, you are not taking my trials and tribulations seriously. I've got to get out of there. She reminds me of Sister Errol Flynn from high school who used to bitch at me for wearing my skirts too short. I mean, what else can one do to spice up plaid uniform skirts with pleats?"

Shay put her hand up to stop me. "Back up there. Did you say Sister Errol Flynn?"

"We called her that because of her moustache. Looked just the way his did in *Robin Hood*. You know. The one with Olivia de Haviland as Maid Marian? Who was a wimp. I mean really, the woman had to rely on her damn nurse to get her out of every situation with Claude Rains and Basil Rathbone. Actually Sister Errol Flynn also looked a bit like Basil. But the moustache was all Flynn. Where was I? Ah, yes. I have had enough nuns to last me a lifetime. I need a life. I need an apartment. My hotel hunting has not gone well either."

Shay looked shocked. "What hotel hunting? You didn't tell me you were getting that desperate."

I waved my hand in front of her face. "Shay! Where have you been? Haven't you been listening to me? Focus, girl. Desperate is an understatement. I've been hitting every women's hotel in the city. At first it seemed like a good plan. I don't know, seems like I saw some old movie one time with all these classy women from Ohio and Vermont living happily at the Barbizon. But I'm telling you, those girls must have had a major career or a big inheritance before they ever moved in. Those places cost more in one week than my salary at *Numbers Up* for a month. And you wouldn't believe the assortment of perverts hanging out on the corner every night. I had to kick one down a flight of stairs to keep him from trying to kidnap me."

A wicked gleam appeared in Shay's eyes.

"Abby. Abby! This is so perfect. You need out of your present living space. I know this because that's all you've talked about for weeks. Ta-da! You, my friend, are now in luck. My crummy landlord has upped the rent again because he painted last month and called it a major renovation, and my current roommate has decided we need a third. You need to save money as much as we do, and we can keep the perverts away. Wanna move in?"

After much groveling and foot kissing, I instantly agreed. She took me by to see the place and I had to admit it was perfect for my needs.

Seven-D was a decent space by even Texas standards. The bay windows with built-in seats overlooked 79th Street, not an alley. There was a real kitchen; not the typical New York pull-down shelf. The subway was just down the corner, Central Park was about three blocks away and Riverside Drive was one block west. The bedroom was pretty small and Shay's antique furniture (courtesy her great-grandmother) filled it, but there was a day bed tucked into the corner and it seemed

more than capable of withstanding my 103 pounds and 5'2"
frame.

This third girl had not been there the day Shay had given
me the tour. I got my first glimpse of Miss Ripe as I stood in
the doorway of Seven-D with all five of my suitcases in hand
and no convent to return to.

I focused back onto what Shay was saying while I still
reeled from my introduction to Cherry Ripe.

"And, Abby, you know you're going to stay. Didn't Sister
d'Agostino say you were about to be bounced from the convent
for breaking the curfew?"

"That's Sister *Agnes,* not *d'Agostino,* you dimwit. She's
not a grocery store. What she is though is scary. The woman
looks like she was sent over from central casting to play Mrs.
Danvers in the St. Katherine's Residence version of *Rebecca.*
Or a thin Kathy Bates in *Misery.* And, yes, I am in trouble
for coming in on a frequent basis past the appointed hour.
I keep trying to explain that rehearsals for a way-the-hell-
Off-Broadway show don't even end 'til eleven, and that it's a
ridiculous curfew for anyone over the age of fourteen, but she
doesn't want to hear it. She thinks all you can be doing after
midnight is having sex somewhere. I should be so lucky. Ha!
In a word: Ha!"

Shay was pacing in circles.

"Abby, you can't go back to St. Kate's. One more week
with the nuns and you'll end up fighting the bag lady on the
corner of 79th Street for her space. We talked about this. You
love the apartment. You're already *here* in the apartment. The
cab is long since gone from the apartment."

She grinned wickedly at me. "Uh-huh. I see those wheels
turning. You *do* need us as much, if not more, than we need
you. And it's very safe here. Think about this. Men hit on you
even at women's hotels. You're tiny and you're cute. What
are you, five two on a good day? Perverts love tiny and cute.
You need protection. If you make friends with Cherry, she'll

volunteer Vito and Guido as your bodyguards. The Mariccino twins will love you."

"I don't even want to know. Vito and Guido?"

Cherry suddenly came tearing out of the bathroom

"What about 'em? Did they call? They still comin' to get me at five?"

Shay smiled sweetly at me then threw a robe at the now totally naked Miss Ripe.

"Sorry, no, they haven't yet. I was just telling Abby to take a message for you if they call and you're still in the tub."

"Oh, okay. I gotta take my bath now. I just came out for another cigarette."

She grabbed a pack off of the window seat, dropped the robe and headed back to the bathroom.

I looked at Shay.

"I've moved into an apartment with a topless naked bimbo. Watch. Cherry will probably set me up on dates with both Vito and Guido. I have no money. Minette, the champion worrier, will call here and Cherry or Vito will answer and she'll immediately call the NYPD to come and get me. And they'll do it for Minette, I swear. She hypnotizes people. I'm in deep trouble. I should go back to the nuns."

A vision of Sister Agnes in her black robes wagging a finger at me, telling me I was headed for the farthest reaches of Hades while I knocked with bleeding fingers on the convent doors at the ungodly hour of 11:31 (and twenty seconds) drifted in vivid Technicolor before my eyes.

I took my suitcases into the bedroom and began to unpack.

TWO

THE NACHOS AT O'Malley's Ale House weren't quite up to
Texas standards, but they'd do in a pinch, and I needed that
pinch. It had been a long week of classes and auditions. I felt
totally down about both.

"Damn."

"What?"

"Oh, nothing. I'm still upset over not getting in the chorus
of *Illumination*. Maybe Minette's right and I'll just never
make it. And since she's gifted, or cursed, with second sight,
which I also got, I'm afraid she'll be proven right."

"Second sight?"

"Don't ask. And I won't tell. I'll just sit here and be miserable
in my nightmare that stars me returning to Texas a dismal
failure."

"Oh, great attitude, Abby. Listen, do *not* let your dear
mother con you into believing that you're not good. Hey, even
Ricky, who admittedly teaches the hardest dance class in all
Manhattan, stopped you yesterday and told you he wanted you
to audition for his company. That says something. His dancers
are the best in town, bar none. So get over this whiny baby
routine and let's dive into a tall glass of something trashy.
Red wine by the glass. House vintage."

I started laughing. Shay was the ideal friend. She took no
prisoners, she was blunt and she'd be loyal to the very end.

A silver-haired gentleman in a three-piece pinstripe suit
waved from three tables over.

"Shay. Do I know him? Is he the one who bought us drinks last week after the three o'clock class?"

She squinted.

"Don't think so. I don't even remember him ever being here before. Looks like you've made a conquest. No, wait. He just got joined by that very young guy in the black leather and chains. Hmmm. I wonder if anyone's told them the gay bar is on the other side of the street."

I watched the interaction between silver hair and black leather with great interest. The cynical side of me was thinking that money can do a lot to keep a young stallion in the pasture, while the romantic side was applauding their courage in bucking the age barrier as well as the gender issue. Then again, this was Manhattan, not El Paso. My attention was suddenly drawn to another table directly behind the gay couple.

"Shay! Look at the table in back of theirs. See him?"

"Who? What? Which?"

"Him. The one who looks like an Irish bandit on his way to Communion services. Red hair, snub nose. He was in Ricky's class today. I was checking him out during layouts. Then I got too busy trying to avoid Miss B-Movie-Queen when she was slapping her multi-ringed fingers in my face pretending to do pirouettes during the combination. Otherwise I would've tried to talk to him. I'm in love, I tell you, in love."

Shay turned back around and stared at me like I'd pointed out an alien from planet Vulcan. "Abby, you dimwit. That's, oh hell, I can't remember his name. His real name, that is. On *Endless Time,* he's Gregory Noble."

"Huh? Gregory Noble? *Endless Time?*"

"Don't they have television in cowboy land? Where have you been?"

"I have been backstage. I have been onstage. I have been in class preparing for stage. I don't watch television except for reruns of *Dark Shadows* and *Forever Knight* and that's only because Minette adores Barnabas Collins and Nick Knight. You and Minette have that in common, you know? Fascination with celluloid vampires. Of course, I have often wondered if my genteel mother was once bitten. She roams our house like some Belle Vampire at all hours, searching for new ways to draw blood."

Shay stared at me.

"Sorry. I'm still upset at Minette's latest phone call exhorting me to marry Elmer Whitacker and produce small versions of Abby and El. Now, that said, who is this man I am destined to marry?"

"Elmer Whitacker? Who the hell is...? Never mind. I don't want to know. Anyway, your new best beloved happens to be the hottest soap star around. He joined the cast of *Endless Time* about a year ago and their ratings shot off the proverbial charts. All that Irish charm I guess. He's just finished doing a revival of *Carousel* because not only can he act he's also got a gorgeous baritone voice. I think he was also in *Les Miserables* a few years back. Anyway, I can't believe you didn't know this. And I can't believe I can't remember his real name. Come to think of it, I don't watch soaps either and he's only been in the beginner class until today and I've just heard everyone call him Gregory Noble. That's his character."

"Well, *I* can't believe my pulse rate has gone somewhere over two hundred. And I'm sweating. I never sweat. I can go through an entire jazz class in July with no air-conditioning and just feel a glow. It's October. One look at this man and I'm drenched. What is it with that semi-leprechaun look that just gets to me? Is that a word? Miss Dad-Who-Owns-English-Department-in-Wisconsin?"

Shay snorted.

"To sum up in one real word: 'No.' Honey, I'm telling you. Stay away from this man. He is poison."

"Poison? Sorry. He looks more like serious eye candy to me. And I'm hungry."

Shay remained silent. I sighed.

"Okay. I'll bite. Poison? Got it. Why?"

Shay let out a large breath and inhaled a new one.

"Every girl he meets falls instantly for him because he is a soap star. Consequently he is bound to have the world's biggest ego and not deign to talk to the peasants—i.e.—us. Add to that the word that he is on a major career fast track and has no time for the hordes of drooling rich bitches, much less the peasantry. That's us, remember. Add to that something about his dad, who's some bigwig at the D.A.'s office or something. And I think I heard somebody said Gregory Noble's real father has a rep for liking very young drooling rich bitches himself. Is that enough for you, Miss Innocent?"

I was trying to listen while watching him almost surreptitiously at the same time.

"Uh-oh. I think you can add something to the list."

"Yeah? What?"

"Her."

The lady who was now sliding a hand territorially across my adored's sweater and brushing off imaginary lint was clearly wealthy and clearly confident. She had that sophisticated elegance only attainable by women with money. Brunette hair that was so expertly coifed it screamed "expensive celebrity stylist!" cascaded over a mink coat. Her perfect make-up screamed "I spend my days at Elizabeth Arden!" and the necklace casually draped over a white cashmere sweater screamed "touch at great peril to your life, you worthless mugging swine!" Surprisingly, Gregory Noble did not seem thrilled with this screaming attention. He looked depressed.

I winked at Shay.

"Think I'd get in trouble for going over and dousing that fur with a glass of red wine and screaming 'Animal Rights Forever'?"

Shay spit out a mouthful of wine as she laughed.

"Oh, yeah, that'd do it. He'd undoubtedly notice you as the handcuffs were being slapped on and you were banned from ever entering O'Malley's again. I think I'd hold off on the activism right now."

I turned back to my glass, lifted it and took a large swig.

"Oh well. If she's his type then he wouldn't notice me even if I danced on the table top in one of our roommate's more exotic costumes."

Shay snorted. "He'd notice. He's a male, isn't he? You're a female? From my experience that means you're his type. The problem would come in the commitment stage. That's when drooling rich bitches win."

"Hmmm. Got any money stashed anywhere?"

Shay tossed a quarter on the table.

"That's it, kid. Although, of course, I think my *Swiss* account could match Miss White-Fur-Coat's any day. You?"

I batted my eyelashes and assumed an exaggerated drawl.

"Well, since ah'm from Texas, and ever'one knows we have all that oil money there, ah'm sure ah could find an ancestor with a raht tall well."

We lifted our glasses and clinked them together.

"In other words, neither of us drool with green. Therefore we must beat out the rich bitches with nothing but our charm, wit, talent and incredible beauty. Or learn to spit better than they can drool."

Shay nodded, then brightened.

"Ah, hell. Forget men and romance. We're going to be the hottest combo of choreographer and dancer this town has ever seen. Incidentally, that reminds me. I've got an interview for the doughnut commercial gig."

"I want to see you hired for that one just to see how you encapsulate the job on your résumé. Also, if you get to choreograph, you'll bring me in as a dancing cruller or something, won't you?"

Shay nodded. "Definitely"

We toasted.

"Abby. Look. Your Irish outlaw and the babe are leaving. Wanna say hi?"

"What? Are you nuts? Even if I got him to say hello, that woman looks like she could rip me to shreds with one elegantly manicured nail. Oh, my God, Shay. He's looking this way."

He was. Unfortunately, so was she. I could hear her strident tones all the way across the bar.

"Are you coming? Hey, are you listening?"

"What, Tracy?"

"The car is waiting. We're expected at your father's *now*. Quit flirting with little bar chippies and let's go."

He winked at us. Then he left. Just before he turned to go, he waved and called out,

"Bye, Miss Dancer."

Shay and I watched in awe as the pair left O'Malley's.

Shay lifted her brows.

"Bar chippies? Did she say bar chippies? What bad movies has she been watching? *Godfather 'Twenty'*?"

I ignored this statement, grabbed Shay's hand and dragged her over to the nearest window.

"Quick! Look over there."

She did.

"Holy Sweet Saint Sebastian! That's a white stretch limo your new buddy is folding his enticing bod into. New and nice. The car, that is."

She turned back to me. "Whatcha think? His or hers?"

"Hers. Take a look at the chauffeur. I can't see his face from here, but I'll bet he's a serious hunk. The big blonde with Aryan Nation stamped all over him. That is *not* a guy's chauffeur. Definitely hers."

Shay said rather cattily, "Think she's hired him for other than driving through Manhattan traffic?"

The smart remark I had prepared dissolved into mush as the room began to spin around me. I was having hot flashes and cold chills simultaneously.

I could see a locale far away from O'Malley's. Specifically on a street in lower Manhattan. A man was bouncing off the side of a car. A limo. I stood frozen, horrified.

"Abby! Abby! Yo! Snap out of it. Are you okay?"

I blinked. I focused on Shay's worried face and the tables around us, then on the street outside again.

"Shay. I just had like a psychic flash or something."

"What do you mean?"

"I told you. Second sight. Sort of. It's a genetic trait. From Minette's side. The Dumas women are all gifted with second sight. Comes down from her Granny Dumas many, many generations ago. ESP and hallucinations of the future. Well, that's the claim. This is actually the first big vision I've ever had. I wonder if red wine is a trigger?"

"No offense, but I don't care if your great-granny envisioned where the Confederate Army hid their gold or something and you have to drink a bottle of Merlot to find out. What just happened to you? You zoned, girl. Where to?"

I looked into her eyes and took a deep breath.

"I saw that white limo, or at least a white limo that looked the same. Which is sort of redundant since I guess a white limo is a white limo."

"Abby. Get on with it."

"Sorry. Shay, it was running down a man. I don't know who he was but in that vision I clearly saw a limo deliberately run him down. Looked like it was on a street way downtown. I could see the courthouse in the background."

"Oh, crap. That's not good."

"Well, that's putting it mildly. What should I do? Do you think I need to tell the police or something? Run after Gregory Noble and tell him he might be in danger?"

She shook her head.

"And say what? That Grandma Dumas has passed down this talent or curse or whatever and that you had a vision of a white limo committing vehicular homicide down on Centre Street? Oh yeah, the cops'd send out a citywide APB immediately for runaway white limos after hearing that. After decking you out in an equally white straitjacket and arranging for chauffeured transport to Bellevue. Rent-free for the next year. As for Mr. Noble, he'd just write you off as a demented fan and blackball you from ever getting to audition for the soap."

I tried to smile.

"I guess it'd be pretty hard to convince anyone of something this vague, wouldn't it?"

She nodded as we returned to our table and quickly downed what was left of our wine.

I mused, "Actually the police would probably tell me limos of all colors are constantly trying to run down men in front of the courthouse. Lawyers, you know. With disgruntled clients."

Shay mumbled as she munched through the last nacho on the plate. Her voice was garbled but I understood enough to set me shivering.

"Then again, maybe you really did have a vision of Gregory Noble getting hit by the Nazi chauffeur and the rich bimbo."

I shuddered. "That's what I'm afraid of."

THREE

"Wait! Shay! Keep it there!"

Shay turned, remote in hand.

"Why? It's the news, Abby. *Endless Time* is over. Credits and all."

"Then why am I hearing Gregory Noble's voice from all the way in the kitchen?"

We both stared at the TV. A good-looking man with salt-and-red-peppered hair was talking into the microphone stuck in front of his face.

"Damn. He's like an older clone of your buddy. Prosecuting attorney, right? Hey, who's the blonde fox next to him? Holy Barrister! Throw me in jail and send him in to negotiate a plea."

"Turn it up, will you? What are they talking about?"

Shay clicked the volume up about three notches. The older Gregory Noble look-alike was addressing a group of reporters.

"I'm afraid that's about all we can tell you at this time. I promise you, the district attorney's office is working closely with New York's finest to get to the bottom of this latest atrocity."

"What atrocity?"

I shushed Shay.

"Will you be quiet? Maybe we can actually find out."

A raven-haired beauty thrust her chest along with a microphone into the handsome face of the man Shay had labeled, "Fox."

"Mr. Jaffert? Gina Giardeli for 'New York News at Noon.' Is there any reason to suspect that this murder has any connection to last month's shooting death of Dominican immigrant Juan Hernandez? Or the two deaths last summer?"

The blonde attorney flashed a set of perfect white teeth at the reporter. Shay oozed off the sofa and moaned. Gina Giardeli appeared as if she felt the same. I poked Shay.

"Hush!"

The man she'd addressed as Mr. Jaffert was in the process of answering Ms. Giardeli's question.

"At this time we are unable to either confirm or deny any direct correlation to Mr. Hernandez' death."

The older attorney took over the press conference again.

"Or that of Benito Domingez or Miguel Santos. Be assured of this, Ms. Giardeli. And all of Manhattan. Our office will do everything in its power to get to the truth behind these killings. Thank you."

"Does this have anything to do with the deportation of the five men who worked for Nick Toblaroni?"

The hunk smiled and gave the last word.

"I believe we've stated all we can at this time. Thank you."

I started humming "Razzle Dazzle" from the show *Chicago,* then held up my hand for Shay's attention.

"Attorneys. Master Side-steppers everyone. Truly Shakespeare's inspiration for *Much Ado About Nothing.* And what exactly happened? Who is this poor man who was shot? Nothing really said about it, just lawyers yakking and playing political games." I stopped. "Hold it. They're about to change stories." I yelled at the TV. "Give us his name you ignorant bimbo! Gregory Noble's father, that is, not the eye candy!"

As if she'd heard me, Gina Giardeli faced directly into the camera.

"This is Gina Giardeli, live at Chelsea Piers, site of the most recent killing of a citizen of the Dominican Republic. We've been talking to Chase Jaffert and Assistant District…"

The phone rang. Shay immediately shut the TV off, jumped up and ran to answer.

I screamed. It had been at least two weeks without any Gregory Noble sightings. He hadn't been in class or spotted drinking at O'Malley's. I still didn't know his name because his daytime drama, *Endless Time,* was one of those frustrating shows that lists all the actors lumped together during the credits without matching them directly to their characters. And I was not going to act like a starstruck teenage groupie and buy a fan magazine to see if he might be featured in a story. The humiliation would be too great. Now I'd lost another chance to get even a last name and then attach it to one of those on the credits.

I lay on the sofa and stared up at the ceiling for the next ten minutes cursing life and my roommates.

Shay hung up the phone fuming that she wasn't a damn fax machine and why the hell was someone calling as if she were.

She finally noticed I wasn't answering.

"What?"

"I am depressed. I have no life. I will never get to dance anywhere. I will never know who Gregory Noble really is. Now, go away. But hand me a chocolate bar first."

Shay sat, lotus style, on the floor in front of me and frowned. "Abby. You need to get your tiny rear end in gear. You need to quit worrying about elusive anonymous actors and their shyster parents. You need to check this week's *Backstage* for the latest auditions. You need to get in a show! That's what you're here for, isn't it? Aha! By George and Gregory Noble, I think I've got it. I will restrict how often you can watch *Endless Time* until you audition for at least three shows."

I growled at her.

"I have not been watching *Endless Time.* Only the credits

for all the good that's done. And I've had it with auditions. The last three I went to were horrible. They stuck us in nasty studios that must have cost their producers a whole eight bucks for the day. I was pushed and mauled by snooty girls who looked at me like I'm dirt because I'm short and I have a Texas accent. They sit there and turn themselves into pretzels warming up, then can't dance a lick because they have no rhythm and no energy. All they can do is stretch. And look tall. But do *I* get cast? Hell no!"

I brightened up and smiled at Shay. "But all this worry about auditions has made me creative. Have I told you about my brilliant bullet theory?"

"Brilliant bullet theory. No, I don't believe you've conned me into listening to that one. Until now. What the hell are you talking about?"

I motioned for my roommate to take a seat. I'd been working on this idea for the last couple of days. I needed a willing ear to try it out on and Shay at least looked interested.

"Okay. You remember the old soldier's adage that goes 'You never hear the one that gets you'? Bullets, that is. Know what I'm talking about?"

Shay nodded.

"Well, I've been so disgusted with the auditions I've been going to that I have come up with a plausible theory to explain how fate takes a hand when we go after jobs and don't get them."

I paused for dramatic effect.

"I call this the Bullet Theory of Auditions."

Shay was intrigued. She'd just been turned down to choreograph that commercial for dancing doughnuts and was afraid that she'd never get a job. That one had gotten to me, too. I'd been ready to play a tapping, kicking, glazed cinnamon bun whenever she needed me.

Shay unwound her body from its lotus twist.

"So this 'sound of gun' bullet theory now somehow extends

to auditions. Would you care to tell me exactly what you mean by that? You can use the doughnut commercial if you need an example."

I stood.

"Your name wasn't on the bullet."

She stuck her tongue at me. She was getting frustrated.

"Excuse me?"

"Just listen. I swear it will all come together. Semi-logically. Oh yeah. It also applies to men as well as auditions."

Shay picked up her favorite embroidered pillow and held it in a way that suggested I'd be hit with it soon. Or smothered.

"Don't muddy the waters, Ms. Fouchet. Just stick to this theory as applicable to jobs. We have enough trouble with you getting all goo-goo eyed every time you see that actor. Or don't. Forget the male species for the time being and get on with this thesis."

"Okay. No men. By the way, I don't think they exactly qualify as a separate species."

Shay grinned.

"You obviously haven't met Cherry's latest sleep-over. But go on. Bullets. I reiterate. Theatrical casting *only*."

"Okay. Ready? Here it is: If the bullet has your name on it—it'll find you. If it doesn't—it won't."

Shay did throw the pillow then. It missed by a foot.

"And this is supposed to explain why the doughnut guys didn't hire me? You just lost me. Explain fully, please. Hey, Cherry! Bring me a diet soda from the fridge will you? Abby's getting philosophical and I'm getting thirsty."

Cherry popped in balancing three sodas, a pack of cigarettes and six of my latest batch of homemade chocolate chip cookies. I may not admire Cherry's taste in costumes, men, or careers, but anyone who can balance all that and not spill a drop has my utmost respect. Especially when I'm on the receiving end of the drink and a cookie.

Cherry and I have gradually declared a truce the last week or so. I wouldn't call us friends, but I wouldn't call us enemies either. She has the street smarts I'll never have, but would love to cultivate. She fears absolutely nothing. I have to admire that along with her waitressing skills. For her part, she has admitted I'm usually pretty easy to get along with and I make a fabulous pot of chili.

I smiled at her and took a bite that left chocolate stains on my teeth. Shay raised her voice a notch.

"Abby? Auditions? Fate? Bullets?"

"Oops, sorry. Stuffing my face. Okay. First, let's take this from the military standpoint since we're talking about bullets. During the American Revolution, George Washington spent half his time dodging British musket balls. When he wasn't sleeping somewhere around the colonies. Fine. Quit laughing."

Shay gulped her soda and gave me a suspicious look.

"What has George Washington got to do with why I'm not showing hordes of little doughnuts how to leap and twirl?"

I munched my cookie and mumbled, "Will you quit interrupting? Let me finish. Washington never got shot, right? Why? Because the bullets flying around never had George's name. Is this making sense? Now. Take this same theory and apply it to theatrical casting. Um. Here's an example."

I thought for a moment while I swallowed another bite.

"Okay. Let's imagine the performer's nightmare audition. You forgot your monologue. Your tap shoe bounced off the director's head! But, oh my, just look! Your name is etched on that particular casting bullet? Hello, Broadway."

Shay was getting excited.

"I'm catching on. Let me see if I can take it from the opposite side to be sure I've really understood the concept. Let's see. You have a great audition. You even nail the singing part by hitting high 'C' twice. You kicked higher than a Jets field goal kicker on a good day. Your name may be Ethel Merman, but if that bullet says Mary Martin, tomorrow Mary's crowing, and Ethel's back on line. Is that right?"

Cherry applauded.

"I got it! I got it! That's why every time we get raided, I don't get picked up. My name's not on one of them bullets. I gotta tell Vito and Guido about this. They'll just die."

Cherry headed off for the bathroom (her private telephone space) and Shay and I looked at each other. Shay sighed.

"She's amazing, you know? Understands things in a way no one else ever would or ever could. This is good, Abby. I think you're on to something that could put performers' analysts and shrinks out of business. No more miserable dancers drooping in to cry that they didn't get cast. Sort of like no-fault divorces, I guess. It's just fate."

She popped the top off another can of soda.

"So, genius. If you believe all this, and you have those wonderful genetic traits of second sight to guide you, why aren't you out there auditioning like mad? After all, the more auditions, the more bullets, right? The more bullets, the better chance of actually getting cast!"

I rolled my eyes.

"Okay, fine. I'll go out tomorrow and do the audition for the *Hair* revival that's supposed to make the original look tame. Just watch. This will be the bullet that hits. I'll have to do a nude scene and Mother Minette really *will* come up and drag me back to Texas in chains."

Shay threw a cookie at me. I caught it with one hand and immediately devoured it.

"Go to the audition, Abby." She added all too casually as I munched, "By the way, your friend Gregory Noble is supposed to be there."

That perked me up.

"How do you know that?"

"He was leaving Ricky's beginner class the other day. Remember when you were a tad late for the advanced? Anyway,

I heard him tell Ricky he hoped he'd get out in time from *Hair* auditions for some publicity shoot for *Endless Time*. Apparently, he's interested in playing Claude."

"Damn. The man never comes to class, which I realize is part of a daytime actor's schedule, but the one time he's finally skipping around doing blasted single pirouettes and I'm not there. Talk about bullets flying away from me."

I shivered and reached for something to steady me. Shay was quick to see my reaction.

"Abby? What?"

"I just had a quick vision of bullets zooming past my ear. I'm in Central Park and I'm with Gregory Noble. Or whatever his name is. And there's snow. Never mind. Probably have bullets on the brain."

She grinned at me.

"I would stay here with you and try to keep you from zoning into Granny Dumas' precognition land if I didn't have an interview with another producer about a jam commercial. Maybe I'll have a better chance of choreographing raspberry preserves than powdered doughnuts."

I grinned right back at her. "I wonder if they give freebies?"

I was glad Shay had left me with the image of dancing red jelly the next day when I got my courage up and headed down to the 44th St. Theatre hoping one of my bullets would be fired for *Hair*. And yes, I must also admit I was hoping to see Gregory Noble.

I'd come to the audition directly from the health club that morning. Shay had gotten me a job there teaching exercise a few weeks before. After I finished with my class, I helped out at the front desk, then changed into a nice burgundy corduroy blazer and pants to impress the clientele. When I left the club, I'd had to bundle into a parka, knit hat and gloves even though it was early November. It felt like February. I was freezing.

I sprinted from the club on 61st and Lexington to West 44th

for noon auditions. I was stunned. There was a line inside. There was a line outside. For three hours I hopped up and down in the icy street to avoid frostbite and cursed Shay for suggesting I go to this one. I did earn fifteen bucks though, retrieving quarters tossed by tourists thinking I was a street performer.

I finally got inside the theatre and didn't know whether to laugh, cry or take pictures. The auditionees were dressed up as though they were participating in the Village Halloween parade.

I saw dreadlocks, love beads and flowered headbands adorning unisex hippie wannabes stuffed into tie-dyed bell-bottoms and midriff tops. Afros hidden since the mid-60's graced every ethnicity. Granny gowns, granny glasses, possibly granny herself, had been raided from Salvation Army bins. A whiff of *Eau de Mary Jane* lingered in the air.

I started talking to myself just to calm down. "I'm hallucinating. And it's not a vision thing. Must be the cold."

Ignoring the masquerade around me, I vocally warmed-up. Then I waited for another two hours. Two hours that were filled with listening to ghastly screeches emanating from the theatre house. Finally, at 5:35 p.m., one of the audition monitors, who appeared to be impersonating Jimi Hendrix, called my name. Apparently the staff had to look like 60's rockers to work here.

I walked into the theatre, up on to the stage, and gave Fleetwood Mac's "Gold Dust Woman" (audition notice had stated: *old rock song required*) to the accompanist. He resembled Paul, my dad. I felt a little more reassured.

I took a breath and prepared to start my song.

A very nasty voice sliced through me.

"Sorry, honey. You don't need to sing. You can leave now."

"I beg your pardon?" I asked. "Is there a problem? Are y'all taking a break?"

"Nope, you're just not right for *Hair*. You're far too sweet looking."

I glanced into the front row where a kid not much older than I sat gnawing away at a hamburger and fries while tossing headshots into a trash bag next to him. I'd just spent hours freezing for this chance to sing. I was ticked. It takes a lot to get me mad but when I do, I lose it like a drunken banshee going cold turkey.

"Have you ever heard of make-up?" I raged. "Or, God forbid—acting? I've been outside waiting in the stinking cold to sing sixteen bars—and I'm gonna *sing* sixteen bars! And you can shove my résumé and headshot up—well—into that disgustingly greasy hamburger if you don't damn well agree."

Shaking, I nodded to the accompanist before anyone could stop me. The stage manager (who looked like Twiggy sans make-up) started grinning. The accompanist started grinning. I finished sixteen bars. He kept on playing. I kept on singing. Twiggy kept on grinning.

I sang the entire song and stormed back into the lobby.

I heard footsteps. Twiggy the stage manager grabbed me.

"Hey," she gasped, "I had to tell you, you're the only person I've heard today who could actually sing. It's a horror show."

"I can see that. What on earth is going on?"

She looked embarrassed.

"The twitty, underage casting director's enthralled by costumes, not talent. But the accompanist and I just wanted to say 'thanks' for having guts and a great voice. You were wonderful."

"Bless you. That helps."

I might have known the day wouldn't end there. The next person I ran into was Gregory Noble. Well, *ran* might be a bit of an overstatement. I'd seen him walking into the theatre wearing jeans and a *Carousel* show jacket. I almost called out to him to forget it, he looked too normal, but decided to let the great soap star find out for himself. He was right up there in my bullet theory. Apparently, my name wasn't etched on his gun either.

I stopped by my favorite pastry shop, La Mirage, on my way home, bought a dozen chocolate éclairs and ate three of them before Shay got back to the apartment. When she got home she grabbed one and asked what had happened.

I told her everything, including the appearance of a snooty Gregory Noble. When I got to this part of my story, Shay started laughing.

"You were just miffed because he didn't notice you."

I glared at her.

"I wasn't concerned with him, thank you. My sole focus was on that audition and the fact that I was beyond furious at how horrible it was."

"Yeah. Right."

We smiled at each other. She knows me too well.

"As you see, I did not fare well today."

"Sounds to me as if no one did. Including me. I did not get the jam commercial. Guess the bullets were flying elsewhere."

She smirked. "I'll wager, though, that the revival will be in need of serious medical attention if they aren't casting good voices."

(She was right. Four months later *Hair* opened. It closed the next night. Critics said the singing and acting were atrocious.)

Shay took another éclair. So did I.

"So, Abby, did you see the notice for the *Jesus Christ Superstar* revival? Of course, with your track record on revivals this may not be something you'd care to know about. But it is headed for Broadway after a brief tour. And I've heard 'Mr. Noble' might be *already* cast in it."

I ignored the last part of her statement. Actually meeting that man was hopeless. Having a relationship if I ever did meet him was doubtless impossible.

"Yes, I saw it. I even circled the listing in *Backstage*. Whatcha think? Should I do this one? Test those bullets again after today's fiasco?"

Shay handed me my copy of *Backstage* so I could take another look. She grinned at me.

"Hey, other than the fact that Minette will probably shoot you for being in something more modern than *The Sound of Music,* I think you should go. At least there is no nudity in *Superstar.* Really, Abby, what have you got to lose? If nothing else, you'll get seen by some top people. Dewitt Dwyer is doing the choreography. I've heard he's a nutcase, but if you can live through a show of his, you're on your way."

"I've heard the same thing. Shay. Look at the notice. Is this on the up and up? I mean they're having it at that awful space on 43rd between 9th and 10th."

Shay nodded.

"I heard it was a last-minute mix-up with the Cort Theatre. The rehearsal hall on 43rd was the only thing open."

I grinned at her.

"Watch. They'll add a live sex dance using the temple whores and Minette really will come up and drag me back to Texas in chains. Or send me back to Sister Agnes for reprogramming. I'm not sure which would be worse."

I TRUDGED DOWN TO the rehearsal studios on 43rd and 9th Ave at the appointed day and time. It really was a nasty place. I was just putting on my character shoes to dance when they called me in to sing. I wasn't quite ready, but one doesn't mention that fact to a casting director.

I'd chosen "I Don't Know How to Love Him" which I'd hastily memorized the previous night in case I got my nerve up to attend this audition. A song from the show had been requested for the audition and there are only two that are women's numbers. I considered doing one of Judas's songs since they're in my range, but decided the director might not appreciate a female bass interpretation of "Damned for All Time."

I gave my picture and résumé to a smiling young man with a ponytail, crossed over to the piano, stood as tall as I could and overemoted, feeling more and more like an untalented dolt.

They called me back to dance.

Dewitt Dwyer, the choreographer, taught a routine from Hell. That's the only word for it. I'd heard he was a bit bizarre, and he was quickly living up to his reputation. Fifty dancers frantically tried to repeat his steps. Fifty dancers hadn't a clue. That included me. Two hours later, the audition was over.

I went home, cried, and ate doughnuts the rest of the afternoon.

Three days later the phone rang.

"Abby Fouchet?"

"Yes?"

"Tommy Greffazi here. Stage manager for *Superstar.* Are you still available to be in the production? Lead dancer/tormentor. Rehearsals start in two weeks. We'll be in touch with the schedule and place."

After thanking him more than profusely, I got my courage up and went for the one other thing I wanted to know,

"Tommy? I know this is a horrible thing and probably illegal to ask, but do you know if the guy who plays Greg Noble on *Endless Time* got cast? Uh. He's in my dance class and I wondered."

"Sure. He's playing Pilate."

I stared at the receiver for a good minute until the operator's voice informed me to hang up. I carefully replaced the phone and walked over to where Shay was sitting. Then I began jumping up and down in sheer glee as Shay grabbed the breakables from the coffee table.

"Shay! Shay! I got in! I'm in *Jesus Christ Superstar!* Headed for Broadway, babe. And guess who's playing Pilate?"

"You don't mean?"

"I do."

Shay had been watching a vampire movie on TV when Tommy Greffazi called. She immediately switched it off and hugged me as we twirled around the room together.

"This calls for a celebration! Where do you want to go?"

"Anywhere but O'Malley's! I'll be rich soon. Let's be wild and crazy and go to the Russian Tea Room."

Shay had her coat on almost before I had decided on the famous New York restaurant. We left a message for Cherry to meet us there if she could get off work, then we got ready to enjoy a victory dinner.

Shay was searching for her bag. She found it behind the sofa, lifted it and then started to laugh.

"Hey, Abby?"

"Yeah?"

"You realize you just got shot with one red-hot bullet?"

I felt queasy. I had a feeling that statement would become reality in a very few weeks. I focused hard to remember the vision I'd had earlier about being in Central Park in the snow as bullets whizzed past me. I could clearly see a man who looked very much like Gregory Noble throwing me to the ground.

Perhaps I needed to stay inside for the next few months until the snow thawed. Or 'til summer.

FOUR

It was the fourth day of rehearsals for the revival production of *Jesus Christ Superstar* and the first day the entire cast was present. We'd had three days of dance rehearsals only. The choreographer was as much of a tyrant as I'd been told. He hadn't even taken the time for introductions to the rest of the cast. Dewitt called the leads by their character names. The dancers were still, "Hey, you." Except for the dance captain, an Amazon Austrian blonde we all called Helga. Her real name was Marietta Marguerite Matilda Mannheim. Hence, Helga. Helga had a confusing lisp, which meant we were translating instructions more often than not.

We rehearsed in a space that should rightfully have been condemned twenty-five years ago. I kept worrying that the floor would collapse and we'd end up in the diner three floors below. Or that someone would forget to completely stomp out their cigarette and we'd be visited by the brave men and women of the New York City Fire Department; ladders and hoses and axes, oh my. I only hoped that the producers were planning to use all the money they were saving by upping cast salaries.

We were smack in the middle of doing "Everything's All Right." Mary Magdalene was singing away. Jesus was getting his temples massaged (the ones by his ears; not the synagogues), the disciples were singing and dancing and writhing and throwing palms and flowers at everybody onstage.

Helga was yelling, "Writhe, writhe!" Dewitt was yelling, "Rise, Rise!" Most of the cast was going with Helga since the scene seemed to call for writhing. I wasn't doing either. I was waiting for my music cue to enter and toss a few flowers while doing *grande jetés* across the entire length of what would be the stage. Consequently I leaned up against the strongest wall and stretched my leg up by my neck. I'd just brought the left one down when Dewitt Dwyer motioned to me.

"Hey, you. Start from stage left, then run directly over to stage right and leap into the arms of Judas."

I'd been cast as lead dancer/tormentor. What that had to do with jumping at Judas was beyond my comprehension. Maybe that was part of the torment. At any rate, the role of Judas is *not* that of a dancer's. Judas is not *supposed* to be a dancer—he is a screaming rock tenor. This particular Judas was a screaming rock tenor with no depth perception.

He did catch me. Yes indeedy. Then he ran slap into the wall, turned, and threw me at the rehearsal accompanist, who screamed in terror and promptly dropped me. I can't really blame him. I'm sure I'd have the same reaction if a flying object in three-inch-tall character shoes came hurtling at me across a piano.

I landed in a heap and began screaming louder and higher than Judas himself. And my guardian angel took pity. Pilate noticed me. After all how could he help it? I was writhing in pain on the floor and the apostles were still writhing around Mary. The pianist was writhing at the piano, and Judas was just writhing. Pilate was the only non-writher around.

The next thing I knew strong arms were cradling me and a gentle hand was brushing my hair away from my eyes and smoothing my forehead. A warm jacket advertising *Carousel* in red letters on the back was wrapped around me. I could hear an angry baritone yelling at the entire cast.

"Coffee! Somebody get coffee. She's going into shock. Give me the damn coffee and get out of my way. I'm taking her to the doctor. Now!"

I was lifted into those strong arms. The last thing I heard

was that voice yelling at Dewitt Dwyer that *he* should have been the one to take a flying leap. Although I believe the final word was not "leap."

I blanked out, then woke up at the podiatrist's office just in time to hear Pilate yelling at the nurse that this was an emergency. Someone in white was spraying my foot with something cold, wrapping a bandage tightly around my ankle, pouring Percodan tablets down my throat. Then I was listening to instructions I knew I'd never remember.

I was back in the cab with Pilate. I looked up into deep green eyes. Irish eyes. I started to sing the famous song about those eyes smiling. He smiled at me.

"How are you feeling?"

I tried to smile back.

"Been better. I'll be honest, it hurts. A lot. Actually, in a word—*oooowww!*"

He was quiet for a second. Then he lightly touched my arm.

"I know. I heard the snap of the ligament all the way across the room. But listen, I talked to Dr. Murray while you were sort of out of it. He said in about a month you should be up and dancing again. It's not broken and he said you have great tendons." He laughed. "I immediately agreed with him. They're very attractive."

I blushed.

"Thank you so much for taking care of me."

"My pleasure."

"This is probably a stupid time to ask this, but what's your name? Your real one?"

He grinned.

"Johnny. Johnny Gerard."

"Aha. Irish! I knew it. And I have no idea why I said that. I've seen you in dance class at Ricky's and at O'Malley's last month, you know. In a white limo driven by a guy straight out of a Wagnerian opera. That ran over somebody. But all this time I didn't know your name. Just Gregory Noble. Or Kieran Attorney's son. Or Pilate. It's a nice name. Johnny, that is. I'm not making sense am I? I think the Percodan may be hitting."

"Well, you're a bit, shall we say, scattered, in your thoughts, but I understand every word." He lowered his voice to seduction level. "I remember you from class, too. You're really good. And you were gorgeous to watch at rehearsals up until that idiot Dewitt forced you to go charging across stage at Judas. I'd love to dance like that. Ricky just tolerates me. At least I haven't had to do any serious dancing in any shows."

He winked. "I think I got hired in *Carousel* more for my skills at baseball than singing anyway. I took the team to finals when I was in the show."

"I doubt it. Wait. That isn't right. Let me try and clarify that. What I mean is I don't doubt that you didn't take them to the finals, but I think that's not the reason you were cast. I've heard you sing. You're wonderful. Actually, this is rude, but why are you even on an inane soap opera when you should be just doing Broadway and making CD's?"

He laughed. "Money. *Endless Time* has taken care of my entire student loan from college and allows me to live in something other than a studio with five other guys. But I admit I'm hoping the singing career will take off a bit more."

"Didn't big lawyer Kieran Gerard help?"

My hurt foot had just made its way into my mouth.

Johnny frowned.

"The soap magazines like to play up the fact that Gregory Noble is the son of the Kieran Gerard who has just announced he's running for District Attorney of Manhattan County in the special election coming up. But let's just say Mr. Prosecutor and I are working on our father-son skills."

"I'm sorry. That was tacky of me to ask."

He shook his head.

"No. It's fine. I'll tell you about Kieran some time when you're not about to pass out from pain and painkillers."

The cab screeched to a quick stop in front of my building. Johnny helped me out and carried me up the large stoop in the front. He steadied me as I tried hobbling through the lobby on the unfamiliar crutches, then he signaled the elevator, pushing the button for the seventh floor. Just before the doors closed he leaned over and lightly kissed the tip of my nose. He propped me against the back of the elevator, then turned to go.

"Can you make it from here?"

I nodded.

"I have to get back to rehearsal, but I'll come by tomorrow and see how you're doing. Okay?"

I smiled happily.

"Okay."

"Bye, Miss Dancer."

The elevators closed behind me as Johnny waved.

I limped down the hall to my apartment, then tipped my keys out of my dance bag onto the floor as I tried, and failed, to balance on the crutches. I finally gave up and started banging on the door with one crutch until Shay opened it.

She took one look at me and ruefully shook her head.

"Jumping turnstiles again, were we? Abby. Abby. My miserly little buddy. I told you if you didn't stop cheating the New York subway system, you'd come to a bad end. Just pay the extra nickel and be done with it."

I poked her gently in the stomach with one of the crutches.

"I'll have you know I was engaged in perfectly legal pursuits. Stupid, perhaps, but legal. If you'll pick up my keys, and help me to any spot that's not covered with Cherry's crap and pour me a large glass of Tanqueray, I'll give you the gruesome details. Oh yeah, where's the rest of the Halloween candy?"

Shay dumped a pile of clothes, records and cigarette cartons onto the floor, then helped me stagger to the sofa. She fixed a reasonably tall glass of Tanqueray and tonic and delivered it into my hands along with a small sack of leftover orange-wrapped chocolate miniatures. I managed a weak grin as I fell back against Ringo, my three-foot tall stuffed giraffe.

Shay inspected the wrappings binding my left foot and ankle.

"Can I sign it?"

"No, you moron. It's not a cast, it's a bandage, and if you get anywhere near my foot I will be forced to strike you with Ringo and he will not be pleased."

Shay plopped next to me.

"So, what happened?"

"I'm going to sue that twit choreographer, Dewitt Dwyer. Dewitt the twit. I don't want money, you understand. I want his solemn oath that he will leave New York and find the next cruise to Antarctica or something. Perhaps go shuck corn in Iowa. Illinois. Idaho. One of those "I" places. Anywhere far away from Manhattan."

Shay looked slightly concerned.

"Do I sense hostility here? Do I sense impending murder? This sounds good. So does Idaho since I understand that's where all the great-looking cowboys hang out, but I guess that's not the topic, is it?"

I glared at her.

She smiled back. "Oops. So sorry for interrupting. Please. Do continue."

I did. Shay looked impressed with my story and only interjected one comment. "Sounds like a nice dodge by the pianist. He'd make a great first baseman."

I ignored her and went on.

"Did I tell you? Johnny wasn't originally going to be able to be in the cast because of his soap, but the director kept holding out for him and wouldn't cast anybody else, and after much negotiating through his agent he's able to do *Superstar*, because they're going to have him laid up in a coma on *Endless Time* after skydiving and getting his parachute tangled up and…"

Shay screamed. "Stop! I can't take it. Just tell me what's going to happen with rehearsals now that you're lame."

The thought struck me for the first time that I was now probably out of the show.

"I'm not sure. I'm supposed to be able to dance in a month. I doubt they'll be able to hold my place. I'm a quick study, but they don't know that."

Shay shook her head.

"I knew they should've hired me to choreograph. I would never throw my dancers at the tenors; any idiot knows that's just not done in polite society."

I held out my glass.

"Hey, can I have some more? Please?"

"No, Oliver. You've had enough. If you die from a gin and Percodan mix, you'll have to explain to St. Peter that you're at heaven's gate because Judas dropped you, Pilate tried to save you and your stupid Episcopalian roommate watched while you overdosed on drugs and gin. I don't think it makes for a good first impression, and you've probably been blackballed by Sisters Errol Flynn and d'Agostino anyway. Damn. I can't believe this. My roommate literally picked up by the great Gregory Noble. Excuse me. Johnny Gerard. So, what about him?"

I smiled with kindness on my lesser mortal roommie.

"He had to go back to rehearsal, but said he'd be over tomorrow to check on me. Shay, he was just so wonderful about everything. He stayed with me the whole time at the doctor's, brought me back home in a cab and walked me to the elevator."

Shay had a pillow in her hand. There was a gleam in her eye that worried me. I ignored it.

"Where was I? Oh yeah, he only had to leave when he

realized he'd just walked out on rehearsal for the last two hours. Did I just say that? Am I being redundant?"

I was feeling loopy. I kept sipping my drink.

"Hey, what's that ringing sound? Are we being raided?"

Shay glared at me in disgust.

"It's the telephone, you soused out useless excuse for a dancer."

"Oh. Well, get it, would you? I don't think I can move."

She *did* throw the pillow at me then as she rose to grab the insistent sounding phone.

"Hello? Oh… Yes… Actually, she is home, but I'm not sure she's up to talking right now."

I waved frantically, then hissed, "It's Minette. Tell her I died. Or got deported or something."

Shay shook her head at me, then hissed, "She knows you're alive and still in Manhattan."

She turned back to the phone.

"Yes, Minette. Let me see if she's available. Hold on one second."

I glared at Shay. I did not want to talk to my mother while still feeling the effects of the painkiller, the Tanqueray, and the high of being in Johnny Gerard's arms for the time it took to be carried to and from a taxi. Shay smiled sweetly, then handed me the phone with the long cord attached. At least I didn't have to hobble over to talk.

"Hi, Minette."

I made myself sound as alert and upbeat as I could.

Her voice dripped with concern.

"Abby. What's wrong? Why are you home in the middle of the afternoon?"

I figured I'd circumvent her.

"Why are you calling in the middle of the afternoon if I'm not supposed to be here?"

Shay started laughing. I frowned at her. A snort came from two thousand miles away.

"Abby. You're being silly. I had a feeling something was wrong, so I decided to take a chance and give you a call. Now talk to me."

That damn second sight passed down from Great-Granny Abigail Dumas who was noted for her tea-leaf reading abilities back in Georgia, as well as her love potions and visions of the fall of the Confederacy. Great-Granny Dumas passed these abilities on to Grandma Giselle, then to Minette, and finally on to me. Minette claims she lost some of those when she moved to El Paso because "the dust makes envisioning too prosaic" (her words), but she still retains enough to be spooky.

I had to tell her the truth. The abbreviated version.

"I hurt my ankle at rehearsal and went to the doctor and now I'm home."

Shay burst out laughing.

I covered the receiver with my hand and barked: "What?"

"I think you're leaving out the good details, Sweetie!"

"I'm not telling her about Johnny. There are some things she'll just have to guess at. If she knew I had the hots for an actor she'd be on the first plane here with a dog crate to nail me into for the flight to El Paso so I couldn't escape en route."

I was back on the phone.

"Yes? No, Minette. I do not need to fly down to Texas tonight. There are wonderful doctors right here in Manhattan, believe it or not. Yes, I will call if I can't walk. Yes, Minette, I will call if I *can* walk. Thanks. Yes. Miss you, too. Love to Dad. Bye."

I hung up and sighed.

"Where were we? Oh yeah, I was begging for more Percodan or something. Hey, did I sound remotely sober talking to her?"

Shay grinned evilly.

"Oh, yeah, right. About like Ben the wino at the corner of 78th and Broadway after a run-in with Thunderbird and Strawberry Ripple. Abby. Go to sleep. You're not rowing with all of your oars. You're not drumming with all your sticks. You're not tapping with all taps. You're not bowing with all strings. Um you're not…"

"Okay! I got it. I got it."

I curled up with Ringo, the blue stuffed giraffe, and felt like I really could fade out, when I suddenly realized that Shay was not in her stay-at-home sweats. I gaped at her.

"Why are you in a dress? A real dress. Wedding or funeral? If it's a funeral, I hope it's Dewitt's."

Shay casually got up and headed towards the cart with the Tanqueray bottle on it.

"Wedding."

"Whose?"

"Mine."

"That's nice. Who? Wait a minute. Who? Did you just say you're *getting married?*"

"I did. Well, not yet. Today we're getting the license."

Suddenly, I felt quite sober. This was not a normal occurrence around the apartment. (Marriage, not sobriety.) Our third roommate, Cherry, had had more husbands in her twenty-one years than I'd had dates in mine, and she had a tendency to bring in every low-life scum she could find, but Shay hadn't had a date in two months at least. Marriage?

"I didn't even know you were seeing someone. Just who are you marrying."

"Whom."

"Oh, crap, don't start with the Abbott and Costello grammar routine. Who is this guy?"

"Fuji."

I racked my brain. "Fuji who?"

"You know Fuji who."

"I don't. Do I?"

"Yes, you do. Fuji, from the desk at the health club where you and I teach exercise to wealthy women executives while we wait for our big Broadway break. Fuji. The one who doesn't speak much English."

"Fuji from the health club who doesn't speak English."

I thought about it.

"Oh! *That* Fuji! Jeez, Shay. When did you two start dating? And when did you learn Japanese?"

Shay looked offended. "I can say *arrigato*."

"That's nice. Do you have the remotest idea of what it means?"

"Well, of course. It's either 'congratulations,' 'thank you,' 'hurry up,' or 'where's the toilet?' I'm not totally sure."

"I hope it's the last. Much more useful. You're avoiding the issue. Y'all've been dating since…?"

Shay hid her face over the Tanqueray bottle. Her response was muffled, so I had to strain to hear, nearly falling off the couch to do so.

"Well, we didn't really date. We're just getting married as soon as we get the license and the blood test results are in."

"It must be the drugs. I seem to be missing something here—like an entire courtship. Damn. Time flies, doesn't it?"

Shay glowered at me.

"You know that he's a baseball player."

"I knew that, yes. I didn't know that meant he was good husband material or that you were even looking."

Shay sipped from my bottle of Tanqueray.

"Don't be impertinent, wench. Be quiet for once and allow me to explain. Fuji came over from Japan and has been trying to land a spot with the Yankees or the Mets. He's a very good pitcher."

"I'm sure he is. So why is he marrying you and not Sammy Sosa or somebody?"

Shay roamed around the room, picking up the tossed items from the sofa, emptying ashtrays and plumping pillows.

"Well, he hasn't been picked up by a real club yet and he needed to either find a spot with a major-league team or become a citizen. I'm his ticket to citizenship."

"You're his ticket to deportation! Or jail. You can't get married to give somebody citizenship! They investigate these things. *Men in Black*. Illegal aliens."

I giggled.

"Get it? *Men in Black?* Illegal aliens?"

Shay sighed. "You are too Percodanned to even explain this to."

"You just have no sense of humor. Go on. Tell me why you and Fuji are risking jail time."

Shay flopped next to my foot and took another swig from the bottle.

"He just needs this scout to see him play a couple more times and he'll be set and nobody will snoop in the next couple of months. I'm sure."

I grabbed the bottle from her and took a long swig myself.

"This is starting to sound familiar. He's playing with some farm team in Connecticut, isn't he?"

Shay's head ducked under Ringo's long neck, unsuccessfully muffling her response.

"No. Uh—Staten Island."

I couldn't help it. I started shrieking.

"Oh my sainted grandmother! That's right. The Staten Island Ferries! I definitely need another drink. Give me that bottle. Shay! Shay! You can't do this. It's beyond nuts. It's illegal. You'd have to sleep with him to make it legal and I'll bet you've never even kissed him. Of course, if I remember correctly, he's pretty cute. Never mind. If you get deported with him you'll never get a chance to direct that show in the East Village. And you don't like sushi and you'll be living in

Japan forced to eat nothing but rice. Let's see. What else can I say to convince you?"

"He's paying me $7,000 dollars."

I paused. I carefully poured a shot of Tanqueray into my glass, popped a Percodan and a chocolate morsel into my mouth, curled under Shay's antique quilt and lifted my glass to my roommate.

"Well, at least you'll have bail money. *Arrigato!*"

FIVE

"He's dead, I tell you, he's dead!"

"Calm down, Mrs. Noble. Try and tell me what happened."

"He was absolutely determined to try and skydive this morning. I was in the plane and he put his parachute on and he jumped and the next thing I knew the parachute wasn't opening and he was just falling and falling! Dr. Morgan, we're still on our honeymoon! We've only been married three days!"

"Dr. Morgan! Come quickly! We were putting Mr. Noble into the body bag when we saw a movement. He has a pulse!"

"Are you sure?"

"Yes, Dr. Morgan! I swear he twitched his little finger."

"Oh my word, he may not be dead! He's. He's. He's in a coma!"

A G chord played on a severely out-of-tune organ and the sound of the downstairs door buzzer buzzing jolted me into solid wakefulness. I had no idea what time I'd fallen asleep but since the sun was shining brightly through the window that faced 79th, I knew I'd been out at least fifteen hours. The TV was on high volume and set to *Endless Time*. The buzzing continued with a resolute tone.

"Yeah? Who is it?"

Cherry was mumbling into the intercom. A muffled voice returned the query.

"Who?"

Cherry turned to me.

"Are you expectin' someone named Johnny?"

"Oh, hell! Stall him. I must stink like a bar on Sunday morning and look like recycled trash."

Cherry had pressed the buzzer the minute I let it be known the person downstairs was friend, not foe. I hobbled in the manner of a manic child on a pogo stick into the bathroom and zipped through a short tooth brushing, face splashing and make-up emergency session. I was out in less than five minutes. Cherry had left the door unlocked and gone back to bed.

Johnny Gerard stood in the open doorway holding a bag of something that smelled wonderfully sweet and buttery in one hand and juggling two cups of coffee in a cardboard container in the other. Everything looked delicious—especially the delivery boy.

AN HOUR LATER, the delivery boy still looked good. The muffins were mostly gone. Johnny had been entertaining me with childhood stories while both of us munched and slurped.

"Johnny. Go back. You did what?"

"I tried to jump over the wading pool on my tricycle. Honestly. I'd been watching some daredevil Grand Canyon type motorcycle jump with my mom on television. Then she made the mistake of going into the kitchen to make dinner or cookies or something. I dragged the Ping-Pong tabletop outside, put it diagonally on a chair, got out my super powered trike and revved it up. I went tearing across the lawn, up the Ping-Pong board and splat. Right into the water."

I loved it. I had no brothers. I didn't know little boys were this courageously nuts at the toddler stage.

"What happened?"

Johnny winked at me.

"Like an idiot, I'd left my huge toy tank in the pool. Head plowed right into it. I only broke my nose that time."

I laughed.

"I could just see my mother if I had done a stunt like that. She would have politely grounded me and locked me in my room with a copy of Emily Post for about ten years. Come to think of it, she pretty much did that without any encouragement or even bad behavior on my part. Your mom sounds wonderful."

He nodded.

"She worked as a legal secretary for the District Attorney's office here in Manhattan for about five years. But after I was born and she and my biological father divorced, she moved to Houston. Two thousand miles away from Kieran the Great. Smart woman."

I looked at Johnny and took another sip of coffee.

"Ah, yes. Kieran Gerard. Currently running for District Attorney. Do you see him at all? What's the story? Or am I being too nosy?"

Johnny paused for a moment. He tore a muffin in half and delicately crammed one half into his mouth.

"Off and on. The seeing of my father, not you being nosy." He grinned. "You always seem nosy."

I threw a wadded-up napkin at him. "Go on. Tell me about Mr. Political Hound Lawyer. I love hearing about parents who drive their offspring nuts. Reminds me I'm not the only one. Only in my case, it's my mother. Sorry. I'm interrupting. Kieran."

"Well, for starters, Kieran has quite the eye for the ladies. And they for him. My mother was not immune. But, fortunately for her, she wised up in time to call it quits shortly after I arrived on the scene. Moved out of the city just after I turned a year old. I had no further contact with him until much later. First time I met him was when I went to New York on a choir trip during high school. Called him, met him at some very expensive French restaurant in midtown. He shook my hand, asked me what I intended to do with my life. I told him I was going to become a singer and actor. He immediately told me he thought my idea of singing professionally was the most childish thing he'd ever heard. Then he suggested I follow his lead and go to Yale Law School, introduced me to some snobby colleagues of his, and told me if I needed a hot date while visiting the city to let him know. And that, as they say, was that. I was not impressed."

A thoroughly impish expression swept his face. "I could see why mom originally fell for him, though. He looks like me. That is, I'll look how he does now in about twenty-five years or so. Irresistible."

I could also see why Johnny's mom had fallen for a young Kieran. *Irresistible* was an understatement. Those looks were enough to send any female with a pulse right into orbit. Without a parachute. I had to stop letting Shay and Cherry watch *Endless Time.*

Johnny continued to talk about his father. "I had no desire to get in touch with him when I got to New York to go to college or use him as any kind of backup. I thought, maybe I'll phone if I get run over by a taxi or something. I spent four years at Columbia then five more in Manhattan without exchanging a word with the man."

He began to pace the room. "Then suddenly, last year, he's calling me and giving me the 'we should get to know one another, son' bit. He's not as good an actor as I am. I didn't buy it. I gathered he'd heard from some of his colleagues who saw *Carousel* that I was still in the city and doing fairly well for myself. Then he learned I'd been hired to do *Endless Time.* Why that should matter, I have no idea. But suddenly I'm Numero Uno on his phone list."

"Some people are big on the soap celebrity bit," I interjected. "Even when it's their own kids."

"Well, I don't think being on daytime drama really qualifies. I guess my father does. Maybe he figures it'll bring in a whole new constituency to vote for him. Anyway, I felt like

I should try to establish some sort of relationship with him. And here's Daddy, actually reaching out to me, saying if I need anything to let him know."

"Do you think he's serious?" I asked.

Johnny gave what might be termed a less than graceful snort. "I'm still not sure why he called. I do see him on at least a monthly basis, but to be honest, I feel like I'm no further in finding out who he really is than I knew over twenty-five years ago when my parents split. And I can't tell you how many times he's cancelled lunches or dinners. Work, he says. Now he's running for District Attorney and he's being very choosy about his friends and relatives. Lawyers. I guess they're a necessary evil."

I had to laugh.

"I'm an expert on the subject of attorneys myself. My mother, Minette, seems to collect them for her parties, rather like expensive figurines. But your dad does sound like a piece of work."

"I remind myself daily never to become him. Except for my fine Irish charm, of course."

"Of course."

We smiled at each other. He reached for another muffin, then mumbled around it: "The only good thing my father has done I can think of is find a great roommate for me. When he first got in touch, he said he knew a guy who works as a paralegal on his staff who needed a decent place to live. For once he was right about people. Cookie's really a good friend. He deflects phone calls from rabid fans, cooks a pot of Dominican rice and beans to die for and has a sense of humor about life at the Manhattan Prosecutorial Office I find extremely refreshing after Kieran, the consummate politician. He's also one of those people who can find amazing deals on used cars and DVD players. Cookie pretty much sleeps with a cell phone to his ear which occasionally worries me as to where he finds these deals. I think the operative word could be 'Hot.'"

I smiled.

"Cookie?"

"His real name is Carlos Gutierrez. He's from Santo Domingo. Actually was a lawyer there before he moved to New York. Has to wait for citizenship before he can take the bar, but at least he's able to work as a paralegal."

"Where'd the nickname come from?"

Johnny tried to look innocent and failed.

"I'd love to say it's from some cute personality trait. Like he bakes great oatmeal squares or peanut butter bars. Unfortunately, it refers more to his primary source of sustenance. The man knows every bakery and fast-food cookie stand in Manhattan and uses them for all his nutritional needs."

"He sounds fun. I should introduce him to Shay. They could hunt down all the sweet culinary shops in the city and leave her résumé to see if they want a commercial choreographed. They'd get along great. Unless she decides to get married to Fuji."

His brows went up.

"Fuji? Who's Fuji? And when is this happening? Are you about to be a bridesmaid on crutches?"

I nodded and snorted, "It won't matter. They'll be locked up in Rikers or someplace by Immigration Services. Hopefully she's come to her senses since I talked to her half of the night."

Johnny unsuccessfully tried to hide his laughter.

"Well, Cookie probably wouldn't be any better. I told you he's still working on citizenship himself. You'd think someone in the D.A.'s office could help out, but I gather the bureaucracy of Immigration is somewhat on the order of the Motor Vehicles Division up on 125th Street. Take a number and a tent and be prepared to camp. Maybe your friend Fuji's right about this marriage business being the easiest way."

I smiled.

"Well, if this works out for Shay, maybe we can hook Cookie up with Cherry, my other roommate. Although I'd hate to be at any wedding ceremony where the priest asks Cookie if he'd take Cherry as his lawful wife. The sugar intake in that one sentence would be enough to send all guests into diabetic comas. So. Change of subject. Is your mother still in Houston? I'd love to meet her."

"She died six years ago."

"Oh, Johnny. I'm so sorry. There's a lot of love in your voice when you talk about her."

"I miss her. She was the best." A beautifully wicked smile suddenly lit up his entire face. "Mom was strict as hell about school and manners and stuff, but she taught me to play baseball, Ping-Pong and pool. She also taught me to swim, and ride my bike. And play pool."

"You said that. Pool, that is."

A twinkle appeared in Johnny's green eyes.

"I know. I said it again for sheer emphasis because Mom loved to play pool. If I hadn't decided to become a singer, I'd have majored in pool sharking. I'm extremely talented thanks to her excellent training."

"I'll bet you are. It's that acting ability, Johnny. Don't pool hustlers have to bluff?"

He raised an eyebrow in an attempt to look innocent.

"Now, now. I engage in only honest games of pool. Anyway, Mom also loved opera, so I was raised on the classics from a very early age. It was funny. I was always having accidents—you can see why after the trike incident—and she would calmly drive me to the hospital with the classical station playing full blast on the radio. I'd be holding a bloody tourniquet to whatever part of my body needed it and the two of us would be wailing away singing Wagner or Verdi."

"How often did you have these little accidents?"

Johnny assumed an angelic expression.

"Well, let's put it this way. By the time I was in sixth grade, I'd had no fewer than ten broken bones, three concussions and numerous sutures."

"You're kidding. Did the doctors call child services every time you gave a command performance at the hospital? I'm surprised you weren't removed from your home by a zealous social worker claiming child abuse."

Johnny shook his head.

"The whole crew at the clinic got used to us. I used to entertain them in the waiting room with exciting renditions of numbers from musicals. They didn't worry about me. They just sympathized with my mother."

Johnny's face took on the expression of that Irish bandit I thought he resembled the first day I'd noticed him in Ricky's dance class.

"I remember one time a nurse politely explaining to the hysterical parent of a kid I'd tied up and shot suction-cup arrows at. He had little red welts all over his face. The nurse just said about me, 'He's all boy.'"

Oh, yeah. I agreed with that assessment. I took a sip of coffee then sank my teeth into another poppy-seed muffin. He'd filled the bag so there would be enough for Shay and Cherry as well, if I didn't eat all of them out of the sheer nervousness of having the man in my apartment.

We stared at each other for a moment, quiet for the first time since Johnny had arrived. He'd told me about his childhood. He'd told me about Kieran. What he hadn't mentioned was his relationship with the broad in the white limo who had been all over him at O'Malley's.

I was about to jump right in and ask point-blank when I was interrupted by a female voice about twenty feet behind me.

"Abby!"

"Shay!"

"I smell muffins. Where are you hiding them and how did you get them?"

Shay's voice was strong and fast headed our way from the living room. I had to give her marks for her nose, but flunk her for her timing. She popped her head in.

"Oh! I am *sooo* sorry. I didn't know Abby had company. Abby. How rude. Why didn't you let me know?"

She plopped down on the couch next to me. I grimaced at her. I had told her very explicitly last evening that Johnny Gerard was expected this morning. She was supposed to be in absentia the entire day doing all the things that one must do in order to get the marriage license I'd been trying to talk her out of.

"Excuse me, Shay, but aren't you supposed to be out preparing to marry the baseball player? Blood tests and licenses and all that?"

She waved my question away.

"Oh, that's not 'til later today. If I even do it at all. You made such a persuasive argument against unlawful wedded bliss that I'm rethinking my plans. Anyway, I have no place to go for hours. Hot damn! Not only muffins but roses as well. I'm impressed."

"Don't be. A florist dropped them off about an hour ago while you were in the shower or something. They're from the cast and crew of *Superstar*. I figure Dewitt Dwyer doesn't want me to sue for negligent stupidity so he passed the hat for the roses."

She grabbed a muffin and a cup of coffee as she considered this statement. She nodded.

"Makes sense. I guess it's hard to put out a hit on a twit who sends flowers."

She laughed at her own rhyming humor. I waved a hand at her and tried not to stick my tongue out. That would be childish, embarrassing in front of Johnny, and totally useless anyway. After emitting a very deep sigh, I gave in gracefully to Shay's interruption and bad jokes.

"Shay Martin. Johnny Gerard. Y'all got that? There you go then, introductions done."

Shay took a big bite and started to talk with her mouth full.

"So. Johnny Gerard. Abby told me how you rescued her after the collision with the piano player at the *Superstar* rehearsal. As her roommate and best friend I say 'thank you.' Especially since I wasn't prepared yesterday to go to the doctor's office and bring home a non-walking dancer high on Percodan. Who then proceeded to get higher on Tanqueray. I'm here to tell you it was like a picnic at the Bowery here last night."

Johnny laughed, then looked back over at me.

"You didn't tell me your injury had aimed you towards demon rum as well as drugs."

I glared at my accusers.

"Gin, thank you. Not rum. And excellent gin at that. Hey. You guys need to give me a break. I'll have you know I am in more pain than I've ever hurt in my life except for the time I got two dry sockets after getting my wisdom teeth yanked. Now that was killer. My jaw still aches when I think of it."

Shay and Johnny both winced at that. Johnny quickly changed the subject and turned towards Shay.

"Shay Martin. Shay Martin. Wait. I know that name. Are you a choreographer?"

She preened a bit.

"I am. I am. Although right now I'm not doing a show. Or even a doughnut commercial."

She still wasn't over losing the last one, but we tried not to discuss it too often. I think it was one reason why she was seriously considering Fuji's offer. The money could come in quite handy.

Johnny nodded thoughtfully.

"I saw a show you did last spring. Um. *Jingle?* Is that right?"

Shay and I were both amazed. Her mouth was hanging open and she wasn't trying to stuff it with muffins.

I spoke for her. "What a memory. Yeah. Shay did that. I didn't know her then and I didn't see it. Of course, I wasn't even in New York then."

"Well, I saw it. Damn. The dancing was incredible. Lewis Canton, a friend of mine, was one of the dancers. He adores you, by the way. Said you were the best choreographer he'd ever worked with and he's been a Broadway gypsy for twelve years."

Shay was beaming brighter than a searchlight. Johnny continued. "You said you're not working right now?"

Shay nodded.

"Good. That means you're available."

"For what?"

"*Endless Time* wants several of the characters to get involved in some scenes with lots of extras dancing and they need a choreographer. Some kind of retro-disco sequence. They haven't liked anyone they've interviewed so far. I'm on good terms with the casting director. Would you mind if I gave them your name?"

I do love Shay. She has no inhibitions and no guile. She leapt off the couch and started jumping up and down like a three-year-old in an ice-cream factory. I was grateful she'd chosen not to do this routine on the couch itself. My foot didn't need extra jostling.

"Johnny! Do not go anywhere. Do not move. I'll get my résumé from the desk and bring it back in a super-jiffy."

She took off. Johnny smiled at me. Nice guy all the way around. Another female voice suddenly took up the slack.

"Shay! Abby! I smell muffins. Where are you two? If there's muffins, why aren't they in the friggin' kitchen? And

where's the coffee? Oh, there you are! Oh. Ya got *company.*
Holy Santa Maria! Have you got company. Hello…"

Cherry was looking at Johnny the way Shay had looked at
the muffins. I considered bashing her over the head with one
of my crutches. Johnny didn't need this admittedly enticing
distraction and I didn't need to be planning a "roommate-
icide." I opted to wait 'til the man had gone, then explain that
Mr. Gerard was off-limits. Cherry has her faults, but I must
say she won't horn in on another girl's relationship. Assuming
there was going to be a relationship.

"Well, what's up? Come on, Abby. You gonna be rude or
you gonna make the introductions? Ah, the hell with it. I'm
Cherry Ripe. Nice ta meet ya."

Johnny was staring in fascination at the third member of
Seven-D, as would any heterosexual male over the age of five.
Cherry was wearing her orange negligee with the pink baby
dolls underneath, all of which, one could safely say, were see-
through since the morning sun was pouring into the room.
Johnny averted his eyes, then looked at me, then shifted his
gaze to the poster of a dancing Minnie Mouse from Disney
World we'd stuck over a hole in the wall. He began to study it
as though it were a Degas original. Cherry grabbed a muffin
and plopped onto the sofa next to me. Unless I was prepared
for a *ménage à quad,* my romantic morning with Mr. Gerard
seemed to be disappearing as fast as the food from La Mirage.
Johnny took a deep breath and tried to focus on Cherry's face
only.

"So, Cherry? Are you also a dancer?"

"Sure am. I work at The Squirrel Shot Gentlemen's Club
on 8th Ave. Ever been there?"

Johnny looked at me for guidance. I took a sip of coffee
and stared at the ceiling. He'd charmed one roommate. I was
sure he'd have no problems at all with the other. He didn't.

"I don't believe I've had the pleasure. But I'm sure many
others have."

Cherry beamed much as Shay had. I knew she hadn't caught the double entendre. I dove into the back of Ringo's neck trying to look anywhere but at my roommate or the smart-ass male sitting across from me.

"Ya should come down there sumtime. A course, my shift varies, but ask at the door. I'll see that ya get in free."

"Thanks, Cherry. That's very kind of you."

Fortunately Shay burst in before I laughed and ruined my newly found friendship with Cherry. Shay handed her head-shot and résumé over to Johnny. More coffee was poured; more muffins were inhaled. The four of us were chatting away about which pastries were the best from the French patisserie when the phone rang.

"'Scuse me. I bet that's Vito and Guido."

Cherry jumped up and ran into the living room to answer.

Johnny looked at me. "Vito and Guido?"

I grinned. "In tandem. Always. Even on the phone. I haven't had the pleasure of meeting them yet."

Cherry returned in less than ten seconds with a funny look on her face. "Johnny? It's for you. Some chick named Tracy. Says it's bad news."

He got up.

"Thanks, Cherry."

He left to take the call as Shay and Cherry both gave undivided and unnecessary attention to the sugar bowl. My appetite departed. I started feeling the pain in my foot for the first time this morning.

Johnny marched back into the room like a man preparing to battle the Hun. His face was set and tight at the mouth. He sank down on the couch and buried his head in his hands.

"That was a friend of mine. Tracy. She was right. It's very bad news."

His voice became hoarse.

"It's Cookie. My roommate. He's in the hospital. Hit-and-run. Some son-of-a-bitch ran him down this morning while he was crossing Centre Street on his way to work. Cops don't know who or how or why."

We all stayed silent.

Johnny looked around for his things.

"I'm sorry. I have to go. She told me he's at St. Vincent's." All color had drained from his face. His voice grew tight. "And he's critical."

Shay handed him his bag and jacket. I stood up best as I could on my crutches.

"Johnny. Let us know if there's anything we can do. And," I paused, "let us know how he is. Okay?"

He nodded, kissed me lightly on my cheek and took off.

Cherry shook her head.

"Well. That was just weird. Damn. Hit-and-run. But just who is this bitch, Tracy? Why is *she* the one telling him about his friend? He's pretty cut up about this. Want me to get Vito and Guido on the case and find out who ran down his roomie?"

Cherry has a way of cutting to the heart of the matter. For a second I was tempted to take her up on the offer of siccing the Mariccino twins on "the case." But I was sure the cops would be doing their best to find out why a lowly paralegal had been run down in broad daylight near the courthouse. I shook my head no at Cherry.

"Thanks, Cher, but I think we should wait and see what happens. No use getting Vito and Guido wound up."

Cherry rose from the couch and headed towards the bathroom. That time of morning. She turned back before entering, and looked me straight in the eye.

"Okay. But lemme know if you need 'em. I'm tellin' ya. This Tracy is trouble. Scary trouble. I know it like I know rain's comin' this afternoon. She's got somethin' to do with this accident. And she's gonna cause trouble for you and Johnny."

Shay stared at me after Cherry left the room.

"She's right, you know. The girl has this innate sense about impending doom."

"Stop it. I don't need Cherry and her psychic ability. Mine is bad enough. Tracy is a friend of Johnny's. I guess she's a very good friend since she knew where to call him about Cookie. God, Shay. That is beyond belief. Hit-and-run."

It struck me then. And it struck Shay at the same time.

"Abby. Didn't you have some sort of vision of a hit-and-run concerning Johnny?"

I nodded. "When we watched him leave O'Malley's. But all I saw was a white limo running someone down. Do you suppose a white limo just happened to run down Cookie? Do you think it could have anything to do with that girl and her chauffeur?"

"No idea. No point in speculating either. And I'd watch what I told Johnny. I mean, if they're friends of his, he may not appreciate you being suspicious, especially since you don't have a lot to go on. Look. Why don't you get some rest? I'll man the phone lines and wait for Johnny's call about Cookie. And pray."

I snuggled down on the couch. Shay silently put her grandmother's quilted comforter over me. I fell asleep and dreamed that a white limousine was flying over El Paso. Minette, Tracy the drooling rich bitch, and Dewitt Dwyer sat in the back eating huge cookies as they listened to a big blonde chauffeur singing the "Winter Storm" aria from *Die Walkure*. Johnny and disco dancers from *Endless Time* swirled around them like snowflakes until one by one, they disappeared.

SIX

"ABBY! THEY'RE ON AGAIN!"

"What? Who?"

"Kieran Gerard and the stud muffin, whassisname Jaffert that works with him. On the news."

I sat up and adjusted my pillow behind my back. She was right. "New York News at Noon." Gina Giardeli.

"Turn it up, would you?"

"Mr. Gerard? Can you give us an update? Is there any indication that this hit-and-run murder on one of your workers is related to the shooting deaths of the other illegal Dominican immigrants?"

I got a glimpse of Gerard anger that I hoped was not genetic, or if it were, would never be directed at me.

"Miz Giardeli. Mr. Gutierrez is a paralegal who happens to be employed by the office of the District Attorney. He is not illegal. And, Miz Giardeli, he is *not* dead! Kindly get your facts straight before you poke a microphone in someone's face. As to the gist of that question, as of now, we have no evidence linking the attempted murder of Carlos Gutierrez with any other violent acts. Believe me, we are hard at work, united with the police department, to discover who is responsible for this attack. Thank you."

He and Jaffert whirled around and headed inside the Centre Street offices that housed New York's prosecutors and public defenders. Gina Giardeli looked stricken. Whether it was from Kieran Gerard's tone or the fact that she hadn't had a chance to flirt with his assistant, I wasn't sure.

I turned to Shay. "Wow. I would not like to have that man mad at me. But at least he looks like he's serious about investigating who's responsible for landing Johnny's roommate in the hospital. Which I guess is where Johnny is. I guess. Damn. Damn. And damn."

I hadn't heard from Johnny for at least three weeks. Being the savvy roommates they were, Shay and Cherry tried to cheer me up by bringing me pastries and chocolates, pizzas with tons of black olives, mystery novels and tabloid newspapers. I couldn't even stand to watch *Endless Time,* even though I knew they were about to air Mr. Gerard's last performance on the show for several months, if one wanted to call lying in a hospital bed and reaching an arm up to the heavens while moaning a performance.

"Abby. You've got to stop moping. Johnny's got other things to concern him. Like spending days in hospitals."

That brought me up short. We'd read in the paper that Carlos "Cookie" Gutierrez was still on the critical list from injuries sustained during a hit-and-run. Drifting in and out of a coma. As yet, no suspects, no leads. Shay had spent an hour after seeing that persuading me that going to the police with a vision story about white limos would not help the situation.

"Shay. I understand Johnny is depressed and miserable and dealing with a hell of a lot of angst. But why didn't he call to tell us about Cookie? It's like he just disappeared from my life. And what's with Tracy? The omnipresent presence?"

"I don't know. But look. You're making yourself feel worse than you need to by sitting here and brooding. And you're driving everyone nuts."

"Well, excuse me for being such a burden. Why are you here anyway? Why aren't you out getting married?"

I was being rude but I didn't care. My pain was swinging from physical to emotional. Shay was my closest target.

She growled at me. "I am here because I have the day off from the health club. And I am *not* getting married because

I don't want to go to jail, a possibility you were kind enough to point out to me the night you came crashing home on your crutches. To tell the truth, I might be able to earn a lot more than $7,000 dollars if this thing with *Endless Time* comes through. Also, Fuji is being scouted or agented, or whatever they call it, by some Midwestern ball club."

I snorted.

"He probably bribed some INS official with that seven thou' since you declined to go down the aisle."

She ignored me. "Let's just say he isn't shopping for a bride right now. Now quit whining and have some tea or something. I'll make you some chamomile. That's calming."

Shame and contrition took over for a good ten seconds.

"I'm sorry. It's being worried about someone I've never met that I envisioned getting run over. And let's face it, it's Tracy, too. I know it. You know it. Cherry knows it. Hell, Vito and Guido probably know it. We should all take out an ad that reads: 'Shay was right: The man is poison. Drooling rich bitches win in the end.' Especially when they own white deadly limos. I fooled myself because he showered all that Irish charm all over me and I fell for it. But when he needs someone to cry with, it's Miss Tracy. Oh, nuts. Hand me the Agatha Christie that's on top of the TV, and another chocolate croissant, would you? I need gooey pastries and murder." I choked as I made this statement. I found I was still falling asleep at night envisioning a man under a car. "Well, fictional murder," I amended.

Shay handed me *Murder at the Vicarage* and a double-sized chocolate croissant. I grabbed both enthusiastically.

Shay scowled at me. "Damn, Abby. You keep eating this way without being able to dance and you're gonna get used as a doorstop. I've never seen anyone cram so much junk down her throat in such a short amount of time. I weigh sixty pounds more than you and I don't have that appetite."

I perused page one of the murder mystery and idly

answered, "My weight won't change. It never does. I've always eaten like a linebacker and never gained an ounce. It's the one really great thing I inherited from Minette. And you *don't* weight sixty pounds more. Do not start that crap with me."

Shay gestured to the phone and asked, "Where is Minette, by the way? I've gotten used to the daily call. It's been at least three days now."

"She's gone off to Dallas for her annual pre-Christmas shop-'til-you-drop at Neiman Marcus. It's the most frightening event I've ever witnessed and I've accompanied her more years than I care to think about. She's like some Roman conqueror preparing to lay siege to Britain. A thorough campaign mapped out for each department. She starts at one end of the store and doesn't stop 'til she's hit every square inch. This is at the downtown NM, mind you. I emphasize that point because she refuses to go the one at Northpark Mall. Says it's for the peasants only. The woman is like no one you've ever met before. Did I tell you…?"

Pity and amazement showed through Shay's eyes.

"What?" I barked at her.

"You're rambling. A lot. You care as much about shopping as I do about cleaning the kitchen. You may try, but you can't hide the fact you're delighted not to have to converse with your mother for a few days. Enjoy the peace. Go back to reading your book. If you're still mad at him, substitute Johnny Gerard for the murder victim."

It was as if someone had dumped a bucket of ice over me. I started shivering uncontrollably, and didn't hear Shay for several seconds.

"Abby? You've just gone pale. What's the matter?"

"I just had another premonition. Worse than the limo thing. Not a nice one at all. I want Great-Grammy to take her little gift of second sight back to whatever psychic bull pen she's in, then wait for someone else to step up to bat. Not me."

Shay sat on the sofa and grabbed one of the pastries. I wasn't the only one eating too much around here.

"Tell me."

I had to take a few deep breaths first. This vision had really upset me.

"I was sitting in our apartment. But it was like I was a lot older. And I was leafing through a scrapbook. A newspaper clipping fell out. It had Johnny's picture on it and the words 'shot' and 'murdered' and something to do with a crime boss and his wife. And Shay? I could see the date. Next July. I swear."

Shay looked worried but intrigued.

"Do we need to find some other psychic type for you? A Tarot card reader? Medium? Gypsy fortune-teller? Shrink?"

I shook my head.

"I don't think any of the above could have a plausible explanation for this. Some guru would explain it as a forward life progression or something and make a ton of money writing about it. I'm telling you, it's the Dumas curse of second sight. My grandmother knew my mother would marry a man who'd take her to a far-off Western land. I guess Atlanta to El Paso qualifies? And my mother has yet to vote the wrong ticket for any election. She trusts her instincts and pulls those levers even if she doesn't like the candidate. Hates to lose. Anyway, no shrinks studying me, please. I have enough to deal with healing my foot. My mental condition can wait."

Shay smiled and handed me another chocolate pastry. The door buzzer sounded. Shay crossed to the intercom and pressed the "talk" switch.

"Yo?"

The mumbling of a male voice downstairs waiting to be buzzed in could be faintly detected.

"Who? Sorry, I can't understand you."

More mumbling. Our intercom was the typical Manhattan

brownstone non-functioning piece of rubbish left over from the 19th century. I think it's a law. All brownstone intercom systems work perfectly when the superintendent checks on them with the repair guys, or when he comes to collect the rent in person. The rest of the time, if friends, the mailman or other delivery persons ring, it's a garbled mess. I waved at Shay.

"Let whoever it is in. Hey. Maybe it's the pizza delivery guy. I'm expecting him."

Shay's eyes widened.

"You are one sick woman. Pizza after croissants and chocolate chip muffins and that enormous pancake breakfast you had this morning? Damn, Abby! Take what's left in the bottle of Percodan and go back to sleep."

She obligingly pressed the "in" button and turned back to me. "You are also the most trusting human being I've ever met. You need to take lessons from Cherry on how to have a true New York attitude and believe that everyone is out to get you. All that Southern Belle courtesy crap just doesn't work up here. And why am *I* telling *you* this? *I'm* the one who's so stupid as to buzz someone in when I don't even know who's on their way up here. Abby, I'm warning you, if it's some pervert, I'm hitting him with your crutches, then pouring hot coffee on him."

She opened the door as she stated this. I rudely stuck my tongue out at her.

"Don't tell *me* that. Tell the pervert at the door."

"Thanks a lot" came from the man entering our apartment.

"Johnny?"

I stared at the man holding a bag of something that was obviously not pizza. He grinned. "Thank you for calling me by my given name. It's so much better than being labeled a pervert. By the way, I noticed at least a dozen or more hanging outside the building so be careful who you buzz in."

Shay laughed and closed the door. I stuck my chin up into the air. Shay began politely hanging up Johnny's wet trench coat in the tiny coat closet by the door. She looked at me; then she looked at him. The three of us shared a long moment of silence until Shay grabbed her own raincoat and threw it on over her jeans and sweats.

"I need to go to, uh, the post office. Will you two be all right for a few minutes?"

Johnny helped her with her coat and nodded.

"Sure. I am here to entertain Abby and see that she walks around the room without her crutches for at least five minutes."

Was that a five minute visit or five minutes of my walking therapy? I assumed the answer would be revealed shortly.

Shay left without any letters or parcels for her non-existent trip to the post office. Johnny ambled over to the sofa where I'd been ensconced since early morning and presented me with a bag of croissants. They were hot, they were fresh, and they were from La Mirage. The man had no idea I'd already consumed more calories in the last hour than construction workers chow down in a week, and I had no intention of enlightening him on the subject. I thanked him politely, took one off the top, and attacked the roll as though I hadn't eaten since his last visit.

I had planned on being wonderfully sympathetic to the fact that he was worried about his friend living or dying. I'd planned on asking if there was anything I could do. Or avoid the topic of limos and comas for a few moments. Maybe discuss work. Always a great conversation starter. I opened my mouth to ask him how *Endless Time* was going.

That's not what came out.

"Who in tarnation is Tracy? And why was she the one calling about Cookie anyway?" Oh damn. Foot and crutches had been swallowed whole along with the croissants. I ducked my head down. "Johnny. I'm so sorry. I really meant to ask how Cookie was doing. And how you're doing as well."

"Not great. He's still in a coma. Weird. Sort of life imitating art. If you can call *Endless Time* art. Gregory Noble in a coma. Gregory Noble's real-life roommate in a coma. Crap! Cookie is truly a good friend, not to mention an all-around nice person. Someone who did not deserve to be run over in the street like a can of soda or something. I've been at the hospital for at least six hours a day the last couple of weeks, talking to him, hoping he'll hear something and snap out."

He smiled.

"I've related every dirty joke I've ever known. Cookie loves dirty jokes. Unfortunately, he has yet to respond and fire one or two back at me."

He sat down heavily on the couch. For a moment neither of us said anything. He finally looked at me.

"Abby. As for your first question, Tracy is just a friend. She's helping out with some stuff. Can we leave it at that?"

I nodded. I didn't want to leave it, but I didn't want to press either.

"So, where have you been? I've been kind of worried. It's been weeks since Cookie's accident."

"Sorry. I tried to call. I've literally been held prisoner at the TV studio when I haven't been at the hospital. They wanted to shoot the entire 'jump from parachute, end up in coma' sequence for Gregory Noble so I could be out of the show for the next couple of months. They didn't want *anyone,* make that *anyone* else, involved at the studio, except the writers, a couple of other actors relevant to the scene, and the cameramen."

I was intrigued despite myself.

"What's with the secrecy?"

Johnny smiled for the first time.

"Ratings week coming up. Very important not to jinx the works with leaks about exciting story lines. Anyway, we redid those scenes about a million times. I honestly did try to call you to let you know what was going on, but your phone was always busy. I know that sounds like the standard trite excuse, but it's true."

I thought about it. Cherry stays on the phone at least four hours daily talking to Vito and Guido. I don't know why. She sees the pair nightly at the club. Shay had also been more verbose on the phone the last few days trying to arrange the interview with the *Endless Time* casting agent. I smiled at Johnny and veered off the subject of calls for a second.

"Thank you for giving Shay's résumé to that guy at the studio. She's got an appointment set up for next week."

"No problem. I meant what I say about her being really good." He grinned. "Although I *might* have considered lying since you two are so close and I wanted you to think I'm wonderful."

"Uh-huh. Are you fishing for compliments, here?"

"Not at all. Just admiring the tilt of your nose when you thank me for something."

"You are an evil charmin' man, Johnny Gerard."

For a second or two there was silence. I debated whether to tell Johnny about my nasty premonition involving him and a gun and a mobster. I decided not to. After all, he'd just been through several weeks of hell. And this vision might be nothing more than a Percodan-induced hallucination.

Johnny's tone changed.

"Abby Fouchet. Miss Dancer. I like you more than any girl I've ever met. My life gets a little complicated with the soap, with shows, and now with weird things happening to my friends, not to mention some of the garbage I have to put up with trying to make nice with my father, but please bear with me through all this, okay?"

He started to kiss me again. This was not a brotherly peck. His lips were exploring mine and tongues were getting entangled with tongues when the door flung open. Shay, Cherry and a pizza carton appeared all at once.

"Hey, look who we ran into down in the lobby. The pizza guy! We told him we were your roomies and we even paid. So let's eat."

Shay nodded at Johnny as though there'd been no tension in the room when she left. Cherry tossed the carton onto the coffee table and grabbed a slice.

"Hey, Johnny! How ya doin'? And Cookie, too? Oops. I guess not so good, huh? Should I shut my mouth?"

Johnny looked at her, then at me. A smile lit up his face as he shook his head. "Hey, Cherry! How *you* doin'?"

SEVEN

"WHEN'S THE LAST TIME you went on a picnic?"

"A picnic?"

"Yeah. You know. Sandwiches and fried chicken and out-doors and ants and forgetting napkins and a cooler of beer and sodas."

Johnny stood in my doorway holding a huge hamper in his hand. A huge grin was plastered on his face.

I bit my lip trying not to giggle and answered, "I know the term, Gerard. I even read the William Inge play in college. You know. They made a movie of it in the 1950's? William Holden and Kim Novak. I just don't know why you're asking."

He stepped in and set the hamper on the floor.

"When's the last time you left this apartment?"

"Do you always answer a question with a question?"

He sat on the hamper.

"Do you?"

This wasn't getting us anywhere. I tried to remember the last question Johnny had asked.

"All right. Fine. The last time I left the apartment was yesterday when I went down to 34th Street to see Dr. Murray. He examined my foot and told me I was ready to leap and turn and participate in marathons. Which I have never done and do not intend to. He *did* however say I can go back to class whenever I want and in fact I need to start dancing immediately if not sooner."

Johnny jumped back up and grabbed the hamper again.

"Okay. So your big excitement for the week was a podiatrist's office. I have plans for you. We are going on a picnic!"

Maybe that stunt with the parachute had unhinged him. His mind was obviously damaged.

"Pardon me for pointing this out, Mr. Gerard, but it's December in New York. The temperature is maybe twenty degrees in the sun. And you want to go on a picnic?"

"Yep. Come on. Where's your adventurous spirit?"

"It got left behind a piano at a rehearsal studio when I took a flying leap."

We smiled at each other. He looked very enticing standing in my apartment in his *Les Miserables* jacket, black jeans and a red furry cap with earflaps. I'm a sucker for a guy confident enough to go out in public with earflaps. Or in private.

"Okay. I'm getting my coat. And my mittens and my fake fur hat and my wool muffler. Do I have time to put thermals on under my jeans?"

"No. Quit being a wimp. Anyone would think you grew up in El Paso or something!"

He helped me with my various outer garments, picked up the hamper, and opened the door for me. Within minutes we were outside and walking vigorously towards Riverside Park. We *had* to walk vigorously. If we stood still we'd freeze onto the sidewalk.

The only other maniacs out were dog walkers with their excited canines. Dogs love snow. Several owners had let the happy beasts off and the pups were tunneling through the piles. Seeing them hop and burrow made me feel like doing the same. At least my foot was now healed enough to try.

We found a table with a clean bench. Johnny pulled a red flannel blanket out of the basket and spread out a feast before me. It was like being at the circus watching the clowns pour out of a minuscule car. Crackers and Boisin cheese, pears and apples all came out during the first wave. Steam rose from the middle of the hamper. I gratefully realized my creative picnic-planner had gone to Zabar's and found hot minestrone soup. Packed in the bag next to the soup was a loaf of fresh baked sourdough bread. A roast chicken lay under that lot. From a separate bag wafted the scent of poppy-seed muffins. Just when I thought the hamper couldn't possibly yield another goodie, out came a bottle of champagne.

"What? No chocolate? Or candles on the table?"

Johnny handed me a pile of thick paper napkins. I folded them and placed them by the paper plates. When I looked back up at him, he was holding up a box of Godiva chocolate truffles and grinning.

"Your trouble, Miss Fouchet, is that you do not trust me to show you a good time."

He popped the cork and we both cheered as a stream of bubbly flowed onto the table.

"Hold out your cup."

So much for elegance. He'd brought foam cups and was filling them both with champagne. I started to take a sip before my lips could stick to the cup. Johnny raised his hand to stop me.

"We need a toast."

I agreed.

"Anything in mind?"

He looked into my eyes and held my gaze for a good minute. I suddenly felt much warmer than the December temperature warranted.

"Let's keep it simple. How about 'to Abby and Johnny and a happy life together'?"

I tapped his cup with mine. He hadn't said in what capacity he meant that happy life but I wasn't going to quibble over semantics. The "together" on the end was enough.

Johnny had also managed to pack a portable radio. He tuned it to the oldies station and grabbed my hand.

"Wanna dance? We can test Dr. Murray's diagnosis on the foot."

"Oh, yes. Definitely. Maybe aerobic movement will keep me from turning into a chocolate-filled Popsicle."

Q104 was playing a tribute to Great Britain and Ireland. When the deejay announced "Moondance" by Van Morrison we knew we had our song. We danced around the bench and the picnic table to the delight of at least six different dog walkers and their dogs. Johnny twirled me and lifted me over his head and dipped me into the snow every now and then trying to sculpt images in the powder.

I took a quick breath as he spun me out and back in again.

He held me close for an instant before spinning me out again. My breath stopped. I stumbled. Johnny caught me and smiled.

We stopped dancing long enough to devour nearly every bite Johnny had packed. We sat and talked until the cold seeping into our bones proved to be too much for even the hot-blooded actor.

"Hey!"

"Hey, what?"

"Let's go to Central Park."

"Johnny, we're already freezing at Riverside Park. What makes you think the five or so blocks east of here will be warmer?"

His eyes danced like a four-year-old sitting under the Christmas tree on December 25th.

"It's not the blocks. It's the activity. I'm taking you ice skating at Wolman Rink. Dancing is only the beginning, ma'am."

I must not have heard correctly. I shook my head to clear any icicles stopping up my ears.

"Do you realize you're talking to a girl who has never, I repeat, never, been on ice skates in her life? Who happens to have wrappings around the foot she sprained. And since when do *you* skate? Don't tell me since you were a kid in Houston, 'cause they get less snow than we do. Unless your mom packed you off to skating rinks in the mall when she wasn't dragging you through pool halls."

He finished packing the remainder of our lunch.

"You forget. I've been in New York nearly ten years now. Not to mention that we did a whole month's episodes on the soap that were supposed to take place at the Olympics. Gregory Noble fell in love with a figure skater and played hockey with a pack of Russians. Honey, I learned how to skate like a pro."

I groaned. I might have known his alter ego from *Endless Time* would have done something outrageous on ice. He tugged at my hand like a toddler towing Mom to the candy store.

"Come on, Abby. Believe it or not, the fact that your ankle is still wrapped will help with your balance while skating. It's not like dancing. You'll be well supported. You may even want to wrap the other one."

With my luck I'd end up lying on the sofa for another month after executing a spectacularly ungraceful fall in front of an audience at Wolman Rink, but I dutifully followed Johnny as we headed back towards Central Park.

Wolman was crowded. Kids were whizzing around showing off camels and spins and flying tours. Adults were gliding with precise movements in neat circles. One or two beginners were primarily engaged in grasping on to anything that looked like it might provide stability. They had my sympathy. I hoped I'd have theirs in return in a few minutes when I landed on my not-nearly-padded-enough behind.

We gave the picnic basket to a curious attendant, rented two pairs of skates, and bought two cups of hot cocoa. At an empty bench near the rink, Johnny knelt down in front of me and laced my boots up. He finished tying the last knot in the boot and took my hands in his. I assumed he was going to help me up. Instead he pulled me to him and kissed me. His lips were warm and tasted of chocolate.

He slid his arms around me as we kissed. Both of us had completely forgotten our surroundings. Suddenly a shrill female voice split the air with a pitch so high I thought it would shatter the ice on the rink.

"Oh My Sweet Heaven! It's Gregory Noble! Look, Margaret, it's Gregory Noble!"

We drew apart as a horde of women descended on us. (In reality it was only three, but they were so noisy and enthusiastic it seemed to constitute a horde.) They encircled Johnny in a claustrophobic embrace.

"May we have your autograph? Please?"

Johnny graciously assented. He was embarrassed about their shrieking and I was just ticked off about the end of our embrace, which made two of us in a less than generous frame of mind for dealing with rabid fans. But he signed his name and even wrote a few brief messages into the autograph books that had magically appeared out of pockets, purses and even hats.

The woman who'd first noticed him turned her attention to me with a sharp look and sharper question.

"Who are you? You're not Carla. And you're certainly not Letitia."

These fans who insisted on thinking Johnny and character Greg Noble were one and the same were almost frightening in their intensity and devotion. I tried to think up a suitable response to her inane question. Nothing came. Then, from nowhere, a soap demon overtook me. I smiled and fluttered my lashes.

"I'm Vanessa. I'd been hot-air ballooning and landed on the beach when Gregory's parachute crashed but I couldn't help him because I was in a wheelchair at the time and also suffering from amnesia. I'm Carla's long-lost illegitimate daughter."

Johnny buried his face in his cap. I could hear muffled choking, coughing and laughter. The women merely nodded as I recited this absurd bit of creative characterization. The fact that the actress who played Carla was at most three years older than I didn't seem to bother them. The lady I'd heard referred to as Margaret walked around the bench scrutinizing me from all angles.

"You don't look much like Carla, but then, we all know her reputation with men. Who's your father?"

Johnny nearly crawled under the bench on that one. He grinned at me and waited to see what kind of brilliant response I could come up with. Inspiration suddenly came from the Muzak playing over the rink's loudspeaker. An oldie from the seventies. "Could it Be Magic?" Ricky used that song in class all the time for six-minute long stretches. I knew it well and knew the composer and singer also. I smiled at the ladies.

"Um. My father is royalty. He's a baron. Uh, Baron Manilow."

The women all formed little "OH's" with their mouths.

"We don't know him."

It was time to put an end to the farce. I wanted Johnny all to myself again for my skating lesson. Besides, I didn't know how much longer I'd be able to keep up the pretense or how much more tripe my devious mind could provide.

I nodded, adding with great conviction, "Well, you haven't seen him yet. To be honest, it's a secret. In fact I shouldn't have told you this much. But you're obviously loyal fans and I know you won't reveal a word to anyone else. In fact, please pretend you haven't even seen us here. If the news got out about Vanessa and Gregory, well, I don't even want to imagine!"

They nodded, hugged each of us in turn, and went off in

search of popcorn and hot beverages. Johnny again covered his whole face with his floppy hat to hide his laughter until the ladies were out of sight.

"You are an evil woman, Abby Fouchet. Have I ever mentioned that I love evil women?"

"I believe that was understood from the get-go."

He pulled me to my feet and kissed me once more. Then we resumed the tentative circle around the rink. Johnny kept one hand under my elbow and the other on the small of my back. After about three times around I felt daring enough to take a glide on my own. "Vanessa Manilow" might end up wrapped around a tree at the end of the rink, but if she was going to learn to skate, she had to go solo sometime.

I loved it. I sailed across that ice as though I'd been skating daily for years. Having a dancer's balance helped. Johnny clapped and cheered when I made an entire lap by myself as though I was his kid getting ready for junior Olympic tryouts. He grabbed me and hugged me. Then we skated off together, arms linked.

After about an hour of this vigorous exercise we needed refreshments. We headed towards the snack bar. Johnny turned back to ask me what I wanted, then his entire demeanor changed. He stiffened.

"What's the matter?"

"Nothing. I mean, nothing to do with you. Just saw someone I didn't expect to see today and would have preferred not to see at all."

I looked around. Standing outside the rink by the bridge was the girl who'd been with Johnny at O'Malley's last fall. Gotta be Tracy. Next to her was the most gorgeous man I'd ever seen in my life. A familiar image. Tracy's chauffeur? The man should be hired at the Met as an extra in Wagnerian operas. I could envision him wearing horns on his head and holding a huge spear in his hand. Intensely blonde, with shaggy hair lightly dusting his shoulders, he also had a body rivaling an Olympic-class bodybuilder's. The cold apparently didn't faze him. He wasn't even wearing a coat. Probably didn't want to hide that superb physique currently stuffed into his black suit.

Johnny's expression was tight.

"I think we're done skating. Let's collect our stuff and maybe head for a warm pub somewhere."

My delight in the day had turned as chilly as the weather. I'd been teasing about being cold earlier, but this was really the first time I noticed.

"Sure. Okay."

We silently took off the skates then returned them to the attendant. Johnny retrieved the picnic basket. We walked slowly out of the rink and crossed through the park towards West 79th. All I could hear inside my head was Shay's voice saying, "The drooling rich bitches win."

Something whizzed past my ear. Johnny pushed me to the ground and I gasped out, "What the hell was that? A bee? In winter? Talk about your survivors!"

"*Shsshh*. Abby, keep down. That was no bee. That was a bullet."

I'd never felt this kind of terror in my life. Of course I'd never had a bullet fly by my face either. I suddenly, and quite irrelevantly, recalled my conversation with Shay about casting bullets and auditions. What was that original military theory? Oh, yeah. "You never hear the one that gets you." Well, that was a good sign, then. I had *very* clearly heard that bullet zip by. Guess that meant I wouldn't die of gunshot wounds. Not yet.

I was also remembering my vision. Central Park. Snow. Gregory Noble. Bullets. Yep. The whole enchilada.

"Johnny? What's going on? Is it cops chasing a mugger or something?"

"No. They wouldn't shoot with innocent bystanders close

by and they don't normally take aim at muggers anyway. Abby. Stay down."

I did. I knew the idea of cops shooting at muggers was dumb. But I liked it better as a possible scenario to the reality that someone was intentionally shooting at Johnny and me.

We stayed on the ground for another few minutes. I heard a voice yell, "Over here!" then two men dressed in gray jogging sweats with Columbia University logos dropped down beside me and started checking my pulse.

"You okay? We saw some guy with a gun about a hundred yards from here. Tried to follow, but lost him at the edge of the park. Thought you might have been hit. Whoever it was is long gone. I think it's safe now."

They helped us up. Johnny brushed dead leaves mixed with snow off our clothing while I tried not to fall back down in a faint. Johnny assumed his Gregory Noble hero façade and bravely reassured our rescuers.

"We're okay. Really. Did you guys get a good look at the shooter?"

"Not good enough. Bizarre thing, though. He was dressed in a suit. Not your average mugger."

The smaller of the two men looked at us both. Suspicion described both his expression and his tone.

"You know anybody with a grudge against you? From what we could see this guy took direct aim at you."

Johnny shook his head. So did I.

"I have no idea who it could be. Probably some nut looking to mug somebody and too stupid to ask for the wallets up front."

Johnny's explanation bordered on puny, but I liked it better than the other theories still lurking in the back of my mind. I smiled tentatively at the pair.

"This may be crazy, but Johnny here is on one of the soaps and he gets noticed a lot. In fact people mistake him for his character all the time. I wonder if this might be some lunatic fan out for publicity. Maybe even revenge for something his character did on the show."

They both stared at Johnny.

"Wait. That's why you look familiar. A bunch of the guys in our Abnormal Psych class watch your show. I've seen a couple of episodes on the tube at the Student Center."

(Oh no, here it comes. He's going to say, "You're Gregory Noble!" and ask for his autograph.)

Instead, the young man looked back at me with admiration in his gaze.

"You may be on to something there, you know. The obsessed fan theory. I was reading about the cops hauling in some kook with a knife just two weeks ago. He'd been stalking an actress from one of the prime-time detective shows. Some of these people truly are deranged."

He smiled.

"If they weren't so dangerous, it'd actually be lots of fun to deal with them and figure out what goes on in their heads. We're both Psych majors. Crazy people are going to be our business!"

I thought perhaps that might not be the best way to refer to one's future clients, but I wasn't going to argue with a rescuer.

Johnny looked intently at the taller of the two.

"You said you chased him? Did you see where he went?"

"Not really. I lost him when he jumped into a limo at the edge of the park and tore off down 6th Ave. Blended in with about six other cars waiting at the light. Interesting. What kind of kooky fan rides around in a white limo?"

Johnny turned ashen white. He stuck out his hand and nodded to the jogging future psychologists.

"Thanks for your help. I think we're okay now."

They shook hands with him and looked again at me.

"Miss? Are you sure you weren't hit? You're bleeding."

I glanced down. Blood was seeping out from a small tear in my jeans. I hadn't felt any pain until they noticed it. Now it hurt.

Johnny knelt down and examined my leg.

"Oh, crap. It's your knee. It's not a bullet. Looks like you may have fallen on something really sharp. I'd better get you home and get this thing cleaned. Doesn't look like you need stitches, but the sooner it's washed the better."

"What the heck could have done that?"

We all looked around. The culprit was immediately visible. An old sundial with broken hands lay gleaming in the afternoon sun. One of the hands had spots of blood.

I began to laugh uncontrollably.

"This is great. First I'm shot at by a rich lunatic, then I'm scarred for life by a sundial. Done in by time. In my prime. What's next? A bolt of lightning will suddenly zap me where I stand?"

I was getting a little hysterical.

One of the joggers nodded.

"Delayed shock. Just now hitting, I imagine. You'd better get her someplace warm and find some hot tea with lots of sugar."

Johnny nodded at the diagnosis. I snorted.

"I'd prefer Tanqueray. Perhaps in hot chocolate."

Johnny quickly grabbed my hand and began to lead me off.

"Thanks again, guys."

"Hey, no problem. We didn't do much of anything, though. Sorry we couldn't catch the creep. But we'll watch for you on the soap. Wait'll we tell the guys at the dorm."

They ran off back into the park, and Johnny and I slowly started walking towards my apartment building. He stayed silent. I tried to make the situation a bit lighter.

"Well, looks like you just built more of an audience for the show. The producers will be happy."

His jaw set. He stopped and slammed the hamper onto the ground and kicked it once. "I'm sorry. I'm just so damn angry I can't even talk. Some goon takes a shot at us and I can't do a thing to stop it. And I don't know why it happened in the first place. I'm so sick of being on this stupid show anyway!"

I stopped and faced him directly.

"Johnny. I saw that blonde man with Tracy at the rink. I know you think he's the one who let loose those bullets. And he's no fan. Please tell me what's going on. Why would someone shoot at us?"

He shook his head.

"I can't. For one thing, I don't *know* what's going on. And I honestly can't believe that he'd be shooting at me. There's just no reason. And I wish I could tell you more about Tracy, but I've promised her and someone else I'd keep quiet about— well—certain things. I can't go back on my word."

"Fine."

I matched him now in anger. I didn't know what this woman's hold was, but it must be pretty tight. We continued our walk. When we got to the stoop at my building he turned and tried to take me in his arms.

"Abby. Please believe me. Tracy is not a threat to us. She has nothing to do with you."

"Not a threat? The fact that her chauffeur is using us for target practice isn't a threat?"

He smiled.

"I meant that in the romantic sense of the word. I know you. You're more concerned about my so-called affair with Tracy than you are about bullets flying! She doesn't mean anything to me. Believe me. We're not sleeping together and never have. As for the other, maybe your theory about some nut is right. It doesn't make sense for Siegfried to be trying to hurt me."

"Siegfried? His name is Siegfried?"

"Yep."

"Jeez, he *is* poster boy for the Aryan Nation. How perfect! Does he speak anything but German?"

Johnny burst out laughing. "Come to think of it, I've never heard him speak."

He gazed at me with admiration and affection.

"You're quite a brave little dancer, Abby Fouchet. People shoot at you and you still crack jokes. You're also still bleeding."

I glanced down. He was right.

"Oh, hell. I wonder if I'll have a scar. I wonder if that matters. I guess only if I have the chance to do another *Hair* audition and this time they ask for the nude scene. What am I saying? I guess I am in a bit of shock after all."

Johnny shut his eyes for a second.

"Look, I need to get you home. You sure you're okay? Going to be able to handle life without me as of tomorrow? Could be dull, you know. Especially after today."

"I'll survive. I have dance class and my job at the health club and at least five auditions coming up. I'll stay busy."

Johnny was heading down to Philadelphia for the out-of-town tryouts for *Jesus Christ Superstar.* He'd be gone a month but I already had visions of the two of us wandering arm and arm around Independence Hall and snapping pictures by the Liberty Bell when I came to visit.

We walked home in silence. Johnny left me at my stoop after depositing a nice brotherly kiss on my cheek.

"I'll be in Philly by tomorrow afternoon. You have the name and number for the hotel. But if you get scared during the night, give me a call. Abby, I think this was just a fluke. Really. Probably a crazy soap fan just like you said out to see if he could get some publicity. Or just because he doesn't like Gregory Noble. Don't worry about it. I can't see it happening again."

I didn't buy the fluke or the fan. But I said nothing. How

could I explain that those Granny Dumas genes screaming "This isn't over" were stronger than any reassurances my uncertain actor could provide?

EIGHT

I WAS HAVING TROUBLE dialing our home number, perhaps because the tears splashing down my face were blinding me. I punched the coin release, retrieved my quarters, and tried again. At least this time I got a ring. After three of them, I heard Shay's voice.

"Yo."

"Shay?"

"The one and only. What's up, babe?"

I started sobbing. Her voice changed to immediate concern.

"Abby? Abby? What's wrong? Are you hurt? Have you been mugged? Abby!"

I managed to subdue the loud sobbing into mere sniveling.

"Shay, this has not been a good day."

"I can tell that. Are you hurt?"

"No."

"Have you been mugged?"

"No."

"Are you in jail?"

"No."

"Abby. Talk to me. First of all, what are you doing back in New York? You're supposed to be visiting Johnny in Philly."

I began to sob again.

"Uh-oh. Is Johnny okay? Is he hurt? Has he been mugged? Oh, hell, this is nuts. Abby? Damn it. What's going on?"

"It's Johnny. We…I…it's all off. I'm not doing too well. Uh, could you meet me here?"

"Sure."

There was a pause.

"Where's here?"

I looked around. I hadn't even noticed where I was, just found the first available phone booth that contained a phone in working order and didn't have a flasher trying to entertain me.

"I'm at 75th and Central Park West. I'm gonna run some errands and I'll see you at the bench closest to the Park."

"Errands? What errands? Abby, what are you doing?"

I hung up. I knew she'd be there.

Twenty minutes later, Shay found me sitting on a moderately clean bench just inside Central Park. She plopped next to me and stared.

"This is not good. It's January. You're wearing nothing but a teensy little jacket over your teensy little T-shirt. You are draped over a bench with a bottle of Tanqueray in one hand, a pack of Mavericks in the other, and a king-size bag of M&M's in your lap. Putting aside the fact that you don't smoke and seldom drink, how can you swig gin and eat M&M's at the same time?"

"It helps with the digestion," I informed her with solemn dignity.

"How much booze did you consume before you bought this bottle?"

I was deeply offended. I said as much.

"I am deeply offended, Shay Martin. My friend. What did you ask? Oh, how many drinks. Not many. I think it was two at the train station in Philly and three at that little bar on 73rd. It's a nice train station."

"Jeez, Abby, I've never known you to drink like this. Even when you tore your ligament you stopped at like two glasses. What the hell happened?"

"I told you. Johnny and I are off. *Kaput. Ixnay.* No more."

"Yes, you said that. The question is why and how?"

I considered this as carefully as my addled brain would allow.

"That's two questions. Have a sip. You're gonna need it. Hey, have a cigarette!"

Shay took both. She too was neither a smoker nor a drinker.

"Good Lord. What is this?"

"Issa, 'scuse me, *it's* a Maverick. Generic ciggies. I figure since I don't smoke, why pay for expensive stuff? And it sounded Texan. I miss Texas."

Shay reached for the bottle again without answering. For the next few minutes, we sat and sipped, smoked without inhaling, coughed and crunched chocolate-coated peanuts.

Shay finally crushed out her cigarette and took a long drink. "Spill it. Tell me the sordid story."

"He's having an affair with Mary Magdalene."

There was silence.

"Would you mind repeating that?"

I began to cry. "He's having an affair with Mary Magdalene. You know what I mean. With the girl who plays her."

THE COMPANY OF the *Jesus Christ Superstar* revival was still enjoying pre-Broadway tryouts in Philadelphia. Johnny had gone to Philly with the company the day after our skating date. A week later, I'd gotten cast in *Escape,* an Off-Broadway show preparing for its own tryout here in Manhattan.

Midway through the music rehearsal yesterday, our stage manager announced that the director had come down with mumps. Anyone who hadn't had them as a kid needed to be checked. An expression of sheer panic spread over the face of the musical director, a newlywed. He ran out of the room without another word. The cast was given ten days off before starting rehearsals again. Those that hadn't had the disease before were exhorted to not only see a doctor, but stay quarantined.

I've had every childhood disease ever invented. I remember cute pictures of me with huge little cheeks playing under the Christmas tree when I was about five. I was healthy. Free to roam the country if I so chose. I decided to use my unexpected vacation and pay a surprise visit to Johnny in Philadelphia.

Johnny had been phoning me daily while he'd been out of town—a total now of three and a half weeks. I assumed he'd be thrilled to see me. I also assumed I'd watch a rehearsal, we'd go off and play tourist for a while, admire the various historic buildings of Philadelphia, possibly find a nice club for dancing, and end up in a thoroughly delicious and compromising position back at his hotel.

After telling the stage manager of *Escape* my destination, I went home, packed a light bag and took a cab down to Penn Station. I boarded the late-afternoon train to Philly. Two hours later I was in another cab on my way to the downtown hotel where the cast was staying. The desk clerk kindly and illegally gave me Johnny's room number and I hauled myself and my bag upstairs to Room 502.

The door was slightly ajar and I could hear voices, so I thought I'd just pop right in and reacquaint myself with whichever cast member he was talking to. I flung open the door. The first thing I saw was Johnny Gerard, sprawled ungracefully on his stomach on the bed. His bare back gleamed in the early evening light.

It took about three seconds to see why it was gleaming. A statuesque blonde was pouring oils over it and massaging them in.

The pain hit in the pit of my stomach. I took in the scene; Johnny half-naked, the oils and the bed. Then I took immediate action. There was a lamp on a table close to the door. Admittedly, it was an ugly lamp, but it probably didn't deserve the treatment I gave it. I threw the lamp with all possible force at the pair, who had yet to notice me. That got their attention.

I screamed something on the order of "You double-dealing copper-headed oily Irish snake!" then whirled out of the room and literally ran out of the hotel. A cab was sitting right in front of the lobby outside. A nice-looking elderly couple had just finished depositing their bags on the sidewalk. I nearly ran them down, but had enough presence of mind to yell an apology before jumping in and screaming at the driver to get me to the train station with all available speed. He did.

I had to wait forty minutes for the next train to Manhattan, which was just enough time to down the first batch of gin and tonics in a nice little pub. I didn't see much of the scenery on the trip back. It had nothing to do with the late hour. My eyes were filled with tears and my vision with Johnny and that woman. I remembered her. She was playing Mary Magdalene in the show. Probably stole the damn oils from props.

Once back in New York, I stopped by a nameless bar on the corner of West 73rd and Amsterdam, ordered a few more gin and tonics and tried to discourage three overeager gents from escorting me to their apartment. There were peanuts at my table. The bartender refilled the bowl twice. I decided that meant I'd been eating enough to offset the booze. I still had enough presence of mind to find quarters in the bottom of my bag and call Shay from a booth near Central Park. The drugstore was only a block away, so I purchased candy and cigarettes. Then I headed over to the liquor store and spent my few remaining dollars for a quart of Tanqueray. I carefully made my way to the park and found an empty bench. Shay was not long in arriving.

"I was going to surprise him," I sniffled. "Ha! I repeat. Ha! *Surprise* wasn't the word. Maybe *stupefaction,* or *incredulity* or…"

Shay tapped me lightly on the head.

"Stop going through the Thesaurus. What happened in Philadelphia?"

"I walked into his hotel room, which had stupidly been left unlocked and found Serena Ballinger massaging his body. That mindless bimbo doesn't even have the ability to find the correct pitch for 'I Don't Know How to Love Him,' but she sure has an idea of how to interpret the song—oils and all."

Shay was staring at me.

"What?"

"You never cease to amaze me. You're tossing M&M's into your mouth like popcorn, swigging gin, choking on Mavericks, drunk as the proverbial skunk, and you're making remarks about 'correct pitch' and 'song interpretation.' For God's sake, Abby, your boyfriend was making it with another girl! You should have thrown your suitcase at him. You should be screaming. You should be mugging handsome men in retaliation."

I got up and walked unsteadily around our bench to breathe in a bit of fresh air. The fact that the fresh air was freezing did not deter me. My voice even sounded sober in my ears when I responded to Shay's comments.

"I do not do any of those things you juss meshoned. To begin with, throwing a suitcase would be not classy. In fact, it would be tacky. Minette raised me better'n that. And what is this obsession with mugging? Are you changing careers and becoming a cop? Or a thief? Hand me the bottle. Please. An' 'nother cigarette."

Shay handed me both and tried to suppress her laughter while I shakily lit a cigarette, inhaled, then coughed until tears ran down my cheeks.

"Don' laugh at me. I am having a crisis."

I sat down again. I couldn't seem to stand without the world tilting.

Shay continued to snicker. "I'm not laughing. Well, maybe a little, but not at your love life. Oh hell, give me the damn bottle. If you're gonna get drunk then I'm joining you. I mean, *my* romantic attachments aren't much better than yours."

"Well, your romances are faithful. I mean your attachments are faithful. You know what I mean. Fuji didn't speak English, but at least he wasn't playing the whole outfield. So to speak. I swear I don't know what's going on in that company. For a religious show these people are just shameless. Herod is having a fling with Judas, and Caiphus, who is supposedly married to Nina—'member her? The one with the 'normous boobs? Anyway, Caiphus is rumored to be engaging in un-natural acts with one of the female lepers, and one of the chief priests became a Unitarian last week. Maybe it was a Libertarian. I don' 'member anymore."

I looked at Shay.

"What?"

She was staring at me. The corners of her mouth were twitching uncontrollably.

"What?"

"Nothing. I just don't think the chief priest becoming either a Unitarian or Libertarian is relevant to the issue of sexual misconduct within the ranks of the *Superstar* cast."

"Oh, shut up. My love life has gone further south than Juarez on a Saturday night and you're lecturing me about non-sequitory things."

Shay finally broke out with a series of ear-splitting laughs. "Damn, you're amazing. Drunk and lucid at the same time. Is that what they teach you in the bars in Texas?"

"Excuse me, Ms. Martin, but at least I am not howling like a hyena on a park bench attracting the attention of the passersbys. I mean passerby that are passing by. I think I'm gonna be sick. Hand me the bottle will you? And a couple more M&M's? Especially the red ones. I like the red ones. I still can' b'lieve they make purple at Easter. Who wants a purple M&M? Stupid."

For the next hour we passed Tanqueray, M&M's and

Mavericks back and forth. We didn't talk. We critically, but calmly, watched people crossing in front of our bench under the lights, not even blinking at the pink-haired teen with the Semper Fi tattoo zooming by on roller skates holding a Picasso print. I was so depressed I didn't even notice the tall, bald-headed black man in gold lamé who was walking a chicken on a leash. (I take that back—him, I noticed. Well, at least the chicken.)

I broke the silence when I saw two joggers in Columbia University sweats heading towards us.

"Are we being shot at again?"

"What? Abby, did you say shot?"

"Yeah. Oops. I didn't tell you about that, did I?"

Shay grabbed the bottle from me and took a large swallow.

"No, you did not. When did you get shot at? This is nuts!"

I closed my eyes for a second. That was a mistake. The world started spinning. I opened them.

"It wasn't jush me. It was Johnny, too. Ashually, 'scuse me, actually, it was prolly Johnny all along. The day we had a picnic."

I told Shay what little there was to tell about the blonde man taking potshots at Johnny and me after we'd been skating and being helped by the two college kids.

"Abby! Why didn't you go to the police?"

I glared at my roommate.

"Because it wouldn't do any good. Besides, Johnny's father is a dishtrick attorney prosecuting machine and he will look into it."

I stated conversationally, "It was Tracy's chauffeur."

"What!"

"Don' you 'member? From O'Malley's? The big blonde in the tight suit. Straight out of opera or something. Running down Cookie I'll betcha. Should'a been wearing horns. That's what the psychologist shaid."

"You're seeing a psychologist? When did this start?"

I tossed an M&M at her. It was orange, so it didn't matter.

"No! The kids who rescued us were majors in psychological crazy shtuff. Don' you listen?"

"Not to this. This is just beyond shtoopid. And quit throwing chocolate at me. I swear, for a sweet Texas girl who's shupposedly well brought up, you are one heck of a tosher. Throwerer. Oh, hell, I'm slurring worse than you. Abby, why is Tracy's chauffeur shooting at him?"

I sniffed. "Because he's a rat. An unfaithful, Libertarian-wannabe rat." I burst into tears again.

Shay silently handed the bottle back to me.

It was past midnight when we finished the booze, the chocolate and the cigarettes. We weren't feeling too swift, but figured we needed to leave and make our way home before some overzealous cop decided to haul us in for unauthorized bench warming and public intoxication. With much tottering and clutching of shoulders and elbows, we helped each other to stand and began what seemed like an extraordinarily long trek towards our apartment. We could have sworn it was only five blocks away. We'd gotten to the corner of 76th and Central Park West when Cherry met us, sporting a micro-mini skirt, a long black cape and five-inch spiked leather boots.

"Abby! Hey! You okay or what?"

"I am just lovely. I am schnockered, but I am lovely. And lovelorn. And lovesick."

Cherry may not be the smartest babe on the block, but she does know a little something about male-female relationships. She understands "upset over men" the way I understand auditioning for summer stock. Both concepts are nothing short of brutal. She chimed right in with her opinion. One I shared.

"Johnny's a slime. Hey, ya want Vito and Guido to pay the

creep a visit? Listen, they'll take care of that whole stupid company. Aren't they the same people who broke your foot?"

I snuffled a little.

"'Ssokay. There's prolly a long line of chauffeurs taking aim at him out of revenge for their drooling rich-bitch passenger ladies! In their made up make-up."

Shay ignored my less than coherent comments. She was gazing without blinking at our roommate.

"I don't think we'll be quite needing the schervices of the brothers Mariccino, Cherry." She giggled. "Never minus. But I wanna know how you know wha' happened."

Cherry smiled. "Johnny called. Said Abby found him with that slut Serena. Well, he didden say slut, but I did."

She shook her head at me. "He knows you're pissed. Said he tried to explain she does therapy in the off season, but you wouldn't listen. I told him considerin' that he never explained away that Tracy girl, why should you listen now? He told me to mind my own business. Then he said tell you not to worry 'bout reimbursin' the hotel for the lamp. He's got it covered. Oh yeah. He don't got no concussion."

Shay tapped me politely on my shoulder.

"I thought you shed throwing things wasn't genteel. *Tacky,* I believe, was the exact word."

"I didden throw the lamp directly at Johnny the creep. I was aiming for one of those awful landscapey arty things cheap hotels seem to buy. Can I help it if Johnny happened to be lying underneath? You want good pitching, hire Fuji the heterosexual Ferry. By the way, whatever happened to him? Good ol' Fuji. Did the Men in Black get 'im?"

Shay sighed. "I told you this before. He got hired by the Cleveland Indians two days after I called off the wedding, thanks to your clever comments about jail. 'Member? I'm still grateful to you that I didn't get married and move to Cleveland and get arrested, especially since I have just finally been hired by *Endless Time*. Did I tell ya that? They called today! Want me to do the dishco, 'scuse me, the disco-scene thingy. Fuji still wants the Yankees, mind you, but maybe this way he'll get to play against them now and then and they'll think he's so great they'll hire him."

I wasn't really listening anymore. I began to lurch forward. I felt my elbows being lifted by my two roommates. My feet were off the ground and my body was in a cab in less than a minute. We were home in less than three.

The rest of the night Shay, Cherry and I watched Bela Lugosi vampire movies on Channel 11. *Dracula. Son of Dracula. The Return of Dracula.* I remember vaguely wishing Bela would make a visit to Philadelphia to a certain actor, but when I voiced this all I got were sweet pats on the head from my fellow television viewers.

I don't remember much after Dracula returned for the third time, but when I woke up it was 10:00 a.m., the sun was shining with a fervor and someone was insistently ringing the buzzer. I knew it couldn't be the famed count. Vampires can't exist in sunlight, unless they're female singers with a yen for baritones.

NINE

SHAY WASN'T SPEAKING TO ME. It wasn't as though she was being rude; I might add that Shay wasn't speaking to anyone. Shay was nursing the hangover of the century and silently cursing me because I didn't even have a headache. Her first words, when I gently wrapped her fingers around a steaming mug of coffee, were to point out this obvious bit of inequity in the universe. She glared at me, red streaks piercing through the white area of her eyes.

"You don't even have a headache. Even with all the flippin' buzzing of the damn buzzer this morning *you* don't even have a headache."

"I know. I'm sorry."

"I hate you. You realize that, don't you?"

"I do. Here, have a croissant. Aren't you happy the bakery delivered them this morning after I called? That's why all the buzzing was, well, buzzing. They're nice and fresh."

"I still hate you. But I will take one and then I will maybe start to think about forgiving you for including me in your debauchery yesterday."

I handed her the croissant and curled up in the corner of the sofa.

"Would it make you feel better to know that I am incredibly depressed, totally miserable and completely heartsick?"

Shay's expression brightened considerably.

"Oh, yeah. That helps. Here. You might want to grab one or two of these yourself. Croissants were made for broken love affairs. As well as hangovers."

We sipped and chewed in comfortable silence for the next few minutes. The buzzing started again.

Shay groaned. "Damn. What is this? No one comes to visit for weeks, and when one is in pain for delving into too many vices at once, the stupid bell rings and rings ad infinitum."

I snorted. "This makes twice this morning, Shay. I wouldn't quite call that ad infinitum."

I pressed the buzzer, as usual, without bothering to see who was there.

Johnny Gerard stood in the doorway with an armful of red roses. I was highly tempted to shut the door in his face. But the sight of the roses proved too enticing. So did the sight of Johnny Gerard.

"Before you slam the door, may I please come in and talk to you, Miss Lamp-Tossing-Champ-of-the-Millennium? That's some right arm you've got. The Yankees should hear about you. By the way, these are for you. An early Valentine's Day gift."

I sniffed. Flattery was not going to help. Neither was a bunch of thorn-filled flowers, no matter how fat, red and gorgeous they were.

"I suppose if you must come in, you must."

I stood back from the door. He opened it wider and came in. He handed me the roses. I accepted them. I then took the opportunity to leave him standing in the living room while I searched the kitchen for a vase. When I returned, he was quite at home on the sofa playing with Ringo's ears. It's hard to stay angry with a red-haired Irishman who looks manly with an enormous stuffed animal in his arms, but I was determined to try.

I sat down in the antique rocking chair across from the sofa and began rocking with a fervor that sent the chair inching across the floor. If I didn't still my manic motion, I'd be out the window in less than five minutes. I slowed it down to a manageable tempo.

"Okay, Johnny. I'm listening. What have you got to say?"

"First of all, that you are one hell of a conclusion jumper. If they gave Olympic medals for the sport you'd win the gold. Why didn't you stay for thirty seconds in Philly to hear me out?"

"Because I didn't care to stand in your hotel room with Mary Magdalene and her oils lying on the bed. You are one low-down, filthy, tumbleweed ridden, horny toad!"

Johnny stared at me.

"You have the most amazing descriptions of anyone on the planet. Did you learn those in El Paso? I never heard them down in Houston. There we call people oil-stealing renegades."

"I don't give a damn what you do in Houston! Everyone knows there's so much chemical pollution down there it's no wonder they spawn cheating S.O.B.'s like you."

"Damn it, Abby. You're starting to get my Irish up. You are the most distrustful, non-listening imp I've ever had the pleasure to get involved with."

"Well, then you don't have to stay involved do you? And don't call me an *imp*. Imps are cute, lovable demons who are smart enough to keep away from Irishmen with more blarney than a score of stones put together. Why don't you just trot back to the city of Brotherly Love and Lord knows what other kind of love and hit on the rest of the *Superstar* cast. At least I didn't get shot at while you were playing oil-me-up with Mary Magdalene."

Johnny's ears turned red.

"Thanks. Thanks for not only not trusting me, but blaming me for the shooting incident as well. I really needed that."

Before I could respond, the phone rang. Johnny frowned.

"Let it ring."

"No, it might be important. I'm waiting for a call about a commercial I'm up for. Excuse me."

I knew darn well that call wasn't going to be about any commercial I'd auditioned for before going to Philadelphia. (Another dancing-pastry thing. Quick Oven Apple Turnovers, I believe. Shay hadn't even bothered to send in her résumé as a possible choreographer after the last two doughnut rejections.) The casting agent had told all of us who auditioned it would be at least two weeks before he called anyone, because he was going out of town and didn't want to leave people waiting by the phone.

But I needed to get away from Johnny's upcoming excuses about Serena the oil masseuse in Philly. I needed to get my breath back and clear my head from the scent of the roses and the more intoxicating scent of Johnny Gerard. I knew very well who was calling but picked up the receiver anyway. Wrong move.

"Hi, Minette."

"Abby. Why haven't you called? Didn't you get my message?"

I sighed. "Yes, Minette. I got your message. Shay told me this morning."

This was worse than trying to keep my equilibrium facing Johnny. Minette has got the worst timing of anyone I've ever known. Or the best, depending on point of view. She has the uncanny knack of insinuating herself into situations that are none of her business. She calls this protective mothering. She'd been leaving messages for the last two months about a teaching job in El Paso she'd heard about over Christmas. Apparently the last time I'd told her no, she hadn't bothered to listen.

"Well? Are you or are you not accepting Mr. Orlando's offer? He's called ever since I told him about you again at the fund-raiser for the mayoral race. I'll be hosting an Easter party soon and we could announce it then. It's lucky that Easter is early this year."

For just a moment that last sentence stopped my thought

processes. I actually understood it. Then the frustration of Minette's insistence on running my life took over.

"Minette. I thought we had this settled. I was going to wait until *Escape* was over and see how I felt then."

"Abigail. He told me this morning that another girl is interested. She's just gotten her Masters in Dance from TCU and has been pestering him about the job. You need to act quickly before he gives it to her."

"Minette? Look, uh. This is not a good time to talk. I have company."

Oops. Mistake. Never tell Minette you have company. Minette knows that company can mean only one thing— male company. I was in for it. The Inquisition could have used her talent for interrogation and intuitive knowledge of who's hedging and why.

"Who's there, Abby?"

"It's, uh, Johnny Gerard."

I tried to act casual since Johnny was listening to my every word.

"Minette, I told you about him a couple of weeks ago. Remember? He's the one who took me to the doctor when I hurt my foot."

"And he's the one who's on that ridiculous soap opera? *That* Johnny Gerard?"

"Yep. That's it, exactly."

I smiled weakly at Johnny who was studying Shay's Beatles vinyl album collection with more intensity than it merited.

"Abby. He's an actor."

"Thank you for sharing that piece of information, Minette. I know that."

"You don't need to be involved with an actor. My word, how completely unstable can you get? Why not just stand at the train station and advertise for hobos? Actors. Artistic men. Losers! All of them!"

"I don't think I want to discuss this right now."

"I don't care. Listen. Put this *actor* on the extension if you want. He might as well hear what I have to say."

Thank heaven for small apartments with one phone and no extensions. The last thing I wanted was for Johnny Gerard to get an earful of Minette's hostility to men in the arts. I have no idea where it comes from. My father is an architect and apparently that's okay, even though it leans heavily towards artistic talent. She calmed down a bit and tried to state her case with her own brand of logic.

"Abby. Do not let this man into your life. Do not fall in love with an actor. They tour, they sleep around, they can't earn a decent living. They're all below poverty level. They are not responsible, respectable people."

Johnny was squatting by my CD collection. I forgot I was mad at the massage-getting, slime-bucket, Tracy-dating actor who'd nearly gotten me killed in Central Park now sitting in front of me. I just wanted Minette to eat some of those slanderous accusations.

"Johnny?"

He looked up.

"What kind of salary do the regulars on a soap make?"

He looked a bit confused. "Let's just say a lot more than college professors and less than oil barons and computer moguls."

I repeated what Johnny had said to Minette.

"Does that sound irresponsible? Does that sound like a person not earning a living?"

"Abby. You're obviously not yourself right now. I'll call you back when this Johnny person is not in the room."

"You do that."

I slammed down the receiver and turned to Johnny.

"So? Is my mother right? Just because you're an actor does that give you carte blanche to sleep around and get oily, snaky little massages from overendowed sluts in musicals when you're out of town?"

I was yelling. Johnny bit back a snort and cackled like a bad Halloween witch in a cheap haunted house.

"You are such a dope. A sweet, wonderful, beautiful, jealous dope. My God, Abby. Do you really think I'm such a heel as to mess around with somebody the minute you're out of my sight?"

His voice thickened.

"I'm not my father. I will never be my father. Why am I going into that? Okay. Calm. I tried to explain the situation with Serena the night you went into your lamp-tossing routine after waltzing unannounced into my room, and then tried to tell your idiot roommate what the deal was when I called, but none of you wanted to listen."

"Cherry's not an idiot. A bimbo, maybe, but she's actually pretty sharp."

Johnny smiled. "I'm sure she is. Anyway. Please hear me out now. Okay?"

I nodded, angrier now with Minette than Johnny Gerard, and hoping he'd actually have some reasonable story to justify his abominable behavior. I sat back down in the rocker. Johnny sat back down on the couch.

"Serena Ballinger happens to be a licensed physical therapist as well as a singer. I wrenched my shoulder out of line trying to master the intricacies of the whip that Pilate uses for the thirty-nine lashes. Serena is happily married with two kids and does not harbor a yen for me or any other male in the company. She adores her husband. She was doing me a favor by trying to heal my shoulder since I couldn't find a doctor after hours in Philly."

Johnny grinned.

"By the way, she said to tell you you've got a wicked right arm and that she would have thrown the lamp, too. She felt it showed your good taste in destroying the ugliest piece of hotel décor she'd seen in years."

I was quiet for at least a minute. I've never felt so stupid in my whole life. Johnny flashed a leprechaun's grin at me. I ducked my face into the stuffed fur of Mischa who'd been hiding in the corner of the rocking chair. I came up for air a minute later and stared at the floor.

"Johnny. I'm so sorry. I don't usually react that way. Really."

That was feeble. Johnny knew it was feeble. Johnny waited for the rest of my apology. So I gave it.

"I guess it's the strain of hurting my foot and being upset about not being able to be in *Superstar.* And getting shot at didn't help. Then I get in a show and everyone gets mumps. And let's face it. You're a bit reticent about certain relationships in your life. Then I have to listen to Minette always telling me to marry a lawyer and teach dance in Texas and stay away from any and all male actors. That's what part of that little phone call was about."

I kept rambling to avoid crying. I could feel it coming.

"You heard my end of the conversation? That was in response to her nasty comments about anyone I might date in theatre. Of course, she also doesn't want me dating anyone who's not in the state of Texas right now. But that's another story. You know how you don't want to be your father? Well, I'm trying really hard not to either turn out like Minette or let her rule my life."

I couldn't control the tears that had started streaming down my face. My nose started running in sympathy with the water. I could feel my eyes puffing out.

Johnny rose from the sofa, deposited Ringo on the coffee table, and began to approach my rocking chair. I jumped up and backed away into the kitchen. The look in his eyes warned me that I was about to have physical contact of the most pleasant kind with the man I'd been dreaming about for weeks. Months.

I felt like a seven-year-old boarding her first Ferris wheel at the fair. The anticipation was tremendous. I knew the ride would be beyond joyous, but I was terrified just the same.

I inched away from Johnny until my back was touching up against the refrigerator. The cold was doing nothing to keep the warmth rushing through my body at bay. Johnny wrapped his arms around me and held me. For a long moment I rested against his chest, inhaling and drinking him in. He gently lifted my chin with his fingertips and forced me to tilt my head up. Neither of us spoke. He wiped the tears from my cheeks with a handkerchief (how many guys actually carry them?) and carefully bent down and kissed me.

He ran soft hands through my hair and traced the length of my jaw with his lips, then went a bit lower. Chills on my back from the refrigerator vied with chills down my front from Johnny's touch.

I felt his hands go to my waist then slip under my shirt and softly began an ascent upwards. His mouth was roaming freely over mine. I returned his kiss with the energy of weeks of pent-up feelings. I slowly slid down the length of the fridge to the floor. Johnny eased down as well.

I managed to get myself in a comfortable position on the kitchen mat and Johnny managed to get himself in a comfortable position on top of me. His body was meeting mine in every place guaranteed to set my senses spinning.

"Hey, Cherry! Whatcha got in the fridge? Any fresh Parmesan? We want spaghetti."

Johnny and I hastily broke apart and sprawled across the floor as a pair of intruders wearing red-and-purple Hawaiian-print shirts topped by orange blazers barreled into the kitchen. The two of them stared at the two of us like we were the ones interrupting their foray into fine Italian cuisine at Apartment Seven-D.

"Hey, you guys okay? You hadda fall or sumpin'? Ya need help gettin' up? Anybody hurt here?"

A hand reached down and lifted Johnny to his feet. Another

did the same for me. I was breathless from Johnny's kisses and the thought of what else might have transpired had we been allowed to continue. But I maintained enough composure to get a good look at this pair of Good Samaritans, then immediately stifled what threatened to be a case of hysterical laughter.

The intrusive gentlemen were twins who had obviously never gotten over Mom dressing them alike as kids. Not only were the brightly colored shirts the same, but so were the black horn-rimmed glasses, the brand-new blue jeans, the tennis shoes with laces untied, and the hair slicked back by what seemed to be a gallon of Vaseline. Duplicates in every way. Neither had reached a height above 5'4" or a weight over 130. Johnny was shaking next to me. I wasn't sure if the cause was passion denied or if he was holding back his own merriment. I held out my hand to the newcomers, thankful that I hadn't had to re-button any clothing or put anything back on.

"Hi. I'm Abby. This is Johnny. You must be friends of Cherry's?"

Two hands shot forward with instant and identical politeness.

"Vito Mariccino."

"Guido Mariccino."

Both: "How ya doin'?"

That did it. I had to turn back to the refrigerator and pretend to search for a soda. These were the famous Mariccino brothers. Cherry's bodyguards. The bouncers from The Squirrel Shot Gentlemen's Club on 8th Ave. The pair looked like they'd just come from a meeting of a high school chess club, circa 1956.

Even as that thought zipped through my brain I could detect unusual bulges under the blazers near the palm trees of the shirts the brothers were wearing. I looked at Johnny and knew he'd seen the same thing. I guess what they lacked in height was made up for by way of Saturday night specials. I didn't really want to know.

Vito (or was it Guido?) was staring at Johnny with a growing and frightening intensity. I was beginning to get worried when his twin displayed a perfect set of capped white teeth in a grin larger than the vegetable drawer in the fridge.

"Vito! You know who this is? Right here in Cherry's apartment? This is Gregory Noble from *Endless Time!* Wow! I can't believe the luck here!"

Vito began to pump Johnny's hand with renewed enthusiasm.

"We been watchin' you every day for two years! Loved the whole thing with Carla, the babe on the beach. 'A course, she's no good for you. Letitia is a much better broad even if she is kinda skinny. And now that ya know Abby, that's even better. Cherry likes her and that's good enough for us.

"But we been worried. What happened after the parachute failed a couple of months ago? Are you still in a coma?"

TEN

THE SET FOR *ENDLESS TIME* had been set up for the disco scene in a non-existent club called Retro Survival. A recycled mirror ball hung from the ceiling. Posters of *Saturday Night Fever* and *Thank God It's Friday* were plastered over every inch of wall that didn't already have a mirror hanging on it. The main attraction was the huge green-and-orange platform near the wall closest to the "entrance." A black male sporting a great-looking 70's-style Afro haircut wearing a three-piece John Travolta–style white suit and five-inch platform shoes hunted through a stack of records in the back of the platform. The records were made of real vinyl. Not CD's. The artistic designers were bringing back the age of disco in all its neon-orange-glow glory.

I sat at a small table with three other extras who'd been cast to dance. When Shay had gotten the job as choreographer, she'd put in a good word for me and since *Escape* was still on hold, I was able to do the soap. Johnny, as Gregory Noble, was still in a coma, but this was supposed to be a dream sequence so he'd ended up the main attraction of the scene. The *Superstar* producers had given him two days to come back to New York and tape the show.

Johnny crossed over to my table and held a hand out. I stood and accompanied him to the dance floor.

The deejay waved vigorously. A sign below his grandstand proclaimed him to be "Dr. Heat." Apparently he also played the good doctor who happened to be the specialist taking care of Gregory Noble.

I turned to Johnny and whispered before the cameras began to roll. "The 'doctor' is the doctor?"

He grinned. "I'm in a coma, remember? These are my unconscious yearnings. I'll introduce you later. Our Dr. Heat in the disco is better known as 'Marcus Montgomery,' M.D., super-neurologist, cardiologist and probably proctologist as well. Although they haven't tried any prodding and poking in that area. Yet. Give them another month. Our head writer is wicked. Listen, do you want to go—?"

He was interrupted by the director yelling, "Action." We stopped talking and started dancing.

Dr. Heat cranked up what sounded like the beginning of Donna Summer's "MacArthur Park"—the long version. The one that lasts for at least fifteen minutes. I was hoping Johnny would be able to tell me whatever it was he'd planned to say, but we were busy trying to breathe.

Shay had told us to take to that dance floor like Marines taking the beaches across the world and make it our own. She'd added elements of cha-cha and mambo to the disco swing and then thrown in a lift or two. As long as I didn't have any runs ending in a *grande jeté* at a tenor, I was happy.

Johnny spun me out again and we finished the song in a flurry of lifts and spins and dips. Then we walked back to the table.

The next few hours were a whirlwind of music, heat, sweat and no chance for private talks. Until Johnny and I were able to dance to a ballad.

He was holding me a bit closer than Shay had requested, which was fine with me. This sequence focused more on Dr. Heat, Letitia and Carla conversing by the platform about parachutes and murder attempts. I caught the last part of their scene.

"He's lapsed into a coma again!"

"What happened? Last I heard he was mending nicely."

"I believe he tried to win the disco contest at Retro Survival and it proved too much for him."

A quick cut to a shot on the monitor of Johnny in the hospital bed, hooked up to tubes and smiling. I choked.

"Johnny! Look at the monitor! They've got you looking happier than a clam hiding in the sand at a bake!"

"I know. I know. They taped that last week. Told me to smile and think good thoughts."

"Which were?"

He grinned at me.

"Things Irish choirboys are not supposed to mention to innocent girls from El Paso, Texas."

A movement near the far camera caught my eye. Two people staring at Johnny. I squinted in the dim light. Not Tracy. Not the chauffeur. Two men. One was a replica of Johnny twenty-odd-years from now. The other was a blonde man who could have challenged Tracy's chauffeur in the Olympic bodybuilders of Germany contest. Another hunk. Every female not engaged in speaking lines was staring.

I poked Johnny as we rocked side to side and waited for our cue to start a more energetic dance.

"Who's that? Isn't that Kieran over there?"

Johnny turned.

"Oh, hell. Yeah, it's Kieran. I invited him to watch the taping today. One of the few times the set's not closed to visitors. I didn't really think he'd show up. Although he's probably got a pile of campaign brochures in his briefcase and will pass them out to the cast at the next break. And I see Chase Jaffert is next to him. His latest racquetball buddy. Kieran collects then discards them from the office pool of eager young prosecutors. You will note there is also an eager young female type standing just behind the great Kieran. He also collects *them*."

I looked. He was right. A gorgeous brunette of no more than twenty-three or so was standing to the left of Kieran

Gerard's shoulder, gazing adoringly at the man who was what? Her boss? Lover? Adopted dad?

I started to make a tasteless remark about bimbos in corporate clothing when I spotted another gorgeous brunette coming up on Kieran's right. I stopped. Tracy. Great. Was she now after father as well as son? Or just there as one of the specially invited guests? I said nothing, just kept dancing until a shout interrupted the flow of the scene.

"Johnny! Yo! Cut, everybody. Johnny Gerard! Call for you. Emergency. From St. Vincent's Hospital."

Silence covered the huge warehouse where this disco sequence was being filmed. I closed my eyes and prayed that Carlos "Cookie" Gutierrez hadn't left this life. Johnny's fearful eyes told me he was thinking the same thing. He hadn't said much about his friend lately, but I knew he'd been visiting daily until he'd had to go to Philadelphia.

He followed the stage manager to an office near the back of the warehouse. I joined Shay, standing by a camera operator a few feet from my original table.

"It's Cookie. I'm sure it's Cookie. I just don't know if it's good or bad news. I'm desperately hoping it's the former."

Shay nodded.

"I share your sentiments. Hey. Johnny's coming back. And he's smiling."

He was, indeed. His teeth shone under the lights of the disco mirror ball.

He yelled loud enough for the entire cast, crew and guests and nearby vendors on the street to hear.

"Cookie's out of the coma! Hot damn! He's bonkers, talking about guys wearing black and judges passing limos in the streets and fixing briefcases. But he's talking!"

Johnny grinned and lowered his tone a notch.

"Knowing Cookie he'll be asking for a cell phone and trying to get a deal on a wide-screen TV by tonight. For himself. He mumbled something about the hospital television set not being big enough. But he watched *Endless Time* today. Said he thought I did a lousy job of being in a coma. Thought I looked far too healthy."

The soap's director snorted and called for the cast to resume their marks on the dance floor. Johnny stopped to say something to Kieran and his entourage. His father appeared to be arguing with him. He finally nodded and left, taking the blonde hunk, the brunette bimbo and Tracy with him. Johnny quickly returned to my side. We hugged. He let a huge breath out.

"I can't tell you how glad I am that Cookie's gonna be okay. I really thought the doctors were about to announce pull-the-plug time. And he has no family here in the States. I honestly think it would have fallen to Kieran if such a decision had to be made." Johnny shuddered. "Not even going to go there. Although Kieran would make the right choice. He's a slime when it comes to women, and not great in his dealings with me, but he really likes Cookie. Told me more times than I can remember how valuable he is to the prosecutorial staff."

"Hey, Johnny! Yolanda Barrett's having her party tonight at her loft. Now that your roommie's better, wanta come?"

A pixie-faced, tiny blonde with more tattoos on her neck and arms than a Marine after a drunk sidled up to Johnny and me and delivered the invitation. She winked at me, then at Johnny.

"Bring Super Dancer here. It's time Yolanda had new blood to impress."

Johnny smiled. "Thanks, Mandy. Sounds like a plan. I need to blow off steam."

He turned to me. "Yes? Want to head down to the East Village for a good time?"

"How good a time? What exactly are Yolanda's famous bashes famous for? For that matter, who is Yolanda Barrett?"

Mandy answered before Johnny could say a word.

"Bite your tongue. At least around here. Yolanda Barrett is the six-foot-six-inched head writer for *Endless Time*. She's made and broken more acting careers in her life than I've had marriages on the soap. But she hides in an office behind a computer most of the time. So she and the other writers keep saying they have to have an outlet. Some of them shop. Some take drugs. Not that anyone would ever admit to it. Anyway, Yolanda just gives amazing parties on an almost monthly basis."

Johnny jumped in.

"Yolanda is also married to an ex-pro football player who's been smart enough to parlay his earnings on the gridiron into a multi-million-dollar computer business. They have the money to spend on the wildest soirees Manhattan has experienced since the Jazz Age. And they're usually legal. Lord knows what she has in mind for this one."

He nudged Mandy.

"Whatcha think? Parachute jumps in honor of Gregory Noble?"

He turned back to me.

"My 'attempted murder by unopened parachute' was her idea. Hmm. Let's see. Hot-air balloon rides? Bozo the Clown? Madonna flown in to entertain? Simple charades? Spin the bottle? Tarot card readings?"

Mandy giggled.

"Believe it or not, I think she's hauling out a Ouija board. I heard something about her trying to invoke the spirit of some hooker U.S.O. dancer type from the 1940's who serviced the troops on the docks of what is now Chelsea Piers. She's looking for more ideas for the show."

Johnny lifted an eyebrow.

"Oh, goodie. I'm sure Gregory Noble's next escapade will be time traveling to World War II and falling in love with that hooker."

I fluttered my lashes innocently.

"I like it. Sounds fun. I'm definitely in. At least for the party. And hey. If the soap *does* start casting for that hooker, I'm your girl. Just no nude scenes. My mother would go to Congress and push through legislation to get the show off the air."

ELEVEN

THE SOUND OF a dance party CD I'd seen advertised on TV months before was blaring away. I followed the vibrations. There was no need to ring the buzzer. People were standing in the stairwell leading to the loft and in the front doorway of the loft. People were dancing in the middle of the loft. People were dancing on the balcony outside the loft.

Two gigantic tables had been set up underneath two gigantic windows. Actors, singers, dancers and dates were crowding around the tables that held various enticing eats.

I myself felt an instant affinity for the seven-layer Tex-Mex dip and chips that boasted guacamole and olives and beans and at least two different cheeses. Then I became distracted by the homemade potato salad and the two Crock-Pots of *queso* that bubbled with or without sausage. Yolanda Barrett must have gone all out for her guests from Texas. Which as far as I knew were Johnny and me. For those not hailing from the Lone Star State there were cakes and cookies and pies and lemon squares. My palate and willpower were being assaulted from all directions. It was dieters' hell. I thanked the gods for the gift of the Dumas "eat everything and stay skinny" genes, then waded right in and piled a plate high with everything spicy plus at least three lemon squares.

The third and fourth tables had been set up for drinks. As rumored, Yolanda had not spared expenses. I asked for and was promptly given a huge glass of ice tea. I juggled both food and drink and found a vacant spot near what seemed to be Yolanda's bedroom. It was separate from the rest of the loft.

"Try the dip," Johnny mumbled. "It's phenomenal. Especially with those big chips. Fresh, hot, outrageously delectable. In a word—*yum*. I think I will ask for Yolanda's hand in marriage after the party if this is the kind of food she prepares."

I looked up. Johnny was stuffing tortilla chips into his face with as much delicacy as a dieter the last night before joining a weight club.

"I think Yolanda's husband, what's his name, Roger? Anyway, he might have something to say about that. According to your buddy Mandy. She told me about him the whole way down here. Thanks for hooking us up by the way. Saved me a long ride on the subway."

Roger Barrett was Yolanda's six-foot-eight-inch, gorgeous husband, the ex-pro linebacker. He hadn't lost an ounce of muscle or strength in the fourteen years since he'd retired from football.

Johnny eased his lean, lanky frame onto the floor next to me. "Good point. I'm not ready to die. I think I'll just see if the pair will adopt me."

We grinned at each other.

"So, how's Cookie feeling? Were you able to spend much time with him?"

Johnny had taken off from the *Endless Time* shoot immediately after we'd wrapped for the day and headed directly to St. Vincent's to talk to his newly cognizant roommate in person. He'd left me in Mandy's capable hands to get me to the party. We'd agreed to meet at the nearest food table to the entrance.

"Cookie's feeling better. Really weak and kind of out of it mentally—but, Abby! Just having him able to talk and joke and lift his head up now and then is miraculous. He's bitching about the cast on his rib and the cast on his leg and the fact that the nurses are all ugly. Oh yeah, he wants his cell phone as of yesterday. So I think he's on the mend. But he's really getting stuff mixed up. Kept trying to tell me about the day he got run down and was making no sense. Hopefully tomorrow he'll be better oriented. The police are supposed to go ask a few questions then and I can be there to help translate."

"Translate?"

He stuffed another *queso*-laden tortilla into his mouth and nodded.

"As well as being whacked out on whatever morphine drip they have oozing into him, Cookie has a very pronounced accent. I don't know why they can't just get a translator and let him speak Spanish. But since they found out little Johnny here speaks fluent Spanish, not to mention German and Italian, they decided not to use up city time bringing someone else along."

"Spanish, German and Italian?"

He grinned as I wiped a trace of oozing cheese off his chin.

"Spanish from Texas. The others from classical voice training. Opera nut, remember?"

I nodded.

A tall blonde I recognized as Letitia from *Endless Time* joined us. Johnny introduced her as Barbie. She resembled the doll of the same name to a frightening degree. She also appeared to have the hots for Johnny.

"Johnny, darling! I tried to call you to see if you wanted a ride here. I just got a new car. Jaguar. It's so awesome. I'll have to take you home."

"Thanks, Barbie. That's kind of you but I think I'll be escorting Abby to her place after the party."

She glared at me.

"It's a two-seater. I don't have room for you."

I choked a bit.

I debated as to the wisdom of leaving and letting the pair

sort out this ride-sharing question without me. I put my plate down on the floor and started to rise. Johnny pulled me back down.

"No you don't, Miss Dancer. You need to try this guacamole. It's excellent."

He scooped up some of the avocado dip onto a huge chip and handed it to me, while responding to Barbie's comments about the two-seater.

"Yo. Barbie. Focus. I gave you one ride after one taping of *Endless Time* when I had the loan of Kieran's Jeep. You gave me one after a taping when you had the loan of your roommate's SUV. This does not constitute a permanent carpool. I am taking Abby home via the subway or a cab. Got it? Okay?"

She was wise enough not to pursue that topic. I quickly changed the subject.

"So, what nutty stuff does this Yolanda lady have planned for tonight? Heard anything since you've been here? I keep waiting for helicopters to land on the roof and whisk us all away to Disneyland or something."

Johnny's eyes danced with impish delight.

"Nothing so elaborate, but possibly more dangerous. Remember when Mandy said she might be doing something vaguely occult? Apparently she couldn't find the Ouija board. So she's gone one better. She's hired a medium. I swear. Madam Euphoria will be conducting a séance at midnight."

My eyes popped wide open. My mouth dropped as well. He grinned at me.

"I'm serious."

"Madam Euphoria?"

"Hey, could I make up a name like that? Rumor has it that she's an old friend of Yolanda's who comes from a long line of madams. Sort of like the Barrymores or the Booths in theatre. Reading minds is the family business. I think they have a little shop up in Harlem."

Barbie stood up.

"I don't believe in that kind of garbage and I don't approve of it either. You two can do what you want. Excuse me."

She left.

I buried my face in a taco and mumbled, "Butt-swaying, narrow-minded, bottle-blonde, spandexed water moccasin!"

Johnny looked at me.

"What did you say?"

I blushed. "You weren't meant to hear that."

"Ha! All that dramatic training pays off. You were quite intelligible. And descriptive. Damn. I would pay money to see a spandexed, bottle-blonde water moccasin."

"Sorry. That was rude."

"Hey. She was rude to act the way she was acting. I mean, how nice of her to let us know we can do what we want. I really was anxious for her permission, weren't you? Forget her. Whaddya say? Shall we go summon up some spooks?"

"What is it about that phrase that chills me? Are you cold at all? I've been freezing for the last five minutes. Doubtless some psychic phenomena associated with ghosts. Or perhaps Yolanda has just turned the air down too low. I never have had decent circulation. Forget it. That makes no sense even to me. So. Spooks and séances. Do you know I have never even gone to a palm reader at a carnival? Although I have the Dumas second sight, so I'm probably more qualified to judge this séance than anyone here!"

Johnny's eyes danced.

"This is such a trip! I mean, how can we resist? If nothing else, it's great for the day some director casts us in Noel Coward's *Blithe Spirit*. Think of it as research."

"I don't know about this. Considering that I've had more than one psychic experience lately, I'm kind of afraid to get near anything resembling the occult, much less someone named Madam Euphoria." I grinned then. "Wouldn't you pay any amount of money to know her real name? Probably Lolita Fiona Theodora Kamelia Zibonowsky or something equally exotic. I'm sure Madam Euphoria was simpler to deal with. Fits on the mailbox."

Johnny got up, dusted a smattering of corn chips off of his trousers and pulled me to my feet. I held back for one more moment. "Are we really going in there? I'm suddenly terrified. I'll probably land in the distant past and witness the signing of the Declaration of Independence and either get burned at the stake for witchcraft or asked out on a date by Benjamin Franklin."

Johnny wagged his index finger at me.

"Come on, Miss Dancer. Maybe this is your chance for some answers about your great-granny's gift. So, show some *spirit,* girl!"

He jabbed me in the ribs, then started howling at his own pun as I winced at both the jab and the joke and shook my head. I went willingly, though, when he took my hand in his and led me through the loft towards the room that had been set up for Madam Euphoria's show. We had to pass through the kitchen first, which gave him an opportunity to grab a last taco that was enticing him from a plate near the stove. I helped myself to two more lemon squares and a brownie and stuffed the latter into my mouth as we looked for what Johnny was now calling Spook Central.

The space looked like it must be Yolanda's music room when it wasn't being readied for spectral visitations. Music stands, sheet music, a guitar and a computer with cables attached to an electric piano had all been shoved to one side to squeeze in the dining table that looked like it would hold a group of ten. Six people were already in the room, Yolanda among them. Johnny quickly made introductions. Yolanda stared hard at me and then gestured for us both to enter. She shut the door behind us and locked it. It was five minutes 'til midnight.

TWELVE

THE OTHER SÉANCE participants were Mandy, Mike Taggart (the director of *Endless Time*), Rolf (Mike's significant other), Tim Ashcroft (one of the dancers from this afternoon's taping) and the actor who'd played our deejay from Retro Survival, Dr. Heat. He nodded jovially to us and motioned for Johnny and me to sit next to him. No one said a word. At one minute before the witching hour, a second door opened from the back of the room and in walked the woman who would take us on a trip through Occult Land.

Her skin was a gorgeous café au lait, her eyes were a deep hazel, her tiny nose sported two rings while a third ring casually pierced the left side of her chin. She was wearing a huge pink turban, so I couldn't tell if she even had hair. The turban clashed loudly with the orange peasant top and red tiered skirt. Huge gold-circled earrings dangled from her right ear. Every finger sported a gold ring. Johnny was literally shaking next to me, trying to contain the laughter that threatened to spill out at any time. I knew if I looked at him directly embarrassing little puddles would soon appear under our chairs. The others in the group all looked solemn and prepared. Johnny squeezed my hand under the table and both of us took audible breaths as we tried to settle down.

Yolanda swept the room with a gracious gesture as she introduced the lady.

"Everyone, this is Madam Euphoria. She'll be our guide to the spirit world tonight."

Madam nodded to the group. The group nodded back. I

wondered who actually believed and who was there strictly for fun. Before I could really speculate about the others the lights dimmed. Madam asked for quiet (not that anyone had spoken a word) and instructed us to put our hands on the table, each pinky finger touching the pinky finger of the person they were next to. Johnny idly started caressing my little finger until Madam threw him a sharp look. He winked at me with his right eye while nudging my knee with his under the table.

Yolanda's antique grandfather clock chimed twelve times and I nearly jumped out of my seat. Even with all the Dumas women having second sight I'd never been involved in a séance and didn't know what to expect. Sweat trickled down my neck. I tried to keep my eyes focused but they kept blurring.

Madam moaned and chanted something to Black Hawk Hairy Chest, or whoever her spirit guide was. Probably a Native American from one of those nice old tribes like the First Church of the Pious Psychic Spirit. I banished the blasphemous thought and waited. The moans and groans continued until Madam slumped in her chair.

"Chief Blackie? Are you with us tonight?"

A different voice came from Madam's mouth. It was guttural and very male.

"I am here, Euphoria. I will guide you to those who wish to contact you from other realms of existence."

This was good. Very interesting, indeed. Chief Blackie spoke better English than the majority of the participants.

"Is there one among you named Michael?"

Mike's mouth dropped an inch.

"Yes! That's me! I mean I! I mean, oh hell, I'm Mike!"

I was afraid I'd end up having to perform CPR on the excited director at any moment. Madam Euphoria/Chief Blackie waved at him.

"You must not attempt the show you were considering. It will be the end of your career in television."

"Oh my word! How did you know? I mean, I was thinking

of doing *The Full Monty* in my hometown in Kansas for a summer gig if I can get the rights and we were going to do the last scene without the hats covering, uh, the guys, but if you think that won't work? My gosh, this is just amazing. I'll do *Annie* instead!"

Johnny's knee was pressing up against mine, since he couldn't signal me using his hand without being chastised by Madam. I bumped his knee back. Chief Blackie was explaining to Mike that Mission, Kansas, just wasn't ready for nude men on stage at this point in time and it would hurt his career back in New York. *How* was never really clear. I bit my lip to keep from laughing out loud, a feat that was growing increasingly difficult what with Johnny bashing my knee every five seconds. I threw him a "quit that" look, which of course did nothing to stop the kneesies under the table.

Madame/Blackie then smiled at Mike.

"You and Rolf are the perfect couple."

Mike beamed.

Johnny whispered in my ear.

"I know of at least two male dancers who were doing the disco sequence who think that *they* make up half the perfect couple with Rolf."

Madam/Blackie must have divined from our expressions an ever-growing skepticism because she quickly skipped over to Tim.

"Do you have a Great-Aunt Harriet?"

"Uh. Maybe. My grandma had at least seven sisters and my granddad had five and that was just on my father's side! I don't know who all's in the family."

"Harriet has passed beyond the veil now. She wishes to tell you she wants you to go to graduate school at her alma mater of the University of Tennessee."

Johnny snickered almost discreetly and muttered under his breath, "Beyond the veil? What the hell *was* Great-Aunt Harriet? An Arabian Knights belly dancer?"

I kicked Johnny under the table. "Sshh!"

We were met with frowns from both Madam Euphoria and Yolanda. Yolanda was next on this list of séance attendees. Madam told her to expect a new addition to her family in the next year or so, which seemed to delight the soap writer to no end. Dr. Heat patted her hand and waited to hear what the medium had to say to him.

"You must continue to work as the doctor. You do much good there. And you need to cut a CD with the jazz group where you play piano. But do not give up your day practice. It too is vital."

Johnny's knee was pressing mine so hard I was afraid I'd have bruises. He murmured *almost* inaudibly, "Don't give up your day job? Is that what the Chief just said? To a guy who makes more money playing on *Endless Time* than the mayor of our great city? This is great! I love it!"

"Johnny! Hush!"

I wondered what trite phrases the Chief would have for me. Maybe I'd finally find out whether *Escape* was going to resume or whether mumps would permanently disable the show.

Chief Blackie, in Madam's body, turned his/her attention to me.

Madam didn't even try to use the Chief's voice. She looked at me directly and her eyes widened 'til the whites showed more than those deep brown irises.

"Dear heaven. I see death."

That's it. That's all she said.

"What do you mean, 'dear heaven'? Whose death? Mine? Chief Blackie's?"

I was trying to make a joke and failing. This comment was not like those she'd made to the others at the table.

She shook her head and frowned

"You must make the choice. Are you more afraid of dying

in that little room on Centre Street or of a future after his death?"

She immediately turned her focus on Johnny. If I thought her reaction to me was bizarre, hers to him was far worse. She began to tremble almost uncontrollably. Sweat poured down from underneath the pink turban. The dark skin turned pale. The woman looked ill. Yolanda broke the circle by jumping up, toppling her chair to the floor, and hurrying around the table to shake the afflicted medium. Madam cried out once and then began to breathe normally. The color came back into her face. Everyone stared at her except me. I looked at Johnny. He looked pale as well. I squeezed his hand.

"What's going on?"

I kept my voice low. His lips tightened.

"Let's go. I think the séance is over for the night. At least as far as I'm concerned."

We stood. The rest of the group talked normally amongst themselves. They also studiously avoided both Johnny and me. Madam was sucking down a glass of ice water, but Yolanda had left her side and was now conversing with Rolf and Mike. Johnny and I made a quick exit and returned to the huge room with the music and the food. A dozen or more people were still dancing and enjoying themselves. We didn't even stop for a bite of the fabulous seven-layer dip. We just headed straight downstairs to the street. Neither of us spoke until we got outside. I was shaking as I took his hand and asked him for answers I knew he couldn't give.

"What the heck was that all about?"

I leaned against what had to be Barbie's brand-new red Jaguar and looked into his eyes. He pursed his lips and whistled tunelessly.

"I haven't a clue. Spooky, wasn't it?"

"Johnny, what was spooky is that everyone else in that crowd got the usual trite answers that anyone who knows anything about their personal lives could make up in an instant.

I mean, Mike and his shows. Dr. Heat and his day job. Tripe. All of it. Until she gets to us. I thought at first she might have an inkling of the visions I get, but what was all that stuff about death?"

"Search me. And at least, you didn't make the poor woman sick. I mean, that was just damned beyond bizarre. One look at me and she keeled right over. We're some pair, aren't we?"

A tall shape came up behind us. At first I was terrified. Then I calmed down when I recognized Madam Euphoria. She had discarded the turban and the pink-and-orange costume and was dressed simply in jeans and a jacket. Wisps of brown hair peeked out from under a black beret. She held up her hand.

"I'm so sorry! Didn't mean to scare you. I was going to my car and saw you outside of yours."

I looked at her.

"Which one is yours?"

She grinned.

"The taxi. Off-duty. My brother Jim owns it and I drive occasionally for him. Big enough to handle costumes, a crystal ball, and various smelly implements of the trade such as incense and, well, smoky stuff."

Madame Euphoria smiled but the expression didn't quite reach her eyes.

"I have to apologize for getting so whacked out in there. I know you guys think I'm a big fake. Hell, I admit it. For the most part I am. My family's been in the reading business for generations and there's maybe only two in the crowd that could *really* predict the future. And they lived in New Orleans, which probably accounted for something."

We grinned at each other.

Madame closed her eyes for a long moment. When she opened them again she stared at me and exhaled loudly. "I need to tell you two things. First, I have no idea what I said to you until Yolanda told me after the séance, and I have no idea what it means."

She shifted her gaze to Johnny.

"Secondly. Johnny. I was awake when I looked at you. I don't know how to explain this. I may not have a real spirit guide or be able to predict the future. But I do have an intuitive, you might even call it psychic, understanding about people. I can feel who's sad, who's angry, who's happy, who's lonely. All that stuff. I'm very nearly a true empath. And when I looked at you, I got nothing. As though you didn't even exist."

She again peered deeply into my eyes, which I'm sure were now wide with apprehension and fear. She reached for my hand and squeezed it.

Suddenly, I saw myself in another place, another time. Granny Dumas had outdone herself with this one. (Perhaps with Chief Blackie's aid.)

I was in Seven-D but it wasn't me. Or at least it was me from a future time, like thirty years or so ahead. I was digging through old scrapbooks in a trunk and searching through newspaper clippings.

There was an article about a show called *Boundaries* that had been slated for a Broadway opening. Someone named Jayce Cracknell had the byline. A scandal involving the producers and subsequent death of one of the stars had derailed the production. The future me then picked up a second newspaper. I began gasping for air. Whether that was part of my vision of current reality, it wasn't pleasant.

Staring up at me was a headline from one of the New York dailies, dated July 11 of this year.

SOAP ACTOR MURDERED!

Police are questioning various friends and acquaintances of Johnny Gerard about the popular actor's mysterious death Tuesday night. Mr. Gerard, on hiatus from daytime drama, Endless Time, *was preparing to open in the new Broadway musical,* Boundaries. *Mr. Gerard was found at 100 Centre Street in the office belonging to his father, Deputy District Attorney Kieran Gerard. Fellow staffer...*

The page faded, then came into focus again.

...Gerard's death, and that Kieran Gerard shot the reputed crime boss out of grief and revenge. Gerard is running for the office of District Attorney in Manhattan County. His arrest has put an end to months of political bickering and maneuvering on the part of several candidates.

I saw myself reading the first part of the article again trying to determine what had happened. I could care less about the politics of the New York City prosecutorial staff. I was far more interested in what had happened, or what would happen to Johnny Gerard. In my vision I knew I was avoiding taking more than a fast peek at the picture of the murdered actor until I had my breathing somewhat under control.

I finally took a long look at the photo in this future edition of the *Times.* The face was his. Undeniably his. If this vision held true, Johnny Gerard would be murdered in his father's office down on Centre Street in approximately five months.

My focus returned to two worried faces. I smiled weakly, then promptly passed out.

THIRTEEN

"HE'S LAPSED INTO a coma again."

"What? He was better. He was talking. I clearly remember you saying he was up and rambling yesterday. What the hell is going on? What happened?"

"Poison."

"Excuse me? Are we talking malpractice here? Did something get into the IV drip?"

"We're talking murder. Murder initiated by a basket of fruit with a little extra injected. Diazepam to be exact."

I popped my head out of the bathroom door to yell at Shay and Cherry to turn off the damn soap opera before their brains rotted. I threw a towel around my freshly showered body and barreled into the living before realizing the second voice I'd heard had been male. It had not come from the television.

Too late. At least I hadn't put on the green facial mask I'd been considering (guaranteed to bring a glow, according to the label).

Johnny Gerard leered at me from a spot on the sofa. I smiled back. To hell with modesty. I look good in a bath towel. Time he knew it.

"What are you guys talking about? Are these the latest lines from *Endless Time?* Is Yolanda trying to poison you now?"

Johnny's smile dimmed the moment I mentioned poison.

"Unfortunately, we're not dealing with daytime drama. This is real. Someone slipped Diazepam into the apples delivered to Cookie this morning."

Cherry chimed in before I had a chance to respond.

"Damn. What is he? Friggin' Little Red Riding Hood or somethin'?"

Shay threw Ringo at her.

"You dimwit. That's Snow White. Get your fairy tales straight, would you? Honestly, you can turn any situation into a farce faster than anyone I've ever known."

I held up my hand for silence.

"Will the two of you quit arguing and let Johnny finish? This is serious, guys. Johnny? What happened? Did I hear coma again?"

Johnny nodded to my roommates.

"It would be almost funny if it weren't so horrible. Gregory Noble and Cookie Gutierrez in comas. And this is so crazy. Apples filled with a strong muscle relaxant. Who would ever imagine such a thing? Anyway, the doctors got his stomach pumped, but he's lying there with tubes all over him again. After being out and laughing and talking for what? One day? Damn. Damn. Damn! I never even had the chance to talk to him today. When I got to the hospital, the cops were already there. I thought we were going to interview him about the original hit-and-run. But then I get informed that he's in Emergency. At least somebody figured out what the problem was. Seeing the fruit looking a tad peaked might have been a good clue. Anyway. I'm still somewhere between anger and being stunned this is happening. What the hell did Cookie do to deserve this? I keep wondering if it's got something to do with me. After all, Abby and I did get shot at in the park. But that was weeks ago. After Cookie got hit by the car in the first place. And I really did think it was a loony fan."

I sat down on the sofa and artfully arranged my towel.

"Johnny, think. Cookie got run down in November. Right after I had my foot accident in *Superstar.* Okay. You and I had our little Central Park adventure in December. Cookie comes to; he snaps out of his coma, what? A couple of days ago? And he's talking, right? Then someone attempts to kill him again. This ties together. You and Cookie may both be targets. I think I'm just incidental."

He shifted and scooched down the sofa to sit nearly on my lap. "I agree. Well, not that you're incidental." He grinned.

"Anything but. However, as to the target idea? It's what I've been thinking as well. I keep going over and over stuff in my head. I just wish I knew what he knows and I know that might be worth attempted murder."

Shay and Cherry plopped into the remaining chairs in the living room.

"I think we need Vito and Guido on this. They're really good about murder, ya know."

None of us had any idea how to respond to this somewhat outrageous statement by Miss Ripe. Especially since it was probably true.

As if on cue, the buzzer rang. Cherry ran to answer. The Mariccino twins waltzed in.

"Hey! How ya doin'?"

Johnny sighed and smiled tightly. He explained the situation. The brothers sat together and nodded their heads in unison as he relayed the original events that had landed Cookie Gutierrez in the hospital months ago.

Vito tilted his head back and stared at the ceiling.

"So, like, what you guys got in common? You and Cookie, ya know?"

Good point.

Johnny handed the twins the bag of muffins. "Good point."

I knew we were on the same wavelength.

Johnny thought for a second, then replied, "Lots. Let's see. First off, he's my roommate, so we know the others in our building. But we're nice neighbors. We don't play music too loud, we don't cook up crack in the basement. Um, we help little old ladies, or gents, with groceries and such when it snows and they can't go out. We pay on time. And really, three-quarters of my building is nothing but sweet, tiny, elderly ladies somewhere between eighty and a hundred. Their ages, not the number of little old ladies in the building!"

He grinned and closed his eyes as he thought. Shay coughed, then asked, "What about the soap? Cookie have anything to do with any of the cast? Any girls you both dated and discarded that now have it in for you?"

I was glad Shay had been the one to open up that box. If I'd even gone near the topic, it would have made me look like a jealous female. Johnny was shaking his head no.

"Cookie has met one or two of the *Endless Time* group. Yolanda and Mike, actually. And I honestly can't conceive of either of them trying to murder him or me. Even for higher ratings."

Vito nodded and asked, "Could it be Carla? Since she tried to whack you before with the parachute? Could she be after Cookie, too?"

Johnny shook his head. "Um. Interesting theory, Vito, but I can't quite see it flying. Carla is out of the country for a month. Skiing. In Siberia."

Vito nodded again. I wondered if it was too early in the day to start a serious round of Tanqueray and tonics.

Cherry stuffed half a muffin in her mouth, then mumbled, "What about immigration stuff? Is Cookie in trouble since he's an alien or anything? Those creeps can be pretty mean. They keep coming in the club and busting people out. Pisses me off no end. Seems like the best tippers are the guys they haul outta there before they can leave the bread."

Guido patted her hand. "It's a crime, ain't it?"

None of us could think of what to say to that. I smiled at Cherry and her bodyguards. I wanted to stay on good terms with her. And them. I tried to find something to like in Cherry's theory.

"You might have something there, about immigration,

except for why someone would also shoot at Johnny and me. Unless it really was a nutcase and it's not related to these attempts on Cookie's life at all. Wait a minute. Immigration. Dominican Republic. What is it about that that rings a bell?"

Johnny brightened.

"Hey. It may have nothing to do with *me*. Cookie knows some strange characters from back home. For all I know some mobster from Santo Domingo may be trying to kill him. Probably found out his new SUV was hot or was mad that Cookie couldn't get him a better deal on a Ferrari."

Vito brightened.

"That's a good reason to whack somebody. But I don't know no mob types who run around stickin' needles into fruit. It ain't classy, ya know? Kinda sissy, too."

Johnny barely heard him. He slumped down again.

"I just can't shake the feeling that's wishful thinking. The mob angle. I have this nagging suspicion that I'm to blame. Which makes me crazy."

He looked over at me. "You think you had guilt drilled into you by the nuns? Forget it. I had a principal at my grade school who was a master at making his little charges believe we were responsible for all the world's ills. Including nuclear bombs and bad rock music. I think he equated the two. They have blowing things up in common."

He sat up.

"Hey. I just thought of this. Talking about things in common. We do have Kieran, sort of. I mean, he introduced Cookie to me as a possible roommate. But I swear Kieran likes Cookie more than he likes his dear son Johnny. And why would my father be taking shots in the park and acting like the Evil Queen in the looking glass and putting poison into apples anyway? Doesn't make sense."

I tried to unobtrusively steal Ringo to cover my bare knees (now getting cold) as I gently challenged his idea.

"Remember my vision with Madame Euphoria?"

Johnny moaned. "I've been trying to forget since you told me last night."

"Well. It's still very clear in my head. And I see that newspaper with your name and the story about you being shot. And that was at Kieran's office. So maybe something is going on there? Something both you and Cookie know?"

"Except that I avoid Centre Street as much as possible. And Kieran knows I'm not especially interested in his campaign for District Attorney. And he doesn't discuss cases with me. Maybe Cookie stumbled onto something. And the Central Park shooting was a coincidence. Nothing to do with him."

I really wanted to ask whether Cookie knew Tracy and the silent Siegfried. But I didn't want to shatter whatever peaceful accord Johnny and I had reached regarding other women since my faux pas with Serena Ballinger, masseuse and singer. I stayed silent.

Cherry wasn't as reticent.

"Hey. What about that Tracy dame? The one who called you the first time Cookie got whacked by that car. Does Cookie have a thing for her? Does she want him out of the way so's she can have you?"

Shay, Johnny and I all choked on our bites of muffin at the same time. Shay stared at the ceiling. I casually picked a non-existent bit of lint off my towel and Johnny blinked. Twice. Vito and Guido stared at him.

He offered the bag to the twins. "Cherry, as far as I know, Cookie and Tracy only met once when she came to pick me up at the apartment. I think the sum total of their conversation was, 'Hi, how ya doin'?' and 'What's the weather like in Santo Domingo?' So I can't see a connection. Good thought, though."

I reached for a muffin and stuffed it into my mouth before I was tempted to delve further into the story of Tracy. My towel began slipping. I suddenly remembered I was less than well-attired to be entertaining, even though I was sure Vito and Guido saw far more at the club on a minute-by-minute basis. I carefully readjusted, stood up and started for the bedroom.

"Time to get into some real clothes, gang. Before I catch cold and end up in the same ward as Mr. Gutierrez. Johnny? Are you sticking around, or are you off to the hospital? Or back to Philly?"

He leaned back and sighed.

"I nearly forgot. That was the other thing I meant to tell you today. Before the manic code blue at the hospital I got a call from Bryan, my agent, this morning. *Superstar* has been officially cancelled. Finances just dried up. Immediately after Bryan called, Yolanda rang up. You two should get together. I swear she's psychic. Anyway, Yolanda is now preparing to bring Gregory Noble out of the coma. I just wish she could work the same magic with Cookie."

FOURTEEN

"*WILL HE KNOW ME? He must know me! Doctor, I can't bear this agony much longer.*"

"*I'm sorry. Your face may be familiar to him, yes. But you must understand. He may not recognize anyone even if he does wake up. And I make no predictions as to when or even if that ever happens. He'll be lucky to know his own name.*"

"*But I'm his wife! He's bound to have memories of our honeymoon in Barbados! Snorkeling in the crystal blue waters! Dancing on moonlit beaches! Kisses under starry skies.*"

"*Why don't you add skydiving with an unsafe chute! Oh, yes, Carla. I know you were the one who sent him up there to die!*"

"*Letitia! What are you doing here? Doctor Montgomery, please remove this person from the hospital at once!*"

"*I can't do that, Carla. After all, she's the head nurse and her father owns the Perpetual Merciful Help Medical Center!*"

"*But she's trying to steal my husband! She just doesn't want anyone to know the truth! The truth that she's lusted after him for years.*"

"*Truth? Truth? Funny words coming from an attempted murderess!*"

"*How dare you speak to me like that!*"

"*Dare? How dare you show up day after day in this hospital room pretending you're not the one responsible for Greg's ending up in this coma! I'll prove it, Carla, if it's the last thing I do!*"

CHORDS.

Shay turned to me, sighed and clicked off the TV.

"I'm telling you, Abby, Gregory Noble is about to be torn apart between those two. Carla may be his wife, but she's probably the one who *did* sabotage his parachute. He's married to a murderer. Letitia needs to punch her lights out. I think she's about ready to start fighting for that man. At least she's cottoned to the fact that Carla is probably the one who tried to kill him."

I stared at my roommate. She'd been watching *Endless Time* daily for the last two weeks. I had only joined her this morning to see the first of Shay's choreographed sequences. There I was, dancing with Johnny, a mirror ball spinning over our heads.

The dances were wonderful, but I wasn't sure my roommate even realized it. She'd been sucked into soap opera fever. I waved a doughnut in front of her glazed eyes.

"Shay! Shay! Listen to me!"

"What?"

"This is a soap. Remember? Actors? You worked with half of them, and me, for several weeks teaching everyone to salsa and grind? For a dream sequence for a *character?* Remember? Gregory Noble does not exist except in some writer's imagination. There was no parachute sabotage. There was no parachute. And if you call Johnny 'Gregory' again when he gets here in ten minutes, I will personally see to it that the television is broken into millions of tiny electrons or atoms or ions or whatever the damn thing is made of. What is the matter with you? And where did you get that awful pseudo Texas phrase of 'cottoned to'?"

She grinned and stretched out to fill the entire length of the couch.

"It's okay, Abby. I am well aware of the differences between your boyfriend and the character he plays. It's just so much fun now that he's about to come out of the coma. He's going to get to be fought over by at least two women. As to 'cottoned to,' I heard Johnny himself say it when he was talking about a couple of politicians that were clueless. Maybe it's a Houston phrase that hasn't made it to El Paso yet."

I just groaned. Johnny Gerard was returning to *Endless Time* and the soap had been setting the scene for his miraculous recovery for the last two weeks. Apparently Yolanda Barrett had decided to up the competition between the characters of Carla and Letitia for the heart of Gregory Noble. The writing was getting fierce. As was the race for daytime ratings. And everyone I knew was bugging me about which woman Gregory Noble was going to choose once he woke up.

Johnny wasn't thrilled with having to come back to the show this soon, but since *Jesus Christ Superstar* had been cancelled, he felt he didn't have much of a choice. The soap paid well, was steady work, and most of the perks were good.

"Shay? Not to change the subject, but to change the subject—I thought that last scene went really well. You did a gorgeous job."

She preened and patted herself on the back.

"I did, didn't I? Thanks, Abby. And speaking of gorgeous jobs, you were pretty hot yourself. Hey! Did I tell you the casting director of *Endless Time* is introducing me to the producers of a revival of *Pippin?* It's slated for a Broadway opening in the next six months. I may finally be on my way. No more rejections from pastry commercials."

We both began hugging and hopping up and down. I was glad she was finally getting the recognition she deserved.

I was out of work again. *Escape* had been set as a very limited engagement only. I knew it when I took the job. At least I'd been seen by some good directors and producers, so I was hopeful that I'd be remembered at my next audition and land a longer-running contract. Johnny and I were in somewhat the same boat. At least we were sailing together. Although it seemed like it was with a surprising number of shipmates. We had yet to be alone.

I also had yet to visit Johnny's apartment. It had been undergoing renovations since I met him. I brushed aside the horrible suspicion that the mysterious Tracy lived there with him. I knew from the super in our building that renovating apartments built "pre-war" could be time-consuming operations. It was not unreasonable to assume Johnny did not want to live without bathroom facilities or in a place with walls that had giant holes and floors that gaped and sagged through the neighbor's ceiling. He told me he slept either at his father's or at the apartment of the guy who'd played Jesus in *Superstar*.

The door buzzed. Johnny. I grabbed my jacket, umbrella and dance bag and hit the intercom button once.

"I'm outta here."

"Where you off to?"

"Auditions for a new musical the Notebooms are producing."

Shay's eyes opened wide.

"Wow. I've heard about this one. Cory Elliott is directing and choreographing. He's like a god to me. And the trades are saying this may well be the most expensive musical to be mounted on Broadway. Ever, ever."

I nodded.

"I don't care what it costs. I just want a chance to get in the chorus of a real Broadway show. At least we know this one won't close due to finances. Those people have more money than a cattle baron married to a sheik's daughter."

Shay hugged me again then threw a pillow at me.

"What's that for?"

"Luck. Go get 'em, tiger! Hey. What's the name of this one?"

"They keep changing. Last I heard it was *The Last Trip*. I hope it's not about hallucinatory drugs. Minette will send me to a convent in New Zealand and force me to take vows of chastity and sobriety."

Johnny was waiting down in front of the building. He'd already had an agent audition with the casting director and was pretty sure he was in but didn't want anyone to know until it was set in stone. I hadn't even told Shay. Advance warning could jeopardize negotiations with the producers of *Endless Time* in regards to another hiatus from the soap. He hoped for that or simply them allowing him fewer hours so he could do both projects.

He kissed me, held me close for a moment, then released me and smiled.

"You look so cute. I think you have much more than a shot at chorus with this production. Honey, you sing, you act and you dance like a dream. And Bryan told me they have parts for at least three solid triple threats."

Bryan was his agent. If he was right about the "parts" that was great, but I would be perfectly happy making my Broadway debut in the chorus.

We hailed a cab down to the theatre on 44th Street. I didn't feel like dealing with mass transit when my stomach was churning from nerves and didn't care to walk to the subway or bus stop in the pouring rain.

I checked and rechecked my dance bag to make sure my headshot and résumé hadn't been crumpled, rain-soaked, or coffee stained; to see if my character shoes were still in there and that my sheet music was in order as well. Johnny finally grabbed the bag and held on to it before I lost something.

"You're ready. Quit looking in that thing. Your stuff is not going to disappear between West 79th and 44th Street."

Johnny put his hand over mine as the cab shot down Broadway.

I let out a huge breath. "I know. It's just that I've never been quite this determined to get into a show before. It's really important to me. I feel like if I don't make this one, carrier pigeons will relay the news to Minette immediately. She'll kidnap me, fly me back to Texas, marry me off to some lawyer, and sign a contract for me that will have me teaching at El Paso Academy for the rest of my life. That's the school with the nuns. She'll probably arrange to have Sister d'Agostino transferred from St. Katherine's Women's Residence there to become principle of the damn school, too."

The cab screeched to a halt in front of the theatre and narrowly missed crashing into a stretch limo that was parked illegally by a fire hydrant. I didn't care. I could be stranded in the biggest wreck this side of the New Jersey Turnpike during a blizzard and still find a way to make this audition.

Johnny paid the fare. He helped me gather my stuff and then we hurried to the alley leading backstage. About fifty other female hopefuls holding umbrellas high in the air were lined up waiting for the doors to open. Someone was passing around a clipboard and telling everyone to sign the sheet on top. Johnny held his umbrella over me as I quickly wrote my name on the list and got in line.

"Hey, aren't you Gregory Noble?"

A voluptuous blonde I recognized from more than one audition I'd been to was eyeing Johnny with unabashed interest. He sighed. "That's my *character.* The person I *play.* Yes."

"Oooh, I watched you all the time before your parachute crashed! Are you coming out of the coma soon?"

I started to laugh. The blonde threw me a nasty look.

"What? Is he your private property, Sweetie?"

I could feel my teeth start to grind.

"No, *Honey.* I do not believe in people as property. They've updated the Constitution on the issue. Or did you miss that lesson in school? Assuming you made it past second grade."

Three girls applauded.

"You tell her, Shrimp."

Johnny quickly kissed me. "I think I'll leave this with you. My presence in line may cause more problems than I imagined or that you'd care to deal with." He leaned close to me and whispered, "We've both got to get this show. When even people in the business think I'm Gregory Noble, it's time to get seen as someone else for awhile. So. Call me when you're done, okay? We'll grab some Italian at Luigi's."

I nodded. The doors had opened and the girls were trotting inside the theatre. I scurried to keep up with them. Then I heard a voice yelling, "Johnny! Over here!"

I turned. Tracy was waving at him from the back seat of that illegally parked limo.

I squinted to get a better look. The Valkyrie blonde in the black chauffeur's uniform had exited the vehicle and was holding the back door for Johnny. I didn't see a gun, but that didn't mean he wasn't packing one. I still wasn't sure about that shooting incident in Central Park. Johnny had claimed that it was not Siegfried. He was sticking to the theory that some soap fan had decided to go hunting for celebrities. His roommate lay dying but he refused to consider the blonde man and his employer.

I almost smiled. Tracy *did* have good taste in drivers. This was the closest I'd ever been to Siegfried. I could finally see the face that matched the perfection of the body. He wasn't wearing a cap and his mop of yellow hair inched down below his collar. Blue eyes stared at a spot somewhere far from the car. I couldn't help but wonder if Tracy didn't have some great times in that white limo. Then I frowned. I didn't want those great times to be with Johnny and tried to convince myself that they weren't. I'd feel much better if I knew she was playing footsies and handsies and any other "sies" *only* with the hired help.

I had to push thoughts about his relationship with Tracy into the back of my mind. I had to gear up for this audition and I wasn't going to be able to do that if I was obsessing about Johnny Gerard and his dealings with Miss White Limo and the German Apollo at the wheel. I turned my attention back to the line of girls waiting.

As soon as the theatre doors were opened I marched backstage, removed my jacket and boots, buckled my character shoes, and started my warm-up and stretching routine. In my head I ran over the song I was going to sing if I made it through the dance call. I focused on the girls around me, on the orchestra pit, on the table out front where three men and two women munched burgers and sipped cokes and prepared to decide my fate. I did not think about Johnny Gerard. No more than a hundred times or so.

Thirty minutes after I'd entered the theatre, Cory Elliott, the man taking the dual role as director/choreographer for *The Last Trip* came onstage with his assistant. The pair taught a combination to the 160-plus dancers. They then split us into four groups and let us strut our stuff to a now semi-darkened theatre. I made the first cut. I made the second cut.

A ballet combination was taught.

"Take five!"

We'd finally been given a break. I rested my legs up on the wall of the stage and sipped water from my thermos. The group of 160 had been whittled down to twenty.

"Okay! Back onstage."

They'd been serious about the five minutes. But I was ready. I knew the combination. I found a nice spot downstage close to the audience and prepared to defend my turf to the end. Then Mr. Elliott decided to pull what I call a *Chorus Line* on us.

"Excuse me, ladies. Before we begin the ballet combination,

I'm going to call out your number. I'd like you each to step forward, say your name, where you're from originally and a little bit about yourself and why you dance. Project loudly please. Then, give me a time step, and a double pirouette finishing in *grande* fourth."

Okay. This wasn't normally done, but I could handle it. He called off ten numbers. Mine wasn't among them. I didn't even watch the first group go through the ritual. I marked out the ballet combination in a corner to be sure I'd remember when we *did* get back to it. Then I heard my number, fifty-two, called along with nine other girls. I crossed to the front of the stage, where we were actually standing in a line.

For some reason, I was at the end of that line. It gave me the unique perspective of being able to watch nine other girls self-destruct live and in color.

Three girls didn't know how to do a time step. Ballerinas? Two girls didn't seem to remember their names or hometown. Drugs? Nerves? Three girls didn't have a clue as to what a *grande* fourth was. Then they stumbled through variations on a theme of why they became dancers.

"I want to be a dancer because I love to dance."

The blonde who'd eyed Johnny and called me "Sweetie" got through all of it quite well. Great. She'd make it and forever rub it in the next twenty years I'd be in New York. (Or call me daily at the El Paso Academy.)

Then we got to the girl next to me. The kind that always makes me feel completely inadequate. Brunette, tall, china-doll complexion. Perfect body. Legs to her neck. A bit like Tracy. I had to stop thinking about that. This girl was undoubtedly the most beautiful woman I have ever seen in my life. I could feel my chances at getting into this show slipping away as I tried not to stare at her. She stepped forward.

"Name?"

They couldn't hear her. I was next to her and I couldn't hear her.

"Name!"

Four times they asked. Couldn't hear her.

"Hometown?"

Same routine. She spoke so softly I doubted that a mike stuck down her throat would make a difference. But it *was* a dance call. She didn't really need to talk except to explain why she wanted to dance.

"I want to be a dancer because I love to dance."

Hmm. Where had I heard that before?

"Time step. Then double pirouette, please."

Her time step had no tempo. She literally fell on her rear twice trying to get around in the pirouette. I found myself feeling sorry for her. Apparently both speech and dance were beyond her capabilities. I wondered how she'd gotten this far in the audition, or any audition, then glanced at her again. With those looks, I'm sure she was being given every chance in the world to display some slight degree of talent. Why she didn't just give up and become a model and make a million bucks was beyond me.

I didn't have long to speculate, though. I was up next.

"Abby Fouchet from El Paso, Texas!"

My voice projected clear to Times Square. I tapped out a clean time step and gracefully finished my double pirouette in *grande* fourth with a huge smile on my face.

"Abby. Tell us a bit about why you dance."

"I blame it on Maggie Shea, my first ballet teacher. She showed me from day one that dance is communication. Dance is sensuality. Dance is the breath of life. Dance is an athletic event. And on those rare and lucky moments when time stands still during a performance, dance is one's soul."

"Thank you. Okay, ladies, please listen for your number."

I waited, holding my breath. Ten numbers were called. The last was fifty-two. Me. The other ten ladies were dismissed.

The brunette doll was not called. The bombshell blonde who'd ogled Johnny was.

We sailed through the ballet combination and were told to wait again. A longer break this time, at least thirty minutes. Then the choreographer came out and asked four of us to stay and sing. The rest of the afternoon went by in a blur. I sang "Losing my Mind" from Stephen Sondheim's *Follies* as my ballad and thought about Johnny and Tracy and white limos and poisoned apples and gunshots in the park. I tried not to let the casting director know the reality of that song was more than I cared to admit.

Then it was over. I took the bus home. It broke down on 57th Street and we had to wait at least thirty minutes before transferring to another. Normally, I'd have been slightly aggravated. Today I barely noticed. I got on the second bus and stared out the window and saw nothing but Johnny Gerard heading towards that white limousine.

I didn't even think about the audition or even the fact that at the very end, I'd been told I was *in*. And with a part. Not just chorus. It was a small role, yes, but it was a character with a name. I'd been cast in my first Broadway show. I'd waited my whole life for this. It was my dream. And the only thing I could think about was Johnny Gerard. I didn't know whether I was more upset with myself or with him.

Johnny was sitting on the stoop of my building. I could see him as I trudged down West 79th from the bus stop. I debated about just turning around and riding on the subway for the next few hours. Would he miss me?

"Abby!"

Suddenly, his arms were around me.

"You got in!"

"How the hell did you know that? Are you psychic or did you fly over 44th Street in your busted parachute!"

"Hey, what's wrong? You sound mad. Aren't you glad you

got in? Abby! Your first Broadway show. I found out because Cory Elliott, the director, called me about ten minutes before I got here and told me I've been cast as Jake, the male lead. I asked him if he knew anything about you and he told me not only were you cast, but you have some lines. Way to go! So, what's bugging you? Still mad at the bimbo for asking me if I was Gregory Noble?"

I pulled away.

"Thanks for the congratulations, but aren't you wasting your time with me when you should be riding to some elegant soiree in the white limo with Miss Ritzy-Britsy-Brunette Tracy? Why you even bother to talk to peasantry such as I is truly kind of you."

"Abby! Enough already! Where do you get these ideas? Why can't you trust me? Take my word that she's only the friend of a friend, and she's a pain in the butt, and I will tell you the whole sordid story but I need to talk to this friend first. 'Ritzy-Britsy'? What does that mean?"

"I have no idea. It just popped into my head."

He snorted.

Green eyes drilled into mine. I don't know why the heck I kept on trusting him, but I did. That darn cute nose, I guess. He took my hands and gently caressed the inside of my wrist. He folded his arms around me then and kissed me hard.

"We are going to do this show together, Ms. Fouchet. We are going to be a smash hit. I am not going to have to play Gregory Noble again. And I will straighten out Tracy as to her position in my life, which will soon be non-existent. And we will live happily ever after. And, by the way, have I told you that I love you, Miss Dancer?"

My spirits lifted, the rain stopped and all was well with the world. Until I looked around and spotted a white limo waiting at the curb on West 79th and Broadway.

I looked into Johnny's eyes.

"I wish I could believe that. I wish I could believe you aren't your father's son. But you make that damn hard, Johnny Gerard. Damn hard."

I turned and walked inside. Johnny did not follow.

FIFTEEN

WE'D STARTED REHEARSALS for *Boundaries* a week ago. That's what they were calling it now. Not *The Last Trip*. *Boundaries*. The same title I'd seen in my vision of that future newspaper article about the show being closed before it opened because of the death of the star. I was trying to ignore that. Meanwhile Johnny was trying to ignore me. Since the day of auditions, we had yet to speak beyond a nod and a curt "Hello." The only benefit from the silence was that no one could accuse me of using my charms on the show's leading man to have gotten the job. As far as anyone in the cast could tell, I'd met Johnny Gerard first day of rehearsal just like the rest of them.

He was angry with me for mistrusting him over Tracy and making that crack about his father. I was angry with him for putting himself in the position of earning my doubt and suspicion. Consequently we were both acting like a couple of kindergarten kids fighting over who'd wrecked a finger-painting. We nodded politely when passing each other in the halls leading to the studio. During music rehearsals we sat apart and pretended to concentrate on the notes in front of us. Admittedly, not sitting together while learning music was also due to our differing roles in the production. Johnny only had two numbers with the chorus. I was part of the chorus, with a teensy acting part, and no vocal solos. We would not have been sitting next to each other even if we were still dating.

I was miserable. My only solace was in the hope that Johnny was miserable as well. Preferably more miserable than I. Unfortunately, he didn't look miserable. He looked good. Real good. A fact that was noticed by more than one female member of the company (and several males as well). The blonde dancer I'd accused of ending her education in the second grade always managed to be nearby whenever Johnny was getting a drink from the watercooler, walking around and chatting during breaks or studying his music in a corner somewhere. Johnny didn't seem to mind the extra attention from the woman, which just made me even more miserable.

In retaliation, I did what every female since Eve has done to irritate and ultimately get her man back. I decided to make him jealous. I spent a day looking over all the male dancers to see who might qualify as best looking and most obviously heterosexual. I found him. Six-four, black hair, steely blue eyes and a body that would have made Tracy's chauffeur Siegfried more than a little envious. I banished that thought. I wanted no intrusions of white limousines and their occupants disrupting my battle strategy.

I put my plan into effect the second week of rehearsal during a break between learning dance numbers. A tradition among dancers is the "feet on the wall" pose whenever the choreographer yells "Take Five!" We plop on our backs, and raise our legs up to rest on the nearest wall. It helps the legs, the feet, the mind and the heart. This day it was going to proceed beyond the norm in aiding the heart. Well, one heart anyway. Mine. I kicked my shoes off, threw my legs up and began sucking seductively on a stick of cinnamon. I smiled at that incredibly gorgeous male dancer who'd ended up sharing wall space with me, thanks to some quick and very sly maneuvering on my part. I fluttered my lashes at him.

"Hi. Whadja think of that last number? Wasn't that a killer?"

He smiled back at me, showing incredibly white teeth.

"You bet. I've done two shows with Cory and that's by far the hardest set of steps I've ever seen him do! Especially the sequence that started during the scene with the windmills.

You did great, though! I mean, a quadruple pirouette without warming up. We were all impressed. And you've got great energy on stage. Really nice to watch."

I thanked him. This was going well. Johnny was roaming around the studio with a script in front of his face, getting closer with each step. I turned up the heat and dropped my voice down a notch from merely alto to throaty, husky and nearly bass.

"You're great to watch, too. And you seem very familiar to me. Did we meet before these rehearsals somewhere?"

We went through the "where do I know you from?" game that everyone plays when starting a new show. New York is amazingly small when it comes to theatre people. Either one has met someone at auditions or been in an Off-Off-Off-Broadway disaster, or done some regional theatre gig best forgotten. The hunk turned his head and stared at me. His feet were still holding up his end of the wall.

"I've got it! You were going to be the lead dancer in *Jesus Christ Superstar!* I remember now. That idiot Dewitt had you running and leaping at Judas and you broke your leg or something! That was so awful. We all felt so sorry for you. Isn't he just the worst choreographer in the world?"

Amazingly small world. I nodded. We began to come up with outrageous means of revenge on Dewitt Dwyer. We'd gotten to sending him out to Colorado to fight wildfires with only a bucket of dirt. This whole business of discussing *Superstar* had sent me back to thinking of how wonderful Johnny had been that day. The day I officially met him. Then I started thinking that if my visions were true, my wonderful Johnny Gerard would be dead in less than two months.

I burst into tears.

The hunky dancer was staring at me as though space aliens had just landed on my chin and were tap-dancing to Irving Berlin tunes.

"What's the matter with you? We're talking about Dewitt

Dwyer, and the next thing I know you're crying like a kid beset by bullies and mumbling about gunshots and newspapers. Are you always this strange?"

I had no idea what to say. I didn't want to explain to the hunk I was trying to attract merely for purposes of making another guy jealous that I was in love with another guy. Better he think I was simply weird.

The stage manager was herding us back to the floor. The hunk seemed in a hurry to get to the other side of the studio. So much for Plan A to make Johnny Gerard insanely jealous. The only insanity appeared to be mine.

I eased my legs back down and started to pick up my dance bag from the floor where I'd been using it as a pillow. As I bent down and tried to punch it back into shape, a body loomed over me.

"Problems, Miss Dancer? You didn't seem too happy, and whatever was causing it, your gigantic idiot admirer didn't seem to want to solve it."

Johnny held out his hand and helped me rise. His face held a mixture of concern and amusement. I tilted my nose as far upward as I could.

"My problems are none of your business. Just as whom I talk to is none of your business. As of course, those you choose to associate with are none of mine. Including Aryan gods and their mistresses in white limos!"

I began stretching and warming up. I decided to include high kicks in the routine. I aimed them closer and closer to Johnny's face. In a show of amazing bravado he was staying and arguing even with my flying feet inches from his nose.

"Will you leave that crap about Tracy and her chauffeur alone? Damn. You can take something and worry it worse than my old collie with a bone! I told you months ago I wasn't free to discuss this. And watch it with your foot. I'd prefer not to go back into rehearsal with a black eye or a broken nose."

I smiled and continued to kick. I have excellent control. I was not about to mess up that Irish nose or put rings around those green eyes. After all, the director would kill me if I bruised his star.

"What? I'm not supposed to still be worried about a girl who's being driven around by someone out of a Nazi spy thriller who just coincidentally might have been shooting at us a few months ago? Who might also have put your best friend into the hospital in the first place? This is something I should just file in the back of my head under exciting experiences in New York City? By the way, did I ever tell you I had a vision the first time I saw Siggie and Miss Tracy outside O'Malley's? I saw a white limo running down a man near the courthouse. I guess that was Cookie, wasn't it?"

Johnny pursed his lips together and blew out a huge breath.

"Siegfried did not do that. And he wasn't shooting at us. Tracy wasn't shooting at us. Neither of them would have a reason to shoot at us. It was just some loony kook running loose in the park. Incidentally, Cookie was not run down by a white limo. He kept saying something about black when he was on the phone the one time he was conscious. We've been through this, Abby. Crazy things sometimes happen."

I brought my leg down and started jabbing his chest with my finger.

"It may not have occurred to you, Mr. Naïve, that someone may have been shooting at *me*. Not you. And that those bullets might just be in retaliation and jealousy on the part of your, your—whatever the heck she is. Ex-girlfriend? Ex-girlfriend who wants to be current girlfriend and thinks I'm the reason she's not?"

Johnny grabbed my hands.

"Why is it *so* hard for you to fathom that Tracy and I do not have any kind of romantic affiliation? Please tell me that. I am hoarse with trying."

I crossed my eyes at him. I nearly stuck out my tongue but I thought one childish gesture per conversation might be enough.

"Perhaps the fact that the woman follows you around town and seems to know where you'll be before I do?"

Johnny let out a small woof of frustration.

"You are the most stubborn, plus orneriest, female I've ever known in my twenty-eight years on this earth. Including Bella Winslow who beat me up on a daily basis in fourth grade."

He had me. Curiosity always wins over mad.

"Why'd she beat you up? Not that I blame her."

He winked.

"Word had it that she had a crush on me and didn't know any other way to express her affection. Since she was a foot taller than I at that particular stage of my life, I wasn't interested. Not to mention that at age nine I was more involved with Little League baseball than anyone of the female persuasion.

I snorted. It was not ladylike, but it was effective.

"Seems to me you got over that particular bent very easily."

He bit his lip. Stifling a laugh. Or, at the very least, a chuckle.

"Actually, I still prefer baseball to many irritating young ladies whose names I won't mention. I made home runs every game for the cast of *Carousel*. Of course, that was before I met you. Now, I'm sure I'd be too distracted by a certain dancer with the mindset of a stubborn mule. A chestnut-haired beauty who has many of the same characteristics as Bella Winslow."

I had no answer to this.

He grabbed my hand and dropped to one knee in a pose straight out of a melodrama.

"Could it be that this sweet Texas lady with a mouth that can spout off some of the most bizarre expressions I've ever heard shares more than just Bella's talent for aggression and just doesn't know how to show her affection? Dare I even hope for that possibility?"

I held on to my own laughter. I *had* been acting like Bella Winslow. For whom I felt great sympathy. I knew just how aggravating liking Johnny Gerard could be.

I answered his question with one of my own. "Whatever happened to Miss Winslow?"

Johnny stood up, then looked a little too casually up at the ceiling. "She became captain of a professional women's Roller Derby team."

"She did not! You're making that up!"

He lifted his right hand as if to testify.

"Swear. She did. Married the team's owner and they have two kids now. They live in Hoboken when they're not touring."

We were grinning at each other by then. I'd even forgotten why I'd been so mad at him for two weeks. He lowered his hand and grabbed mine with it.

"Truce, Abby? I miss you. I miss talking to you and laughing with you and kissing you and snuggling with you when I get a chance and never getting that chance because of the crowd of bouncers and club dancers and brilliant but nutty choreographers at your apartment. Do you hear me? I miss you!"

"Oh, hell. I miss you, too."

We kissed, right there in the corner of the rehearsal studio. Thirty pairs of eyes watched us with intense interest. Thirty pairs of hands applauded. As we came up for air the only sour note I heard came from the blonde.

"Well. I guess we now know why Ms. Fouchet got cast, don't we?"

Cory had been watching Johnny and me with the same interest as the rest of the company. He shook his head.

"Ms. Fouchet got cast because she's damn good. No

backstabbing, Sweetie. Or knives to the front either. Ms. Fouchet had *better* be good. Company. Gather. Sit. I have an announcement."

We made a circle in the center of the room and plopped back down on the floor.

"I have just been informed by Petra Johnston's agent that she will no longer be a part of *Boundaries*."

Petra Johnston was our female second lead. I wondered what had happened. She had two songs with Johnny, so this affected him more than the rest of the company. Cory continued his speech.

"I've been in meetings all morning with Sidney Bracco, our constantly worried composer of *Boundaries,* two of the producers, and Jimmy, our stalwart, albeit frustrated, musical director. It was decided that even though Petra has some name recognition we were not going to let that be the focus in deciding how to replace her. We've decided to go with someone already in the cast. Since we had not announced the understudy for the role of Katherine before now, this may be a bit of a surprise."

The cast was sitting up straighter and trying not to stare at every girl in the room.

Cory smiled.

"Abby Fouchet will now be playing Katherine in *Boundaries*. Denise MacGuire will take over Abby's lines. Congratulations, Abby, Denise."

I went into shock. Johnny nearly knocked me over hugging me and suddenly I could hear "Congrats!" and "Cool" and "Way to go, Abby!" from all sides as company members pulled me to my feet and cheered. It was almost too much. Johnny and I had made up with one another, and now I'd been cast to play a very good part in this very good show.

The thought flitted quickly through my mind that Minette was not going to be happy about this turn of events. Then again, she'd probably call every administrator of El Paso schools offering dance and negotiate a salary increase for a job based on my Broadway credentials.

Johnny couldn't seem to wipe the huge grin off his face. He was jumping up and down like he'd just won the Tony Award, Daytime Emmy and a Grammy all in the same year. I felt exactly the same, but was trying to preserve some measure of professional dignity. I also couldn't jump with the crowd around me. I couldn't even move.

Sid, the composer, got up from his perch at the back of the rehearsal studio and pushed through the crowd.

"Abby, my love. I wanted you from the beginning. But the producers were afraid to take a chance on someone just making their Broadway debut. But I'm very happy things have turned out this way. Your voice is perfect for my songs."

I didn't know whether to just burst into tears of joy or faint. This was a man who'd won so many awards for his music I wondered if he had to rent storage space for the trophies. And he was complimenting me. Life had turned sweet in the last ten minutes.

Cory made his way through the throng behind Sidney.

"I'm taking a big chance on you, Abby. You've definitely got the talent and the energy. Just don't let me down. I have some very nervous producers waiting with a rope in case any of us blow it."

"Cory. Thank you so much for this opportunity. I can't begin to tell you what this means to me. It's truly the dream of my lifetime. I promise I'll do everything you ask and not be a diva and I'll work my tail off. I'll even get you coffee during breaks!"

He laughed and gave me a big hug.

"That's what gofers are for, Hon. You just show everybody what you showed us during auditions and we'll be more than happy. You and Johnny are going to be a sure hit."

Johnny had managed to make his way next to me again and put his arm around me with an air of possession.

"We'll do you proud, Cory. Me and Miss Dancer here."

I noticed my tall male dancer friend with the blue eyes was now sitting by Miss Blonde Legs-to-Her-Neck. She had given me a quick, "Congrats, Abby," then twirled around and headed right for the dark-haired, white-toothed hunk. She had that look on her face, the one that reminded me of a dog staring at a five-inch-thick steak. She'd been aiming at Johnny since auditions. Now it was directed at the giant male dancer. I silently wished them both well. I'm a firm believer in love. For everybody.

SIXTEEN

"YOU'RE A WHAT?"

"Triple threat. Dancer, singer and actress. It's been called a triple threat since the beginnings of musical theatre."

He turned to his son.

"Yes, of course. Johnny, would you be so kind as to tell the Governor that I'll be with him just as soon as I check with the catering staff?"

Johnny winked at me and went off ostensibly to search for the Governor, who was chatting with some wealthy constituents at this fund-raiser for Kieran Gerard, Deputy District Attorney for Manhattan County. Johnny and I had taken a cab to Mr. Gerard's penthouse apartment in the East Sixties shortly after today's rehearsal for *Boundaries*. The plan was to try and spark up what promised to be a thoroughly dull evening. And to give me a chance to finally meet Johnny's father face-to-face.

I wasn't thrilled with coming to this party. I'd hoped we'd be out doing something wildly romantic. (So far, the most romantic thing we'd done was paint the kitchen at Seven-D with Cherry and the Mariccino brothers enthusiastically helping by pouring liquid detergent over our hands when needed.) We could perhaps have gone tonight to Nathan's for a hot dog. By ourselves. That alone could classify sauerkraut and franks as an aphrodisiac. We hadn't been on our own for the last two weeks.

Johnny kept assuring me the entire taxi ride over that we'd do the "Hi, how are you, nice to meet you" circuit, then go out to dinner at some posh restaurant with low lighting and obsequious waiters. He mentioned something about a Hansom cab ride through Central Park if the weather held up.

The first thirty minutes at the party hadn't been bad. I'd been introduced to various legal types who seemed to want to impress me with their noble intentions as to crime, criminals and cleaning up the whole legal system. Lawyers love dancers who are tiny and cute. Often, however, when those same dancers demonstrate they have a brain, the attorneys flee, looking for fresh, tiny and cute with lower IQs.

I'd listened to arguments about the rotten liberal legislation and the rotten laws that prevented putting rotten criminals away. There'd been one violent debate about a case currently before the courts and the fact that the judge had thrown out every piece of evidence Kieran's office felt should have been admissible. There was mention of witness tampering and immigration authorities taking bribes and extortion and judges fixing cases. I almost smiled thinking of Shay and Fuji the Immigrant Pitcher and the Men in Black. Then I stopped smiling thinking of Cookie Gutierrez lying silent in a hospital bed a few miles away.

A tall man with a beaked nose and imposing presence was taking the defense side (brave of him in a mob of prosecutors) and trying to explain his position. A short man with an obnoxious cigar and equally obnoxious attitude was attacking him verbally.

"Dammit, Jeff. *You* get murderers, rapists and serial killers off. How can you say those crimes pale in comparison to bribing a judge or fixing a case?"

"A murderer being given a good defense is important. It's that old 'Better hundred guilty men go free lest one innocent man be convicted' deal. And it's true. So I don't feel badly for providing counsel. But if cases are fixed, if judges are taking bribes, then the whole judicial system is in jeopardy. The concept of a fair trial goes out the window. It's a far more serious evil. It means those murderers, rapists and serial killers you're so fond of can get away with anything. If they have the money. It's the destruction of the law."

I almost applauded. A man of integrity amongst the piranhas.

I moved from that conversation to:

"Stinking INS. They've messed me up completely by deporting at least four witnesses I've had primed and ready. Wish they'd just take the first plane out of Manhattan and find a jungle somewhere that wants them."

I finally found a quiet corner and was indulging in a Tanqueray and tonic and some sort of veggie dip when Johnny grabbed me and told me the time had come to meet the great Kieran Gerard.

I'd seen him months before on TV giving a press conference. Then at the disco-scene taping for *Endless Time,* but that was from a distance. Up-front he was even more impressive. A man in his mid-forties, he was undeniably as physically attractive as his son with the same red hair (plus a splash of white streaking through his temples), that cute snub nose and the sharp features. His charm, at least as exhibited in my direction, could use some polishing.

I had decided before arriving that I would be on my best behavior, even though I did not approve of Mr. Gerard's attitude towards women or his behavior towards his son. Kieran Gerard struck me as a user. I don't like users. Johnny once told me during a conversation about agents, fans and casting directors that he doesn't suffer users kindly. Yet he was still determined to try to patch up twenty-odd years of neglect by his father. Consequently, he chose to ignore certain of Kieran's baser characteristics.

Knowing Johnny, I figured he'd grab a few bites of cheese from the passing tray of the first waiter he saw. Then he'd park his frame close by and keep an eye on what would doubtless be a short conversation between his father and myself, the lowly, albeit talented, triple threat currently dating his son. If it looked like I was being drowned in the current of Kieran Gerard, Johnny would be there to pull me out and administer CPR.

I waited for Kieran to complete a conversation with a short and chubby, balding, sweaty man. Perspiration dotted his face and he kept dabbing at his forehead with a sodden handkerchief.

"Kieran. The man's murdered two people. How the hell could he have gotten off? I swear that woman changed her testimony between my examination and the cross. Got to be witness tampering. The question is whether to just charge her with perjury or offer her a deal."

Kieran Gerard frowned.

"I don't think this is the time to discuss the ramifications of the legal system and pros and cons of defense, do you? I'm sure we're boring our little dancer here."

The little man nodded then gave me a sharp look before striding to the table that prominently featured Beluga caviar. Kieran turned his attention back to me.

"So. Ms. Fouchet, is it?"

I nodded. This was good. Mr. Gerard, Esq., had at least taken the time to learn my last name. The fact that he had yet to look me in the eye was not as reassuring. It was somewhat disconcerting to be talking to someone with such a strong physical resemblance to Johnny, including the red hair and green eyes, yet someone who seemed so opposite of his son in every way. Including courtesy.

"Ms. Fouchet. Please. Tell me how you met my son. Oh, hello, Senator! Nice to see you again. How's the campaign coming? I hear you've got some tough competition in Rockland County. Let's lunch Tuesday at 21 and talk strategy."

A distinguished silver-haired gentleman acknowledged both the rhetorical question and invitation with a smile and a wave. The state senator looked amazingly like the man I'd seen in O'Malley's last fall exchanging drinks and smiles with the black-leather-clad male hustler, but I quickly dismissed the thought.

If Johnny's father hoped to intimidate me with his guest list, he needed to employ different tactics. Minette has hosted more dinners for Texas senators, governors and other politicians than this man had clerks at the D.A.'s office. Paul, my dad, has designed homes for every one of those Texas luminaries. Democrat, Republican, Texas Secessionists, Marxist and Fascist. Minette can be a pain in various sections of the anatomy, but I have always admired her ability to have these people in her home simultaneously with never a harsh word exchanged. An ambassador from Mexico taught me to read Spanish when I was seven years old. I babysat for the mayor's kids all through my high school years and led a contingent of pastel-clad ladies down the aisle as maid of honor for the state representative's daughter last summer.

Political gentry held neither mystique nor awe for me. I smiled sweetly at Mr. Gerard's question about my first meeting with his son and regaled him with a condensed version of the foot-injury story and Johnny's subsequent rescue. I thought I detected a smile behind the green eyes when I described the writhing *Superstar* cast, but it was gone before I could confirm my suspicions.

Abby Fouchet was not in the plans Kieran Gerard had for Johnny. Since I myself wasn't sure Abby Fouchet was in the plans Johnny had for Johnny, I was growing more and more uncomfortable.

Johnny had told me more than once about the numerous bimbos his divorced father liked to squire. It was one of the main reasons I'd stayed mistrustful of Johnny's intentions. That ugly specter of genetics kept popping up. I was Minette's daughter and while I didn't share her views on actors and other artistically inclined males, I had doubtless inherited some of her skeptical nature. The fact that Johnny did not always enlighten me as to his own activities with other women hadn't helped. Now I was meeting the District Attorney hopeful and trying to persuade myself that apples falling from the tree can roll far enough away not to become rotten. This particular big tree didn't look pleased to have me anywhere near his orchard.

I wasn't in Kieran's category for babes to boff, (Johnny said he liked them tall and stupid) and I wasn't politically situated in the state of New York to be a help to Mr. Gerard's campaign for District Attorney. I was a non-entity from Texas. Just one of many women his semi-celebrated son had dated in the ten years he'd been in New York. Passing through Johnny's life and soon enough forgotten. Kieran could care less about me. He quickly made that quite clear.

"Please, call me Abby."

"Abby. Just how serious are you and my son?"

Now, that question did throw me. The man was direct. So direct that I had no idea how to respond.

"I. That is, we. Well, we've been seeing each other about four months now. Off and on, that is. Um. He was out of town about a month, you know, when it looked like the *Superstar* revival was still on? And now we're in rehearsals for a new show. *Boundaries.* Did he tell you? Headed straight for Broadway. We're both thrilled. It's my first Broadway show. And I've got a featured role."

The man made no response. I could feel the urge to ramble creeping over my vocal chords. Or perhaps I should break into a soft-shoe routine. I soon wished I'd chosen the latter. My feet don't get me into nearly the amount of trouble my mouth does.

"Um. Anyway. I guess you'd say Johnny and I are pretty steady. A heavy-duty romance?"

"Is that what *schtupping* is called these days?"

"Excuse me?"

I couldn't believe he'd just said that. Aside from the fact

that it was a ridiculous word, I was reeling from the nasty implications.

"Ms. Fouchet. I'm not an ignorant man. And I know my son is attractive to women. They see him on that brain-draining soap opera and dream of having sex with him on a daily basis."

I stared at him.

He continued, "I'm sure you're no different. And since Johnny is a hot-blooded young stud, I have to assume that you and he are doing more than just dinner and a movie now and then. He has his needs, as do most men. If I were you, I wouldn't make too much of it."

I was angry. Let's make that royally pissed. How dare Mr. Hit-On-Everything-in-Skirts insert his nasty little mind into my love life? Make me sound like some soap opera groupie with an overactive imagination and libido. The fact that I had doubts myself as to what I meant to Johnny just made all of his insinuations that much worse.

"For what it's worth, Mr. Gerard, what has or has not transpired between Johnny and me is, quite frankly, none of your damn business. And considering what I've heard about your background with women, I'd hold off on casting those first stones. Sir."

I was taking a breath to let loose a few more salient zingers when a voice came from behind me and thankfully shut me up.

"Key!"

"Chase?"

The tall blonde man with the shocking blue eyes and athletic body I'd last seen with Kieran at the taping (as well as on TV making my roommate Shay swoon with lust) was approaching, hand extended, ready to grasp the hand of the Deputy D.A. Kieran Gerard was instantly all smiles.

"Ms. Abby Fouchet. Chase Jaffert. Recent graduate from Harvard Law, recent resident of New York and recent staffer on the District Attorney's team. He's staying on with me as a Deputy D.A. when I, hopefully, win the election."

The blonde flashed those perfect teeth at me as he extended a hand. I shook it vigorously, grateful for the interruption. Definitely a fox.

Kieran continued to wax eloquent over Mr. Jaffert's talents. "I can't let him go can I, Chase? You're the only man I know who can beat me in racquetball in straight sets. Or could until you pulled that muscle a few months ago. I miss our games. Have to keep him at the D.A.'s office until he heals and I get the chance to get even. Which I will."

The testosterone level in the room was rising fast. For a second I considered telling these two toned (muscle-wise that is) males that dancers are better athletes than racquetball players ever hoped to be. And besides being incredibly good for the heart, ballet training also enabled one to leap tall buildings in a single bound. Well, close. I stayed silent.

Chase was now bowing to the man he obviously considered a god. Responding like a true sycophant he said, "Thank you for the kind words, Key. We'll see how tolerant you are about my racquetball prowess when you become the D.A. Which is a foregone conclusion. Kieran Gerard is the best prosecutor in New York, if not the entire country."

Kieran beamed and shifted almost his full focus to me.

"I believe you and Mr. Jaffert have something in common, Ms. Fouchet. Aren't you originally from Dallas, Chase? Perhaps the two of you can get together sometime and reminisce about the delights of the Southwest."

Chase smiled. "Sounds inspiring, indeed. Abby? Very nice to meet you."

Chase Jaffert gazed at me with some interest. He extended his hand to me again, but this time grabbed mine and kissed the back of it. Very smooth. Too smooth.

They must teach suave at the D.A.'s office.

I needed gin and I needed it now. Perhaps a double.

As I prepared to make a graceful exit from the pair, I suddenly was gifted with a vision that was anything but pleasant. Kieran and Johnny were in an office, arguing. And in the background I could see a hand holding what appeared to be a gun.

I came to and started rambling as I backed away from the two lawyers.

"Nice to meet you, too. Chase. I need to go now. Would you excuse me, please? Um. I see Johnny struggling with more than one glass of champagne and an entire plate of cheese, and I'm going to rescue him before he embarrasses himself."

I could feel two pairs of eyes on my back, doubtless preparing to discuss what an uncouth babe I was, as I turned and made a beeline for a table on the penthouse balcony. Johnny was standing near the edge, indeed trying to balance both glasses and plates for no obvious reason I could perceive.

"Hey! Nice juggling."

"Hey, yourself! I see you escaped the clutches of the beast. And without any help from me, I might add. Did I detect a slight smile on Daddy's face at one point? Or did I just dream that?"

I grinned. "Very slight. I was telling him about Dewitt throwing me into the arms of Judas and I think he thought the idea of a tenor getting flattened was rather amusing."

Johnny laughed. "I'm glad he's learned *something* from me this past year. Look. Are you about ready to leave? I know we haven't been here very long, but I have no desire to stay now that I've showed voters that Kieran Gerard has a devoted son. Which is my whole *raison d'être,* you know."

"More than fine with me. I think I wore out what welcome I had from your father pretty fast."

I took a sip of the champagne. It didn't mix well with gin.

"Johnny? I had kind of a weird flash."

He chuckled. "You're about thirty years too young!"

I tossed a piece of cheese at him.

"Not that kind. Sort of a premonition of something not good."

"When?"

"Just now. Talking to your father and then meeting that other attorney. I sort of zoned for a second and saw your dad and you fighting. Not a pleasant fight."

Johnny squinted at me with more than idle interest in my vision.

"What exactly did you see? Do you remember?"

"Why?"

"I just feel like there must be some reason for this vision. Didn't that newspaper article you saw when Madam Euphoria was hypnotizing you or whatever mention my dad's office? Maybe this is a warning."

I groaned. "It's more than possible. And I don't know if that's good or bad."

"Do these Granny Dumas visions, as you call them, always come true?"

"Not sure. I really didn't start having them this strong until I moved to New York."

I brightened for a second. "I did have a vision just before I left El Paso that Minette would go to Paris last summer. That never happened. And the vision was pretty 'date specific.' So maybe I'm wrong about things. Or maybe I can change the future if I know what's going to happen. I talked Minette out of going. Told her to wait 'til she and Dad could go together."

"So all this 'Johnny Shot in Kieran's Office' stuff could be a crock?"

I shivered and ignored the question. "Listen. Are you ready to leave now? Or will that be too offensive to your father, who incidentally really did come across as a jerk."

Johnny looked slightly surprised, even though he knows I

say what I think. After all, this was his father I was labeling a jerk.

I blushed. "Sorry. That might have been a bit too blunt. Let's just say he sent a few insults my way and I didn't appreciate it."

"Oh, nuts. Was he horribly rude? I figured you had to meet him sometime, and I thought he'd be on better behavior at his own fund-raiser, but I guess I was wrong. Yeah, I'm ready to go. I may not come back. Ever. I'm so tired of his attitude I could—" he smiled "—almost not eat this excellent cheese."

We placed our still-full glasses of champagne on the closest table and prepared to make polite excuses for departure.

"I need to get my jacket and purse from the bedroom. I'll be right back."

Johnny nodded. I found the room. My belongings were cozily lying on a velvet comforter. Kieran had good taste. Minette has the same comforter at home and she's known as having an exquisite eye for décor.

When I came out again, Johnny was looking over the balcony railing. The view was magnificent.

"Abby. I know you and Kieran didn't hit it off, but I need to tell you something. That flash or hallucination you had could be partly right. I'm afraid my father is in for some trouble."

"What's the matter?"

"Kieran Gerard may be about to go down. Big-time. I was talking tonight to one of the law clerks who works with him and the buzz is the proverbial *ca-ca* is about to hit the proverbial ventilator."

My eyebrows arched over Johnny's euphemisms, but I got the point.

"Why? What's going on?"

"Kieran's latest female conquest is a very married lady whose husband is one Nicholas Toblaroni. Ever heard of him?"

"Wait. Toblaroni? Like the chocolate? I love Toblerone bars!"

Johnny grinned at me. "Same pronunciation. Different spelling. Although I've heard Nicholas Toblaroni referred to in some circles as 'Candy Nick.' He's a business tycoon who appears to have serious ties to organized crime. With a capital 'O.' His family has been reputed to be in the mob for generations."

"Ouch. Does Kieran know this? Wait. That's a stupid question. If you know and you're about as observant towards local politics and crime lords as I am, then of course he knows. What's wrong with the man? Is he as hard up for sex as all that?"

Johnny shook his head. "We could have a big scandal on our hands concerning our wannabe D.A. What's really nuts is that Kieran told me he knew she was married before he ever got involved. I don't know if he's actually engaged in illegal activities with these guys, or just messing with the wife. But either way, it doesn't look like a good situation for anyone, much less a prosecuting attorney desiring to be the newest District Attorney of Manhattan County."

"Oh, Johnny, I'm sorry."

"I just can't believe Kieran is so taken with her that he hasn't managed to extricate himself from this situation. And the primary elections are coming up in a couple of months? What is the man thinking? Apparently I'm the only Gerard who understands good timing. All that actor's training. Abby. Come back to the conversation. You have a very strange look on your sweet little face."

I reached for one of our discarded glasses of bubbly and took a long sip.

"I was so intrigued by this whole scandal business that it didn't hit me until just now. Retroactive pre-déjà vu."

"Excuse me?"

I grimaced, then grinned.

"I thought it sounded classier than saying it's just second sight. Anyway, I've heard the name Nicholas Toblaroni before. In connection with your father. But also, somehow, he's mixed up with you. I can't quite remember how, but it's not good."

Johnny shook his head.

"Enough, Miss Precognition. Let's split and go someplace uninhabited by lawyers, politicians and Toblaronis."

He added casually, "I was thinking of my place."

I arched an eyebrow.

"Are you telling me it's out of renovation repairs, home improvement remodeling, etcetera, etcetera?"

"It is. Not only that, but it's vacant. Very vacant. And the whole apartment is ready for a housewarming party for two."

He pulled me close to him and nuzzled against my ear.

"I can think of only one way to warm up what is now a very cold and lonely space."

SEVENTEEN

THE SCANDAL ARROW LEFT the bow much sooner and was aimed in a much different direction than Johnny had initially thought. In fact, it came sailing right at *him*.

We were in the last week of rehearsals for *Boundaries*. As is often the case with putting together any production, professional or amateur, it was one of those days when everything was going wrong.

"Four new songs? Four new songs? Damn it, Sidney, you interfering idiot! The composer does not drop four new songs on the cast a week before opening! Why don't you go back to Illinois or wherever the hell you first came from and write jingles for a local car company?"

Cory Elliott, the hottest director/choreographer since Bob Fosse, was literally throwing sheet music at Sidney Bracco, the hottest composer since Stephen Sondheim. Those of us who might be affected by these changes by having to learn those four new songs stood onstage and tried to look calm and neutral.

Sidney was throwing the music right back.

"Cory. Might I remind you that I wrote the book as well as the music for this extravaganza you seem intent on destroying? And when I want four new songs added to Act Two, then by God, I'll have four new songs!"

I was watching this ping-pong exchange of words with some interest until I heard the lead, Dulcie Evans, screaming across the stage. Just whom she was screaming at was not quite clear.

"My agent is incensed! Do you hear me? Incensed! We

were promised pre-show publicity from the *Times* and the *Post* and Channel Five and have yet to see any of it. If we don't, then my lawyers are getting involved immediately!" Dulcie took a breath. "And those lines at the end of Act One? I thought I made it clear that they were to be changed to suit my character. And I hate to bring it up, but I must. That purple rag the she-devil costume designer has me wearing in that scene makes me look…well…"

"Ugly," Johnny whispered. "Say it, Dulcie. You look like a plump plum. We all know it. You know it. Say it! Ah, hell, she'll never admit to it. Hey, Abby! Having fun in your first Broadway we-open-in-a-week rehearsal? I warned you these people would be nuts."

As Johnny was nuzzling my ear while lightly vilifying Dulcie, I heard the sounds of the fire-door alarm buzzing for the twelfth time today. Brawny men with tool belts had been working unsuccessfully to fix what appeared to be a short in the system. At the same time, five gentlemen dressed in nearly identical three-piece suits banded together and huddled in a corner under the box seats like football players before the final play. All five were shaking their heads in obvious despair. I had no idea what the problem was, but was intrigued by the rhythmic head movement.

I chattered, "I'm having a wonderful time. I love chaos in the theatre. Makes me feel like I'm part of the process. I feel like I did the day of my first dance recital when I was barely six. I just jumped up and down in sheer glee for about an hour. Care to jump with me?"

Johnny grabbed my hand and we began an impromptu jitterbug onstage. Several cast members decided to join us, ignoring the debate still raging between composer and director, Dulcie's diva fit, the gentlemen and the fire alarm. We were all having a terrific time until I heard one of the head-bobbers suits scream. It was not a shout. It was a scream.

He then yelled in a tortured voice, and I quote, "We're ruined!"

The entire company stopped talking, stopped singing and stopped dancing. Something about the man's voice wasn't joking, wasn't the normal sound of creative crisis we heard on an almost daily basis. Something was very wrong. The conservatively dressed men motioned to Cory and Sid. We stayed quiet. One of them handed a paper to the director and composer. From where I was standing it looked like the *New York Daily News*. He kept several other papers in hand. What on earth? Cory and Sid looked at each other. Then they looked onstage. All seven men stared at one person. Johnny Gerard.

Cory was the first to break what was turning into a very long silence.

"Johnny. Could you come down here for a moment?"

Johnny looked at me.

"I think this is it. Kieran's little mob love nest must have been discovered. It's not like it's a surprise. Come on, Abby, let's see how trashy the press is in describing Daddy and Mrs. Toblaroni."

I jumped down with him and we ambled towards the group frowning at us. Cory looked at me with some concern.

"Abby? I don't think you need be involved in this."

"Hey, Cory. Not to be pushy, but if Johnny has to deal with a problem, I'd like to be with him."

One of the five suited men, a small, balding, accountant-type with enormous glasses, thrust a newspaper at Johnny and me. Johnny took the paper and I peered over his shoulder.

The newspaper headline hit me like a fist in the stomach:

Noble Out-of-Bounds
Boundaries Bound for Broadway Oblivion for Notebooms

A second paper was thrust into my hands with a headline that yelled:

Noble Not a Boon to Notebooms!

I looked at Johnny. He looked at me. If the expression of horror and amazement on his face mimicked mine, someone needed to call the paramedics fast. I watched the blood run out of his face, knowing I was similarly pale.

Cory quietly said, "Read the Op/Ed page. Jayce Cracknell's piece."

We began to read as a deafening silence filled the theatre.

Johnny Gerard, winner of the Emmy for Best New Actor on a Daytime Drama three years ago, seems to have been caught with his pants down on more than just an afternoon episode of passion. Rumor has it that the young Mr. Gerard, son of eminent attorney, Kieran Gerard, currently running for the office of District Attorney in Manhattan County, and Mrs. Nicholas Toblaroni, wife of entrepreneur Nicholas Toblaroni, are checking out the bedroom in Mr. Toblaroni's plush penthouse. The Toblaroni's have been linked on more than one occasion with organized-crime figures in the city. Is Johnny bedding Mrs. Toblaroni with an eye to securing big bucks for his latest venture, a show entitled Boundaries, opening next week at the Cort Theatre?

If these allegations are true, it opens a huge can of worms for the theatrical-producing family, the Notebooms. While show biz and crime syndicates have been in league with each other at one time or another in this city for over 100 years, this could present major problems for the Notebooms, who have had, up to now, a spotless reputation when it comes to keeping their finances pure. Money laundering by way of show productions has been an ongoing concern for the

*Manhattan District Attorney's office since the days of
vaudeville and burlesque.*

*When questioned by this reporter, Deputy District
Attorney Gerard had no comment, other than to say
what his son does with his sex life is no concern of his.
Rather a cavalier attitude, but...*

"Holy shit! That son-of-a-bitch! Dumps his little piece of
trash in my lap and walks off into the sunset. I'll strangle the
bastard! What kind of father does that to his own son?"

Johnny's face was as red as his hair.

"You guys don't believe this crap, do you?"

Cory took the newspaper from Johnny's hand.

"I've known you since you first came to New York and
started college. I've worked with you and hit the bars with
you and played more than a few mean games of softball and
pool with you. I also know your father. And it's a good thing I
believe more in environmental upbringing and being responsible for one's own destiny more than I believe in inherited
traits, because I'll tell you something, Johnny. Your old man
is one scheming, hypocritical bastard. And I *do* know you're
nothing like him. Hell, no, I don't believe this garbage. What
I can't believe is that nobody even bothered to check with
us."

Cory was enraged. I was glad. Sid was nodding his head
yes to every word Cory said and I was glad of that as well. I
wasn't quite as sure what the consensus would be from the
suits. The oldest of them, a gentleman I only knew as Mr.
Andrew, was glaring at Johnny rather like one glares at an
army of New York roaches parading across one's kitchen
counter.

"Would you care to explain, Mr. Gerard, why your name is
splashed all over the paper and television in connection with
less than savory people?"

"Now that you bring that up? No! I'd prefer going to the

phone and calling—who the hell wrote this particular piece? Jayce Cracknell? The damn drama critic? Nice of him to contact me. First thing I'm doing is calling and asking a few questions of my own. Then I'm confronting the eminent District Attorney wannabe himself. Excuse me."

Johnny charged off in the general direction of the theatre's backstage pay phone. I was left standing with a group of very unhappy men. I searched their faces. Only Cory and Sid seemed at all sympathetic. What the hell? It was just my upcoming Broadway debut. My whole career. Should I risk being tossed out on my rear for Johnny?

Any day. And it looked like today was that day. I took a huge breath.

"Pardon me, gentlemen, but it doesn't appear that outside of Cory and Sid, any of y'all are willing to believe Johnny Gerard is innocent of that filth the papers are shoveling."

The oldest of the crowd frowned at me.

"Who are you?"

"Abby Fouchet. I'm playing Katherine in this show. And I'd like to state, categorically, unequivocally and for any record that's recording—Johnny has never had an affair with Mrs. Nicholas Toblaroni."

I kept my fingers crossed behind my back and hoped that was true.

"While we're on the subject, Johnny has no ties to any mob. Johnny has been set up and you're—well, you're just total morons if you've ever worked with this man and don't know that."

Silence. A long, scary silence. Finally, "Thank you for your faith, Ms. Fouchet. And thank you for standing up for Mr. Gerard. Loyalty is a nice virtue. Now, you need to go back to your rehearsal and let us look into this."

Thus spoke the youngest of the five suits, a man of forty-five or so, who almost smiled as he waved me back to the stage. The good news was I wasn't being fired for daring to open my mouth and defend Johnny. The bad news was I didn't think for a minute that Johnny was out of very hot water with the producers—or with New York newspapers.

Johnny didn't come back to rehearsal that afternoon. When I finished dancing in all the wrong directions and singing songs in unwritten keys, I left the theatre and headed over to the Times Square station to grab the subway home. I figured I'd try and call Johnny once I got to the apartment and find out if he'd talked to Kieran about this.

As I waited for the train I glanced over at the newsstand near the platform. Maybe I'd grab a Butterfinger or a few Snickers to tide me over before I got home. But instead of chocolate candy covers, the only things attracting my attention were the headlines on every New York rag propped on the counter.

No! Not Noble! Notebooms "No" Nothing!
Story Old as "Endless" Time. Crime and Sex
in the Afternoon!
Soap Star's Act Stained!

I bought a copy of each one, including the *National Enquirer* in case the story was now more than local, and hid them in my dance bag. Absurdly, I didn't want anyone else to see them on the train, but I wanted to get a line on exactly what kind of trash the papers had manufactured.

Most of what was being said had been covered by Jayce Cracknell's front-page article. I skimmed through the story. Mob bride. Shady tycoon. Money laundering. Soap star. Gregory Noble. Johnny Gerard.

I continued my perusal. Nothing new, nothing more startling until I reached a sentence that made me want to just stay on the train until I reached the last stop in Riverdale or

Yonkers or wherever out of Manhattan the Number One IRT train travels.

"Mrs. Nicholas Toblaroni, Terresota Grayson Toblaroni, (Tracy) could not be reached for comment."

Tracy Toblaroni. The Drooling Rich Bitch from O'Malley's bar. The babe who'd called Johnny at my apartment back in November. The girl in the white limousine I'd last seen in front of my building the day of *Boundaries* auditions. The possible paramour to both father and son. Tracy.

EIGHTEEN

SHAY WAS WAITING for me outside our building.

"I saw."

"Shay. This is a disaster. Not only is Johnny in trouble with the Notebooms and backers of *Boundaries,* he could be in trouble with the police as well if they decide there's a connection to the mob here. Then there's the reverse scenario. He could be in deep *doo-doo* with the mob. As in cement-type-overshoes deep. I don't think they like outsiders messing with family members of the bosses. Especially wives."

Shay and I entered the elevator of the brownstone. I couldn't face seven flights today. She handed me the one newspaper I hadn't yet seen. Not one of the rags. Not a cute come-on headline. It was far more lethal. This paper carried weight. This paper could ruin Johnny, the Notebooms and the show itself.

D.A.'s Office Looking Into Allegations of Ties Between Mob and Notebooms

The suits at *Boundaries* were gonna love that. Since the middle suit was one of the famed Notebooms himself, Johnny would be lucky to get a job sweeping the alley behind the theatre by the time tomorrow's paper hit the stoops of New York.

"Damn, Shay. I don't know what to do. I don't even know what to think."

I paused. "Did you happen to notice the first name of Mrs. Nick Toblaroni?"

She shook her head no.

"I don't think the *Times* gave anything but Candy Nick's name. Why?"

"Her given name is Terresota. Her nickname is Tracy."

Shay wasn't quick on the uptake at first.

"Terresota? What the hell kind of moniker is that to drop on a kid at birth? Wait a minute. Go back. Did you say 'Tracy'? As in drooling-rich-bitch-call-our-apartment-last-November-and-follow-Johnny-around-town-in-the-white-limo-possible-connection-to-Cookie Tracy?"

She looked at my face.

"Oops. Obviously it was. Oh my gosh, Abby, do you suppose all this stuff about Johnny and the mob is true? And if not, why isn't his father helping him sort this mess out?"

"Because Daddy Dearest has apparently also been on the receiving end of Miss Tracy's charms and would rather the world think less of his son than him. Well after all, Johnny's just an actor. Who cares? Right? They have no morals anyway. I despise Kieran Gerard."

We'd reached our apartment. Cherry had obviously heard us in the hall and had the door wide open.

"Abby! Ya want Vito and Guido to take this A.D. fellow out?"

"Thanks, Cherry. I think we need to wait and see what's going to happen."

I didn't even have the heart to correct her turnaround of the initials "A.D." and tell her that the year wasn't the problem; the District Attorney was.

I threw my junk on the sofa.

"Cherry? Has Johnny called here? He tore out of rehearsal like the hounds of hell were after him. Didn't say a word to anyone. Just turned so red I couldn't even see his freckles anymore! I gotta admit I'm more than a little worried."

And I'd like an explanation of this Tracy story.

"Na. Sorry. I've been here for the last two hours. No one's called. Oh. Except Minette. She wanted to know if this Johnny character was the same guy you've been dating."

"Has this crap hit the Texas papers? Why on earth?"

Shay answered instead of Cherry. "Price of television soap fame. Think of it. Johnny Gerard, the great Gregory Noble on the highest-rated soap this season caught in a huge sex scandal involving organized crime and theatrical types. What reporter in any state in the union could resist? Sorry, Abby."

"I know. I just am not thrilled with the fact that Minette knows about all this. I'm surprised she hasn't called the governor to borrow a Lear Jet or something and fly up here to rescue her baby."

I started pacing. "This might all be straightened out if that coward of a father owned up to dating Miss Tracy. Terresota Toblaroni. Jeez, what a name. Sounds like a dessert pizza topping."

I was starting to sound like Cherry. I quickened my pacing. "Terresota. If I ever meet up with the witch she'll find out what Terror is. A Texas Terror. I'll rip her little fur coat from limb to limb, preferably with her in it. Then I'll introduce her to Minette. She and her stinkin' blonde chauffeur hit man will wish they'd stayed in whatever hole they crawled out of."

Shay nodded approvingly. "You tell 'em. Meantime, Miss Menace-to-Society, what are you going to do?"

"Find Johnny. This really worries me, his not calling or showing up here or anything. And I tried his apartment before I left the theatre. No answer. Where could he be?"

"Take a deep breath. Now breathe semi-normally and think for a moment. You know him better than anyone. Where could he have gone?"

I thought about the possible whereabouts of the man as calmly as I was able. I grabbed a piece of cold pizza left on the coffee table from this morning (the table itself, not the carton) and absently stuffed it in my mouth. Shay wisely made no comment about this total lapse in good judgment.

"Bingo! I've got it. He's gone to see his father. At Centre Street. Not at the penthouse. I'll wager my new cream-colored sweater on it."

Shay looked at her watch. "It's six o'clock. Suppose anyone's left at Centre Street?"

"Are you kidding? Those people work twenty hours a day. Johnny told me one reason his mother wanted to leave the D.A.'s office even before she got involved with Kieran was the hours. They've never heard of a normal eight- or even ten-hour day. I'm sure Kieran's still there. Probably a great place for the craven little scumbag to hide. He can let his minions talk to the reporters and give himself time to get his lies straight. That's it. I'm headed down there."

"Wait, Abby. What are you planning on doing once you get there?"

"Spitting in Kieran Gerard's face if I can work up a good amount of saliva. Then I'll figure out where to take it from there. Hell, Shay. I mainly want to find Johnny and make sure he's okay. And wring the truth out of him concerning his relationship with Tracy Toblaroni if I have to beat him up to do it."

"Want company? Better yet, want a loyal roomie? You're gonna have to have a tough broad to sock the man in the jaw, you know. Or a tall broad, since you can barely *reach* his jaw. No offense. Or I could send Fuji with a baseball bat."

I nearly said *yes*. Then I grinned.

"That's okay. I have my flying Fouchet feet. Even that Aryan Nation clown Siegfried-the-hulk will be Siegfried-the-small by the time I'm through with him and his snaky employer. Thanks for the offer, though. I think I'll work up a better mad if I'm by myself. And if I do decide to rain down fire and brimstone on the younger Mr. Gerard as well as Tracy, Siggie, et al, I won't be aiming for his face. If it turns out Johnny's been messing with this Candyman's wife, he's going to find out what life is like as a tenor instead of a baritone."

Cherry had entered the room during my rant and now cheered. I bowed to her.

"I'll even take a taxi. That's guaranteed to make me crazy. A cab in Manhattan during rush hour. If my nerves survive I'll be ready to take on the entire D.A.'s office and every reporter camped outside with my little cowboy boots."

I grabbed my bag again and flew out the door before Shay or Cherry had time to acknowledge and applaud the last part of this ridiculous speech. I didn't wait for the elevator, just ran down the seven flights in less time than it took to even press the lift button. I charged out onto 79th Street like a girl on a mission. Which I was. A cab was just dropping off a fare at the building next to ours. I was inside the taxi while the gentleman who'd been riding was still doling out his change.

"One hundred Centre Street, please. And don't spare the rubber."

That was embarrassing. First I was talking like Cherry in the matter of Tracy's given name. Now I was starting to sound like either a character in a B movie or Vito and Guido on a normal day. I blushed in the privacy of the cab. Either way, I knew I had to arrange my thoughts before I confronted the great Kieran Gerard.

My driver turned. She was wearing an orange-and-black African-style tunic top that had more fringe draped on the sleeves and more beads around the neckline than a hippie leftover from Woodstock touring through an Egyptian bazaar. She wore a neon-pink turban over her Raggedy Ann hairdo. She was undeniably familiar.

"Madam Euphoria?"

She flashed a grin at me in the rearview mirror.

"None other. Hi, Abby."

"I hate to ask this, but did you know you'd be picking me up today?"

She ignored my question and drove swiftly through the crowded midtown traffic, expertly weaving a path through buses, pedestrians, horse patrol cops and frantic commuters.

I had to compliment her on her skill and calm demeanor.

"Damn. You're an amazing driver. I'd be crawling into the first vending cart I could find and pulling the lid over me. These people are nuts. How do you do it?"

"I was raised two blocks from Riverside Drive on 139th Street. Learned to drive on the West Side Highway. On slow days I'd go up to Washington Heights and cruise Broadway at 175th. Guaranteed to turn one into a fearless racer!"

She winked at me in the mirror. "I love my neighborhood. Got some great soul-food places and incredible hat shops. You can get anything from Sunday go-to-meetin' to beanies to this big ol' turban I got on now."

"I love your tunic. You look gorgeous in it. I think it would swallow me. And the dreadlocks are great. When they're unbound your hair must reach your—well, butt!"

She grinned. "Almost. If you remember from our talk outside after Yolanda's party, I'm a big girl. Six-six when I stand up straight. It's good to be big in my profession though. Kind of gives one respect."

"What? When being a medium? People who don't like your predictions or don't buy the Chief Blackie bit? Or for when you're driving? I doubt anyone would consider mugging you!"

She grinned and laughed. Huge wooden earrings bounced against her cheeks.

"Driving is just part-time, remember? I take the cab out for my brother when he needs a break and I need some cash. I'm much more comfortable among the tarot cards, palms, tea leaves and crystal balls. Did I tell you every woman in my family is a reader? It's been passed down for hundreds of years. I'd be disowned if I didn't follow in the business."

"I didn't really get to hear much about you when we met before. And let's face it. I was focusing on other things. Like strange newspaper articles in hallucinations. This may sound rude, but do you think you're truly psychic?"

She laughed.

"On good days, girl. On good days. Let's see. I can tell you're from Texas, how's that?"

"You're kidding. How did you know that?"

"Well, to be honest, I can't take a lot of beyond-this-world credit for figuring that out. I'm good with listening to people's accents, and kid, you're from Texas. Besides, Yolanda told me at her party. Which I guess is cheatin'. Seriously, though, I do get flashes about people. I think I told you, I'm somewhat of an empath. I don't see future events. It's more like feelings about things."

Her tone grew almost ominous.

"I've been getting some strange feelings about you since the first time you sat down at that séance. I haven't been able to stop thinking about you and that man of yours."

I didn't know what to think. I hadn't had a premonition since Kieran's party and I wasn't sure I needed someone else hearing strange things from the universe about me. But I'm undeniably nosy. Especially when talking to someone who might just have some answers for me.

"Like what kind of strange feelings?"

She didn't answer. She pointed outside and screeched the cab into a space my old Volkswagen wouldn't have fit into.

"One hundred Centre Street. Are you doing any better? Are you ready to face the dragon?"

I know I must have looked like Little Orphan Annie. My eyes and mouth had formed one huge "O." Huge brown eyes met mine. She smiled, but her eyes registered concern.

"Abby, I hate saying this. I can see dark things hovering around you. I do. And I know you're in for a fight."

I dug in my bag for the fare and placed the money into her hands. I added an extra-big tip.

She held my hand just a second longer.

"Girl, remember. This is *your* life. Fight for what is right in it. And trust your vision."

She repeated.

"Fight for what is right. Trust your vision."

Then she was gone.

I looked around me. Centre Street. Home to hundreds of legal eagles. And legal carrion, which was how I'd begun to think of Mr. Kieran Gerard. I straightened my shoulders and walked up the steps.

NINETEEN

I'M NOT GOOD AT CONFRONTATIONS. I have been known to throw things (ugly hotel lamps came to mind) or speak out (usually without thinking first). But I don't usually stand up to people (especially authority figures) without feeling nasty pains in my stomach and getting panicky. One thing I've always admired about Minette is her expertise in dealing with tense situations with a combination of charm and assertiveness. I've often wished I could emulate this talent. She has no qualms about taking on anyone, no matter how powerful and challenging they are. She does it in that quiet, Georgia-born raised-as-a-belle voice. Never pitched too high, never frantic.

If the need arose, she could face a thief in the very act of stealing the Hope diamond and make him or her feel guilty for ever attempting such a foolish thing in the first place. I tried to remember that exact genteel, steely tone she always used. I'm not a bad mimic. I just hoped I wouldn't lose my temper when I met Kieran Gerard and forget to pretend I was my mother chastising an errant sinner. As Johnny had pointed out to me on more than one occasion I do have a colorful way of expressing my anger. (He was still teasing me about the "spandexed water moccasin" line I'd used on the Barbie doll at Yolanda's party.)

I didn't even notice where I was going after I read the name "Gerard" on the directory list near a watercooler in one of the halls. Prosecuting and defense attorneys were busy making deals in the offices I passed. They ignored the angry Texas dancer that was striding down the hall with her cowboy boots tapping like bullets on the bare floor.

I'd almost made it to the corridor that housed Kieran Gerard's office when I was knocked off my feet by a tall blonde man tearing down the hall. He was carrying a briefcase and moving as if he was going for the winning touchdown. My bag went one way. I went the other. I was dusting off my knees and hoping nothing was permanently damaged when a hand hoisted me to my feet. I looked up into the perfect blue eyes of Mr. Chase Jaffert, lawyer. He began to apologize. Profusely.

"I'm so sorry! I wasn't watching where I was going. Most of the staff left an hour ago and the night-court lawyers are busy sifting through files in their offices. I didn't expect anyone to be in the hall. Which is no excuse, of course. It's Miss Fouchet, isn't it? We met at Kieran's party. Chase Jaffert."

I brushed the dust off my jacket and jeans and started to retrieve the items that had spilled from my bag. My small cosmetic case had rolled under a watercooler, and my wallet was under my foot. I placed the wallet back in my bag and started to walk to the watercooler. One other item had fallen from the bag. It was the newspaper article concerning Johnny and the Toblaroni scandal. Chase Jaffert picked it up. Maybe it was because I was angry at seeing that paper in anyone's hand for everyone to read that I was more abrupt than I needed to be. I put my hand out.

"I want that back—now."

"I wasn't planning to keep it."

He started to hand me the crumpled paper. I snatched it from him.

"Thank you. I'm sorry to be rude, Mr. Jaffert, but I'm in a hurry to reach Mr. Gerard's office. If you'll excuse me. Nice to see you again."

An arm intercepted me and blocked me from moving.

"Miss Fouchet? Abby?"

"Yes?"

"Look, this is none of my business, but I can tell you this disaster surrounding Mr. Gerard is not going to go away anytime soon. I don't presume to know the extent of your relationship with Johnny, but I do remember you quite well from Kieran's party. You're an attractive girl. You seem intelligent and I'd hate to see someone like you involved in this kind of sordid matter. If I may give you a word of advice, stay clear of Johnny Gerard. You might end up very hurt, more so than you even think you are now. It's best if you just go home."

I wondered if he somehow knew Minette. That was a lecture straight out of her quotations from the "this is what's best for you" book. I've heard the warnings too many times. I looked at Chase Jaffert, at his undeniably handsome looks, at his perfectly pressed navy suit and his perfectly coifed hair. I couldn't help wonder if the man had ever known a day of pain in his perfect life. I shook off the thought. He was trying to be helpful, even if his statements had sounded like a cross between a pick-up line and a lecture.

"Mr. Jaffert."

"Chase."

"Chase. I thank you for caring about the feelings of a woman you've only met twice, but I'm a big girl. Maybe not physically, but emotionally I can take care of myself. I have to go where I need to be. Which, right now, is Kieran Gerard's office. Again, thank you for your support and your advice."

I dodged any more discussion by executing ballet split leaps down the rest of the hall. I found a closed door with Kieran Gerard's name stenciled in bold gold letters. It was unlocked. I peeked inside.

Johnny was sitting in a small chair in Kieran's office. Six cans of soda were in the wastebasket and scraps of newspaper were littered all over Kieran's desk. Drawers had also been pulled out and papers tossed on the floor. Files were scattered on top of other files. The surface of the desk that was not hidden by scraps of shredded paper was chipped and cut as though someone had taken a knife to the wood and carved a bit too vigorously.

"Johnny?"

"Abby? What are you doing here?"

"I had a feeling you'd be here. I wanted to know what was going on. Have you seen Kieran yet?"

He shook his head.

"You're nuts, my lovely Miss Dancer. You know that? You should be home practicing your music for tomorrow's rehearsal. Or you're welcome to start singing those songs to me. I doubt I'll get to hear them at tomorrow's rehearsal because I doubt I'm welcome at *Boundaries*. Or anywhere else in the Manhattan theatre community. Maybe I could kidnap Cookie from the hospital, grab a fast boat to Santo Domingo and sing to tourists, while Cookie's grandmother makes vats of rice and beans so I won't starve."

I grabbed his hands and knelt down in front of him.

"Johnny. Are you drunk? Or just crazy? Doesn't matter. For some unknown and probably stupid reason, I'd like to see that you don't get kicked out the show or thrown in jail. And you were so angry this afternoon I could just imagine you sailing in here and doing something rash like punching out dear old Dad. I thought my presence here might stop that."

Someone coughed, then stated, "Good idea, Miss Fouchet. As far as it goes. Which isn't very far because I'd like both of you to leave my office immediately."

I turned. Kieran Gerard, looking devilishly handsome in a striped navy suit, white shirt and navy tie, stood in the doorway and surveyed the damage done. He began to yell at his son.

"How dare you! How dare you waltz into my office and destroy it?"

"How *dare* I? How dare *I?* You sick, rotten, cowardly, bastardly excuse for a parent! You've got the nerve to accuse me of destroying your office when you've taken great care to destroy my life? You won't take responsibility for your own actions. Oh, no. You dump all your sins on me. Was this the plan the whole time? Anything goes wrong with your little illicit love affair and let's have a scapegoat tailor-made in the shape of my stupid son, John?"

"I'm not going to discuss this with you."

"Why? I'm the dupe. Doesn't the dupe have the right to know the reasons for the duplicity? Damn, Kieran, just give me a break and tell me if you're at least going to stand up and take the blame for this."

Kieran wasn't budging.

"I asked you both to leave. I'd appreciate it if you'd do so, before I'm forced to call security. Get out. Now."

Johnny looked as though he would have liked to take a swing at the older man. Then he let his arm drop and took my hand in his.

"We'll leave, Kieran. Because we obviously aren't going to get any satisfaction from you this evening. I have to say something, though. I wanted a relationship with you because I miss Mom more than I can possibly say. But at this point I don't think of you as even my biological father. I think of you as a sperm donor. Nothing more. Which someday you might think is a shame because I'm actually a pretty neat guy. Some people seem to think so, anyway."

He began to lead me out of the office, then turned quickly around to face his father.

"Oh, Kieran? One more thing. About the mess here? I drank six cans of soda today. The empties are in your wastebasket. And that was the sum total of my activities here. Someone else trashed your office. Not me. Think about that while you're congratulating yourself on shoving blame onto others. You're in someone's sights, Kieran. Someone is not happy with you at all. And if that someone is Candy Nick Toblaroni, then heaven help you."

We left the man to his vandalized room and fears and destructible thoughts and walked hand in hand down the hall to the large doors leading back out to the street. Several people popped out of their respective cubbyholes to watch our progress and stare. I felt very uncomfortable, but also very proud. Johnny had stood up to his father. He hadn't made a heck of a lot of headway, but at least he hadn't run away. Neither had I.

We stood in silence for a moment as we waited for a taxi to come by. Johnny squeezed my hand.

"What happened at rehearsal after I left? Did anybody say anything?"

"Not much. They're playing it very close to the vest, as it were. Remember the old saying about 'as nervous as a cat's tail in a room of rocking chairs'? Well, put the suits on the felines and you've got a damn good picture. They all have that look in their wealthy little eyes that says 'I don't want to be involved.' And their little tails are just twitching and ducking under their, well, tails. What?"

He'd been wincing at each word.

"I'm not going to have a job by tomorrow. You just watch. And I've got to tell you, Abby, I'm damned afraid of anything to do with the mob. And that's who's involved here. I'm sure. I'd love to know just what this whole thing has been about on their part. And just where Kieran fits in beyond engaging in sexual activities with the tempting Tracy, excuse me, Terresota Toblaroni."

It was time to ask him just what the nature of his relationship was to Tracy and get a straight answer for once. But I couldn't get the words out. What if part of the reason he was so angry with Kieran was that he felt betrayed that he and his father had been seeing the same woman? What if he was frightened for her? And himself? As well he should be if Nicholas Toblaroni decided to believe the stories from the paper and go hunting with one soap opera star as the prime prey. A broken parachute would be the least of it.

I shuddered. A yellow, checkered cab screeched to a halt. Johnny pulled me to him, kissed me hard once and nearly threw me bodily into the taxi.

"I've got something else to do. I'll call you later. Please trust me."

He whirled around and took off back in the direction of the courthouse. I sat for a minute in the cab, unsure of just what my options were at this point. Follow him? He obviously didn't want me with him or he would have let me stay. Go home? I couldn't face an evening alone in the apartment brooding about this day's events. Shay had said something about plans to see Fuji tonight, but I didn't know the exact time she was going.

I stared at the back of the driver's head while he waited, with more patience than the normal New York cabbie, for me to give him a destination. I sat still and mulled over the fact that the equation of Johnny and Kieran and Tracy and Candy Nick didn't add up.

At the party for his father, Johnny told me Kieran knew this Terresota wench was a married woman. Kieran knew that. If he'd known her husband was a reputed mob boss and sought her out anyway, he must have known her husband would catch on to the affair pretty quickly.

So why would he worry about hiding anything from the mob? He wasn't. He was more interested in trying to kid the public and still get elected. So he needed Johnny as scapegoat if the affair became public. Which might just mean that Kieran Gerard was up to his starched collar in shady dealings with the Toblaroni family. Which meant he had no intention of clearing Johnny's name. Which meant Johnny had to clear it himself. I still didn't know the extent of the Johnny and Tracy relationship, but I knew one thing. Johnny loved the theatre too much to ever bring it down. A scandal involving money laundering and the Noteboooms would do just that. Ergo, Johnny was innocent of any wrongdoing as regards to organized crime.

No matter what happened between us I had to see if I could help clear his name. Maybe it was those years with Minette and her lawyer friends. Most were politicians, some were prosecutors, some were defense attorneys, some worked strictly in corporate and private sectors. They all had one thing in common. They believed in justice. So did I.

Another vision hit me, but this one was based on solid memory instead of shadowy second sights of the future. Two men in identical orange suits and Hawaiian-print blazers with bulges in the pockets kept coming into view. Two men who were staunch fans of Johnny Gerard. Two men who doubtless had a few connections in places I didn't even want to dream of. I'd been given invitations by my third roommate to visit her place of employment for months now. It was time to accept.

I leaned forward and motioned to the cabdriver.

"Forty-fifth and 8th Avenue, please."

I was about to enlist the services of the brothers Mariccino.

TWENTY

THE SQUIRREL SHOT Gentlemen's Club on 8th Avenue was moderately crowded for early evening on a weekday. Cherry had once told me the place didn't start stirring until after eleven. I entered with more than slight trepidation. At least I didn't have to pay a cover charge. Ladies got in free. I guess they figured they weren't going to lose much money that way. The man at the door gave me a strange look as he motioned me inside. I was thrust smack in the middle of what was my first (and hopefully last) foray into the world of soft porn live entertainment.

Sturdy wooden tables using cheap candles as the only decoration were in every conceivable spot in the club. Navigation was a bit difficult. Men of all ages, ethnic groups and professions sipped alcoholic concoctions (mostly beer) and stared at the four women currently writhing atop different tables to the sounds of "Lady Marmalade." I love that song. I found I was singing and swaying to the music as I tried to find a vacant place where I could look for Cherry and the Mariccino twins.

I looked around. It appeared the fleet was in. Guys who looked barely old enough to drive were sloshing each other with glasses of beer and eyeing me with more hunger than I have for a La Mirage muffin with butter.

I told myself I'd best not be gyrating to the music or the boys in uniform would think I was part of the floorshow. I was in no mood to engage in fisticuffs with the Navy or the Marines to save my virtue.

Too late. My small movements to "Lady Marmalade" had been seen and had attracted the attention of a very young, very large kid in shore-leave whites.

"Hey, cutie! Whyn't you dance on over here! Jake, Tommy, look at this one here! Hey, baby, need a lift to the top of our table?"

I didn't want a peach-fuzzed drunk missing part of his teeth calling me cutie, baby, or trying to entice me to entertain them with a lap dance. I tried to move away and was blocked by two other guys. Jake and Tommy, I presumed.

The trio scooped me up and deposited me on top of their table between three bottles of beer and a basket of pretzels. For one ridiculous moment I found myself coveting those pretzels. The last thing eaten today had been that stale pizza slice at home. The pretzels looked fresh.

The music had changed to a new song I'd heard once or twice before but didn't know the title of. I liked the deejay's taste. We had used the song for turns across the floor in Ricky's class, and he'd even choreographed a gorgeous dance to it for an outdoor concert coming up at the Delacorte in August. Before I realized it, I was starting to shimmy a bit.

That stopped immediately when my table of sailors began whistling, clapping and exhorting me to shed a few layers. I jumped off the table, landing in a deep first-position *plié* to save my knees from impact and took a deep breath.

I quickly looked around for an empty table anywhere away from my new admirers. Admirers who weren't keen on losing what they seemed to think of as their personal pet. I kept jumping up and down as they circled me, trying to see over their heads and make my escape.

Claustrophobia was setting in. I needed air. I needed space. Rescue came in the forms of Vito and Guido Mariccino, bouncers extraordinaire.

"Hey!"

Vito lifted "peach-fuzz" clean off his feet although the sailor was at least a head taller. The boy's buddies stared.

"Don't you know who this is?"

All three shook their heads. Guido jabbed his index finger into a broad chest as Vito allowed his victim's feet to touch ground again.

"This is Gregory Noble's girl! She ain't no bimbo, she ain't tonight's entertainment, or tomorrow's breakfast, and she ain't available to none of you!"

That said, the Mariccino twins each took an elbow and gently escorted me to an empty table on the far side of the club. They signaled to the waiter and a gin and tonic appeared so fast I wondered if Madam Euphoria had snuck in behind me and given the bartender my drink preference.

The sailors looked disappointed. But they quickly found fresh meat when a bouncing blonde in a red teddy sashayed towards them and was helped to their tabletop by my beefy tattooed would-be swain with the chipped-toothed grin. The girl began her gyrations above them and I was (thankfully) ignored.

A long runway that curved into a U was vacant about three feet away from my hideaway. Cherry had once explained that tabletop dancing was the order of the day until nine at night when the girls took to the runway for actual routines. "Choreographied and all" had been Cherry's proud statement.

Vito and Guido had gotten called away right after I sat down to unknown parts of the bar. I'd been so busy watching the action in the place, I'd let them go without explaining that I needed their unique services to help Johnny Gerard.

I searched for my roommate through the smoky haze of the club. I found her atop a table shimmying to the music that had now changed to a very old disco song. "Love to Love You, Baby." She was wearing bronze pasties and a leather python striped G-string. I blinked, wondering if I was imagining things. I blinked again. Same outfit. She was plying her trade on the opposite side of the club from where I was sitting. I was glad that Johnny wasn't with me. I had no desire to see his eyes light up when he noticed that Cherry was built, as the saying goes, like the proverbial Brick House. I started humming the old Commodore song about that particular concept, but "Love to Love You, Baby" unfortunately kept intruding.

I downed my drink and replayed the day's events in my head. I was about to get Vito and Guido entangled knee-, or in their case, chest-deep in this sex-mob triangle, rectangle, pentangle, whatever angle, scandal. The pair may come off as characters in a bad play Way-Off Broadway, but Cherry had often told me they had connections no one else in the city does. She had more than hinted on many occasions that the twins could find out the most amazing things about New York's major players, whatever that meant, while staying as discreet as was possible when one or two are wearing neon-colored polyester suits.

I waved again at Cherry to make sure she knew I was here. My hand froze midwave.

A man stood by the bar lighting a huge cigar. He bore a remarkable resemblance to Siegfried. Tracy's chauffeur. Park-shooting gunman? Hit man for Candy Nick?

I dropped a book of the club's matches on the floor and bent down to retrieve them. Same man. Siegfried, the tall and gorgeous. Why was Tracy's driver hanging out here? His presence was making me very nervous. Was he following me? Did he intend on doing me bodily harm? Or was he just a casual customer come to watch the scantily clad girls shake their stuff?

I mentioned earlier I have a problem with confrontations. This includes standing up to both people and situations. Until recently, that's meant my mother. Consequently she's been able to manipulate me into attending her multitudinous fundraisers, and also when I was a teenager, play peacemaker between her and my dad when they were fighting. (Usually about me and my dreams of dancing on Broadway.) I've also had problems going to auditions. There were at least five great auditions I skipped my first month in New York for no other reason than sheer panic. Rejection has not been my favorite thing (is it anyone's?) and I was always worried I wasn't as good as the other dancers. I have long understood that I wasn't the most assertive person in the world. I run away rather than fight.

Why am I bringing this up?

Because this was one time I knew I couldn't chicken out. I didn't know where this investigation would lead. I didn't know if Johnny Gerard was an innocent pawn or the most notorious scoundrel this side of Butch Cassidy. I only knew that Abby Fouchet, generally mild-mannered daughter of Minette Fouchet, had to stay and fight and find out the truth. Chauffeurs, lawyers and drooling rich bitches be damned.

Cherry descended from her perch above a group of sailors tucking bills into her G-string. I winced, knowing that cash usually ended up in the hand of the pizza deliveryman, often by means of a middleman—me. She trotted over to greet me wearing a huge smile and very little else.

She plopped almost wearily into the chair I pulled out for her and immediately lit a cigarette. She jumped into the non-existent conversation without preamble.

"I told you that Tracy broad was trouble. Didden I say that the first time she called Johnny after those *Superstar* people broke your foot?"

"You did, Cherry. You are almost as psychic as Minette and Madam Euphoria, the Harlem cabdriver. The three of you scare me senseless. Great-Granny Dumas would love you all. Listen, I need help. Do you know where Vito and Guido went off to?"

Cherry is often frighteningly quick. She has street smarts that career drug dealers envy. She knew I hadn't come to

The Squirrel Shot Gentlemen's Club on 8th Avenue for the entertainment.

"Sure. They're in the back playing a few hands of poker. Hang on. I'll get 'em."

I thought she'd wander to "the back" and bring the twins with her, but instead she whistled loud enough for every man in the joint to turn his head and continued to take long drags on her cigarette. In less than ten seconds the Mariccino brothers were at our table. I smothered a grin. They'd changed clothes in the few minutes they'd been away from me. Their attire was now white and pink. Pink shirts with white ties and white blazers over. White pants. With hair greased back so the color looked completely black, they looked like vanilla ice-cream cones with a swirl of strawberry and chocolate sprinkles on top.

"Hey, how ya doin'? How's Gregory Noble?"

"Vito, don' ask that. You know how he's doin'. You read the papers. He's doin' crappy."

The pair shook their heads.

"He gotta bum rap, Greg did. Sold out by his old man. Ain't good. Family is everything. A man should understand that, ya know?"

I nodded.

"I know."

I looked directly at Guido.

"I need some help here, guys. Johnny, uh, Greg, is in a world of trouble. He could lose his job at the theatre. He could get hurt. He could get killed."

The pair nodded somewhat sympathetically while I rattled off this litany of doom. Nothing stronger crossed the planes of their faces.

"He could be fired from *Endless Time*."

This possible scenario that Gregory Noble could disappear from their favorite daytime drama forever worked miracles.

The twins straightened their shoulders in synchronized lifts, flinched and looked at me with absolute horror.

"We gotta do sumpin' about this, Vito. We can't let them kill off Gregory Noble. Bad enough that Carla babe was fixin' his parachute to stay closed. Nobody does that and gets away wid it if we can stop it."

Vito's head was bobbing in agreement.

"We know some guys, ya know? We'll do a little talkin' and see if we can find a solution to the problem. Okay?"

I relaxed. For no good reason I could think of, I had confidence the Mariccino twins would come through. They would find a solution to how Johnny and the Notebooms could keep their respective good names. The fact that Vito and Guido didn't seem to know the difference between Johnny the actor and the character he played on the soap would work in his favor. This pair would storm the gates of heaven, hell, or daytime drama network studios to keep their beloved Gregory Noble from harm's way.

Cherry was determined that I stay to watch her first real number of the evening. While I wasn't enthused about viewing Cherry in even less than she wears on her way to our bathroom in the morning, I felt I couldn't refuse. After all, she was lending me the dubious talents of Vito and Guido Mariccino. The least I could do was sit through a four-minute song.

She wasn't half-bad either. I found that I started watching her performance with the eyes of a dancer critiquing rather than a female being embarrassed. She was pretty good, with a nice control over her body. I was garnering an appreciation for a different style of movement, albeit one I would not care to exhibit. Cherry was quite entertaining. She bumped, ground and writhed her way through her number showing lots of energy and, of course, most of her great figure. Her kicks were about a foot lower and a lot more bent than the average Rockette's, and she didn't have the best rhythm, but she made up for it with lots of smiling and waving and interaction with the crowd. The sailors whistled and cheered. I clapped. Vito clapped, whistled and cheered. Guido looked morose.

"Guido? Are you okay? Don't you like Cherry's act?"

"Can I confess sumpin' to ya, Abby?"

"Sure. Hey, you're about to play private eye for Johnny and me. You can tell me anything."

I shuddered as I said that, fleetingly wondering what I'd do if Guido admitted to a major felony, or any possible variety of lusty scenarios with my lightly clad roommate.

"I really like Cherry."

I looked at him sharply.

"You mean?"

"I mean, I really like Cherry. I wanna marry her and move outta the city and start a family in Jersey. But I'm scared to tell her 'cause I don' wanna ruin her career or nuthin'."

I could see it now. Cherry wriggling her way down a crowded school auditorium to accept the honor of PTA mother of the year in East Orange, New Jersey. I never knew what "it boggles the mind" truly felt like until that moment. I smiled at the lovesick bouncer.

"I think that's terrific, Guido. Uh. Just maybe take her out sometime without Vito? So y'all can get to know each other. But, hey. You have my full blessing, for what it's worth."

He grinned, showing nearly all of his perfectly capped teeth.

"Thanks. I think I'll take your advice. You're a good kid, Abby. And don' you worry none about Gregory. I swear Vito and me will set this right."

Cherry finished her number and waved to one and all, then disappeared down the runway to the dressing rooms in the back of the club. I decided it was time to make a clean getaway. I hugged Vito and Guido and told them to let me know as soon as they found out anything. Then I headed for the door and out onto 8th Avenue. Guido came with me.

"What's the matter? You're not going with Vito for the investigation?"

"Cherry just said she'd feel better if ya had an escort home. I volunteered. I'll meet up wid' Vito later."

"Thanks, Guido. I do feel safer having you around."

The air outside felt so pure I inhaled to dispel the smoke and booze smells from my nose and lungs. I smiled at my bodyguard. "Listen, let me get us a cab, okay? I didn't have to pay a cover at the club so I still have some bills left. And I'll treat you to a cup of coffee when we get to the apartment."

"Abby, I got money. I don' wanna take yours."

"Hey. These are small expenses for your detecting services. I can't tell you how much it means for Johnny and me to have you guys on our side."

"No problem. Gregory Noble's my hero. I even taped every episode since he got on."

I sighed. It might well be a long cab ride back to 79th Street.

TWENTY-ONE

GUIDO WAVED DOWN THE only taxi not careening down the street at more than forty miles an hour and politely held the door open for me.

I gave the cabby directions to the apartment. We hadn't gone more than three blocks up 8th Avenue when the driver, an attractive male in his thirties, turned to face us.

"I don't know if you've seen it or not, but there's a white limo that pulled out behind us as soon as I picked you up. He seems to be following a bit closer than these guys normally like to. Almost like a tail. I've been driving a cab for ten years in Manhattan and drivers in limousines like to pass fast and stay in a lane where they won't get scratched. But this one's right on my bumper."

I turned. Our cabby was right. Even at night I was able to clearly see who sat behind the wheel. Siegfried. Whom I'd last seen in The Squirrel Shot Gentlemen's Club on 8th Avenue minutes before. Tracy's devoted chauffeur. I just wished he'd find an Opera Company somewhere, get cast as an extra in each and every Wagnerian performance, and stay away from Johnny and me.

Guido's face set and grew bright red.

"Okay. Time to try the stuff I learned from watching Gregory Noble goin' undercover and shakin' the bad guys. He's amazin', ya know. Got moves that even Vito and I can't figure out."

I stared at him.

"Gregory Noble is a cop?"

"Of course he's a cop! All guys on soaps are either cops or doctors. Don't you watch the show?"

Before I could answer, Guido began tapping our driver on the shoulder. "'Scuse me?"

"Yo."

"Interested in makin' a little extra tonight and helping out the girlfriend of Gregory Noble? The babe here?"

I was about to interject that if I was anyone's girlfriend, or babe, it was Johnny Gerard's, not Gregory Noble's. I waited for the driver to ask if we were both crazy.

I saw eyebrows lift in the rearview mirror, followed by a quick smile. "Hey, anything to help a fellow actor."

I laughed. "You're in the business. Jeez. Is everyone in this city in theatre?"

He smiled. "Seems that way sometimes. Especially at auditions. But I know Johnny Gerard. I was a day player on *Endless Time* about six months ago. Did a few scenes with him. Nice guy. Saw him in *Carousel* a couple years back, too. Super voice. Hey. I know you! You were dancing with him in the disco stuff they did while he was in the coma. You're really good."

"Thanks."

I leaned back in my seat. For a place as crowded as New York, it was incredible how many people knew one another. Not to mention soap opera fans. Guido and the driver (who had given his name as Clancy) had already started swapping *Endless Time* story lines and cast biographies. Then they got serious. Clancy inclined his head towards Guido.

"So. Whatcha need me to do? About your guy in the limo?"

Guido changed his tone to that of a businessman about to make the deal of a lifetime.

"I need to have a nice chat with this blonde-headed clown. Can you stop between those two delivery trucks a block up the street near 56th? I'm gonna sneak out the door nearest the curb, and you're gonna pull out from behind those trucks and take Abby home. While you're high-tailing it outta here, I'm gonna pay a visit to his window. With a friend."

I shuddered. I had a feeling the friend was the bulge that ruined the line of his blazer. I didn't approve of this plan.

"Guido. Wait. What are you going to do? It isn't anything that can get you killed or jailed, is it? Or anyone else killed?"

"'Ssokay. I'm just gonna talk to him. He's Toblaroni's driver, right? You can bet he's got more dirt on Mrs. Tracy than her garbage collector. I'll just persuade him to share it. I'm good at persuadin'."

Clancy pulled in between a huge white laundry truck and a *New York Times* delivery van. Guido opened the door a crack and slid out. Clancy waited to be sure my bouncer guardian was hidden behind the delicatessen truck double-parked on the right side of the street, then he took off with a squeal of tires. We headed north towards Columbus Circle. I couldn't see what was transpiring between Mr. Mariccino and Siegfried. I couldn't even see the limo.

I stayed silent for the remainder of the short ride. Clancy did as well, seeming to understand my need for some quiet.

As we drew closer to my apartment, I thanked Clancy for his help and wished him luck with his acting career. He smiled at me.

"Thanks. Hey, what's your name? Besides 'Gregory Noble's girl.' Or 'babe,' as your colorful pal puts it."

"Abby Fouchet."

"Pretty. Listen, you might be interested in knowing that nobody in the business believes that crap about Johnny. I was at an audition for a car commercial this morning and a bunch of us were passing tabloids around. Everybody agreed what they're writing about him is bull. Feeling is that Johnny is taking the fall for someone else's crime."

"I know. I just wish that other person would own up."

"You stick in there. Johnny Gerard is a good guy."

"Thanks, Clancy. So are you."

"Hey. I'm curious about something. How long have you guys been dating?"

"Oh, since late November. So that's, what, about seven months?"

"Seven fast approaching eight. So how is it you didn't know Gregory Noble was a cop?"

I laughed. "I've never watched the whole show. It's on in the morning when I'm either in class or teaching exercise at a health club. And Johnny never talks much about it. He filmed the episode where the parachute breaks right after I met him, so his character's been in that crazy coma for months now. I did the disco scene a couple months back but that was a dream sequence and Gregory Noble's profession was never mentioned. And every time my roommate has it on and I'm home I seem to get in just for the 'Oh, Doctor, Gregory's in a coma!' scenes."

Clancy's eyes twinkled.

"I wish you two only the best of luck. Unfortunately, what with nasty things being alleged in the paper, you're going to need it."

"Unfortunately, I think you're right."

Clancy waved off the fare.

"Consider it my contribution to keeping Greg Noble's girl safe. Same to Johnny's girl. See ya around."

He took off. It was nice to know there were some good people left in the world. I could add Clancy to the growing list of Johnny Gerard supporters that included a topless dancer, a pair of Italian bouncers with bad fashion sense, two roommates hooked on the show, a too-long unconscious Dominican immigrant and me.

I'd like to say I scampered up the steps to my apartment but that would be untruthful. I crawled up the stoop outside then dragged myself to the elevator. I was searching for the keys to Seven-D when the door was flung open. Shay greeted me with a hug. I needed that hug. What I didn't need was the overly long litany she recited naming the phone calls she'd answered all afternoon. Every one of the calls had been for me.

"Mother Minette has called three times. New York's ace reporter Jayce Cracknell has called twice. Two other reporters from competing papers have called twice. And Gina Giardeli who used to be on 'New York News at Noon' but has been promoted to 'New York News at Eleven' called to ask if she could have an exclusive interview with Gregory Noble's betrayed fiancée. I guess that's you? Let's see. Dr. Murray has called once to say thanks for referring four cast members from *Escape* to him. That must have been one hell of a tough show for feet. Anyway, your father called twice from San Francisco where he's designing a mall or something. Actually, he called once from there, then once from the airport on his way back to Texas. Um. He said, 'Hang in there, sweetheart!' Cory Elliott has called once to say he's with you and Johnny all the way, and not to feel badly that *Boundaries* is now stalled. Some guy named Bernie, claiming to be stage manager, called once to explain that *Boundaries* is indeed stalled until the scandal concerning Johnny can be, I quote, 'properly dealt with.'"

It was late. I couldn't call anyone if I wanted to. Which I didn't. I sank down on the sofa, then sat up immediately.

"*Boundaries* is stalled?"

"Yup."

"Oh, that's just terrific. Not only does it seem that our producers and angels think Johnny's guilty of collusion with the mob, but now the cast is going to be pissed because they won't see a paycheck. This is not good."

The phone rang. Shay looked at me. I lowered my head into my hands and sighed.

"I think I may get a phone service for a few weeks."

"Hmmm. Might not be a bad idea. Meantime, are you going to answer? Could be your mother again. She said she'd call back in an hour."

She checked her watch and grinned.

"That was exactly an hour ago."

"I'd almost rather talk to Jayce Cracknell, that sleazy reporter from the news than to Minette right now."

"Hey, don't blame Cracknell. He just covers whatever is happening in theatre and TV. And this is a big story. Jayce is okay. Really. He gave me a great review last year for the choreography for *Jingle*."

The ringing stopped. I took the opportunity to notice Shay had a jacket on and a purse in hand.

"Are you going out? Wait a minute. You have a date with Fuji tonight, don't you? With everything that's happened today, I'd almost forgotten. Why haven't you gone and come back? You did have plans, right?"

"Yup. But it's not really a date. Well, it's sort of a date. Fuji is playing a special midnight charity exhibition game with the Indians against the Yankees. He got me a ticket. I love baseball."

"Shay. You love baseball *players*. I doubt you know the difference between a fly and a foul."

She looked offended.

"Of course I do. A fly is the front of a guy's trousers. A foul is what you eat with stuffing at Thanksgiving."

We grinned at each other. She tossed her head back and shook her hair around her face.

"I'll have you know, Ms. Fouchet, that I have been a Yankees fan since I was about three. Watched every game they played on TV. And collected baseball cards, too."

"When you were three?"

"Well, maybe a bit older. Hey, are you going to be okay here by yourself? I have to leave in about thirty seconds. But I'll stay if you need me. Or you can come with me. I'm sure

I could get you a ticket at the gate. I doubt that many rabid fans are up for a game that doesn't even start 'til midnight."

I pushed her out the door.

"Offer heard. Offer refused. Thanks. I'll be fine. Give my love to Fuji after he loses."

She shot me a look. I smiled and fluttered my lashes.

"I may be from El Paso, but I too have been a Yankees fan all my life. The Indians don't stand a chance."

TWENTY-TWO

As soon as Shay closed the door, the phone started ringing. There was an angry, insistent timbre to the sound. I picked up the receiver and spoke immediately but with resignation, "Hello, Minette."

"What is going on up there?"

I tried to be cautious and pretend innocence.

"Just how do you mean that?"

"Abby, I am not stupid. And I am certainly not illiterate. La Luna Foods carries the *New York Times*. I read it daily. I do the crossword daily. And *this* day I read that your little friend Johnny is in serious trouble because he can't keep his pants zipped."

I considered slamming down the receiver. Had it been anyone but my mother I would've. Instead, I took a huge breath while preparing to explain the situation. Using a calmer tone than I felt, I began.

"Minette. First of all, Johnny is not little. He's six foot and one inch tall. I don't know why I feel the need to correct that assumption for you but I do. Okay. Next. He was not involved with this mob bimbo."

I prayed that was truthful information.

"His father was the one involved with the girl. And you didn't ask, but no, I have no idea whether Kieran Gerard has ties to organized crime. I just know that Johnny Gerard does not. But, hey, Minette! This should make you happy. My show, Johnny's show? My first break on Broadway? *Boundaries?* Well, we're unemployed until the powers that be can look into all the garbage, proclaim Johnny's innocence, and by extension, that of the Notebooms who are producing this extravaganza."

"Oh, my word, Abby. This is such a pickle. You need to come home, and forget about all these sordid people. Sweetheart, I'm hosting a huge party for the Representative from our district in two weeks. Fireworks, barbeque. The works. We missed being able to do the annual 4th of July party because Paul was still in San Francisco, so this will make up for it."

She paused and softened her tone to a pitch I recognized as the sort of pitch a vacuum-cleaner salesman would envy.

"And Abby? Paul and I are having a lot of problems, but with you around we somehow seem to always patch things up. And I talked to Mr. Orlando from the Academy of Arts again. He was at the wedding for the senator's daughter. He told me again how impressed he was with your résumé, and he said to tell you that the job is still open. Abby, this is such a wonderful opportunity for you. It's as though fate has stepped in with this, well, what I can only call an unholy mess with that boy. You've been given a chance to leave all that behind."

I paced around the apartment listening to Minette's monologue. I wrapped the phone cord around my wrist and slowly unspooled the gnarled twists. I took a long look around the three rooms I shared with Shay and Cherry. I spotted my stuffed animals neatly arranged on my bed and the sofa. Ringo and Mischa seemed to be cocking their heads and staring directly at me. I grimaced at the sight of spaghetti stains on the refrigerator. (Cherry's contribution to the world of Impressionistic art.) I shook my head when I spied Cherry's latest costume, a silver-and-gold concoction that wouldn't cover a toy poodle, drying on top of the radiator.

A soap opera magazine lay on the coffee table. It was opened to the page showing three couples dancing at a fictitious nightclub in Manhattan in a certain coma-induced dream episode of *Endless Time*. Shay's choreography had been captured in a still photo and printed up in bright colors. One of those three couples just happened to be me and Johnny Gerard. My bag was next to the magazine. Sheet music for one of the new songs Sidney composed had fallen out. I stared at it for about ten full seconds. The title was "Dancing on the Edge." I felt good for the first time since this morning when the news article slandering Johnny had disrupted rehearsals and our lives.

"Minette? Are you finished?"

"I suppose I am. So, when are you coming home? I can arrange for Paul to come meet you at the airport as soon as you get a flight. His own flight should be in by midnight our time."

I took a deep breath.

"I'm not coming home. Look. I'm sorry that you and Dad are fighting or sniping or whatever you're doing. But I can't fix that. And I don't like political fund-raisers. To tell you the truth I don't like politicians. And I am not walking away from Johnny. Not just yet. I'm not walking away from our show. It may never open, but even if that's the case, then I'm auditioning for the next one and the one after that.

"I'm a dancer, Minette. I'm sorry. I don't want to marry some Texas lawyer I haven't met yet. Or heaven help me, Elmer Whitacker and his fortune. I don't want to teach kids at some foo-foo academy for spoiled brats. I don't want to end up twenty years from now angry or full of regrets because I ran away from performing. Not to mention I couldn't face myself in the mirror if I dumped someone I love during a crisis. And I do love him. Regardless of how he feels about me and regardless of how messy this situation gets. That's my problem and I'll face it. So. End of discussion. You're my mother. I love you, but I'm unbelievably tired of trying to be the perfect society belle daughter. And I'm asking you to take me, or leave me, for what I am."

The longest silence I've ever experienced in any conversation or debate with Minette since I was old enough to speak filled the phone line with a ghostly noise. After a few dozen lifetimes, I heard my mother's voice.

"I'm sorry, Abby. Honestly. I do know it's your life. I know it's your time to dream. I'm truly sorry if I've tried to make it mine. Let Paul and me know if we can help in any way in the next few weeks. I have to say, though, from what I've been reading in the papers here, you're in for some tough times. But, we're behind you. Solidly. Believe me. I love you, Honey."

"You, too. Thanks. So much."

My throat tightened. Hot tears threatened to spill down my cheeks and my voice grew hoarse.

"Minette? Let me call you in a day or two. Maybe by then I'll know a bit more about this whole situation."

"Night, Sweetheart."

"Night, Mom."

I hung the receiver up as carefully as if it had been good china. That was the first time I'd called my mother anything other than Minette since I was three. The tears splashed onto my chest, then onto Ringo as I held the stuffed giraffe and sobbed. I knew that I'd reached a turning point in our relationship. A good one. I'd stood up to her. I'd told the truth. I hadn't caved in. I'd let her know who I was. And she loved me.

Before I had time to truly process in what new direction Minette and I might be headed in our dealings with each other, the phone jangled again. I nearly fell off the couch since the darn thing was lying by my ear.

"Hello?"

"Miss Fouchet?"

I was wary of male voices calling me anything other than Abby. It could only be a reporter, a "suit" from the show telling me to pack my bags because they wanted nothing to do with a friend of Johnny Gerard's, or a telemarketer trying to sell a subscription to the *Post* or the *Daily News*. At midnight. I was not inclined to invest in either right now or any other printed medium other than fiction books or travel guides that hadn't slandered Johnny. I thought I'd be crafty.

"May I ask who's calling her please?"

That should head 'em off at the pass. Of course, "should" doesn't mean "does."

"This is Jayce Cracknell, Miss Fouchet. The reporter."

"Thumb-sucking, drool-spitting, bare-bottomed anaconda with a pen you mean!"

Silence, then a chuckle.

"Miss Fouchet. You have quite a knack with words. You should have been a journalist."

"No, Mr. Cracknell. What I should have been, what I *am*—is a dancer. Which I will be again when this mish-mashed slanderous piece of crap gets cleared up and I'm able to go back to work on *Boundaries* with the other dancers. Assuming you and your other buddies in the media haven't destroyed any credibility this show had."

"I'm truly sorry all of you got caught up in this. I know it's not your fault. May I ask you something, Miss Fouchet?"

"No, Mr. Cracknell, you may not. What you may do is take a flying *jeté* off a slow boat down a fast river. Do you know what a *jeté* is? I doubt you do. I shall enlighten you. It's a balletic term for *jump*. So, Mr. Cracknell, you can go jump. Is that descriptive enough for you? Good night."

I slammed down the receiver with such force I thought I'd broken the phone. No such luck. It immediately rang again.

"I told you, you lily-livered rancid piece of moldy hog drippings, I'm not talking to you!"

"Ouch. I presume that was meant for the last caller and not for me?"

I was stunned. A new voice making itself heard in the night.

"Who the hell is this?"

"This is Chase Jaffert. Abby, is that you?"

Why in bloody blue blazes was Chase Jaffert calling me at what was now close to midnight? Why was he calling me at any time, for that matter? I assumed a civil tone.

"Yes, Mr. Jaf—uh, Chase. This is Abby. What can I do for you?"

"Have dinner with me tomorrow night."

There had been many shocks this day. This one was about a 7.5 on the Richter scale of what-in-blue-blazes. If I hadn't been so exhausted I might not have been so blunt. But I didn't care about being polite. Not after a day of scandalous news stories, fighting with producers, watching my roommate do a topless routine, hiring amateur detectives, baring my soul to my mother and making an enemy of the *Daily News* drama critic. The only thing I cared about was getting off the phone and making friends with my pillow.

"Why do you want to have dinner with me? Excuse me, Mr. Jaffert, but I've met you twice. Once at a party where we exchanged about ten seconds of meaningless chitchat and once at the D.A.'s office when you suggested I steer clear of Johnny Gerard. A statement I resented, if you must know. Now you're asking me to dine with you as though we've known each other for—well a lot longer. I repeat. Why?"

He laughed. He had a nice rich bass sound to his voice. I figured with that voice and the hunky blonde looks he must do all the closing arguments for the prosecution. The women jurors would have to be either past ninety, life-long lesbians, or newly dead not to respond.

"Ms. Fouchet. Abby. Are you always this difficult to date? I'm asking you out because I think you're attractive and smart and funny and I'd like to get to know you. Does that answer the question?"

"Not really. Mr. Jaffert? Your timing is a bit strange. And my timing right now is that I'm not interested in socializing with the enemy, so to speak. Not to mention that it's really late and I've had a really rotten day. So, I'm going to say 'night, night' right now."

"Wait. Abby. Don't hang up. I do have another motive here. Kieran Gerard is a friend and he's about to go down once the truth gets out about the affair with Mrs. Toblaroni being *his* disgrace, not his son's. I need your help in seeing that what he goes down for isn't criminal, just stupid."

"I'm listening."

"Look, I'm due back in night court here in about fifteen minutes. That's why I'd like to take you out tomorrow so we can discuss all this. Admittedly, I also find you cute and charming, but if you're stuck on Johnny, I promise I won't interfere. Won't you help them both out?"

What could it hurt? If Chase knew that Kieran was Tracy's lover and not Johnny, maybe he could help in clearing Johnny's name. And if Kieran wasn't involved with the mob, if he was just an innocent ninny ruled by an overactive libido, well, no matter how mad Johnny was at him I knew he couldn't bear to see his father railroaded.

"All right. How about if I meet you somewhere?"

"That would be wonderful. I'm handling arraignments in night court all this week. How about a late supper, say around nine-thirty? There's a great pub where most of the attorneys hang out, called Habeas Corpus. Over on Wall Street. Can you find it or do you need exact directions?"

"I know New York fairly well. I'll find it."

"Good. I'll see you tomorrow evening then. Good night, Abby."

I stared at the phone without hanging it up. Was it possible that this gorgeous, rather pompous lawyer knew something that could help? I had to find Johnny. I needed to know how much *he* knew about the affair between Tracy and his dad.

I was excited by that direct statement Chase had made that Johnny had not had anything of a personal nature going on with Mrs. Toblaroni. But since I doubted Mr. Jaffert had been with Tracy and Johnny those times they were alone in that white limo, I needed better confirmation. I needed to wring the truth out of Johnny Gerard.

I got back on the phone and began what quickly became a fruitless search for the man.

I tried his apartment. I tried his health club, even though it was now way past midnight. I tried three guys from the *Jesus Christ Superstar* cast I knew were Johnny's friends. I tried the hospital where Cookie still drifted out past reality. I tried Kieran's penthouse. At least with that number I got a service. A friendly female voice informed me of Kieran's business hours and offered to take a message. I had none to give. No Kieran. No Johnny. I called Cherry at the topless bar in case Johnny had gotten word about my little visit there and tried to find me. She hadn't seen him, but promised to sit on him if he happened to come by. (A thought which made me shudder.)

Vito and Guido were both *in absentia* as well. For some absurd reason this cheered me up. I wondered if Guido had talked to Siegfried, then gone back to the club and picked up his brother to look for Johnny, kidnap him and keep him somewhere safe.

MAYBE MY ITALIAN guardian angels were already watching over him. I could see their little wings made of cannoli pastry shells fluttering around Johnny as he dodged large chauffeurs with larger guns. I tried to call out to him that his parachute was ripped, but before I could get the words out, I heard shots. A man wearing a Toblerone candy box stood over Johnny crying, "Gregory, Gregory! I told you what would happen if I caught you and Letitia together. I can't trust Carla anymore either. It's over!"

The man took aim and shot again. I was drenched in sweat. In that last moment before waking I clearly saw a newspaper headline dated July 11. It screamed: *Soap Actor Shot!* I jumped up from the sofa.

July eleventh was tomorrow. I checked my watch. It was 3:00 a.m. Make that today.

A solid progression of drops of moisture dripped down my forehead to my neck. I threw off the quilt that hadn't been on me when I fell asleep (Shay doubtless being maternal after she'd gotten home from the ball game) and tugged at the window that faces W. 79th from our living room. I leaned out and breathed in the night air.

It was fairly quiet in the street below. A couple walked arm in arm about three brownstones down. A cab pulled up across the street and let out a young girl hauling about three suitcases and a small dust mop of a dog. At the end of the block, with lights off, parked just barely fifteen legal feet from a fire hydrant sat a white stretch limo. I had instinctively known it would be there. Its presence barely raised a hair on my forearm.

I crawled back to the couch and immediately fell asleep.

TWENTY-THREE

I DIDN'T DREAM AGAIN. The smell of fresh coffee awakened me sometime late in the morning.

Shay wandered in wearing an oversized Cleveland Indians baseball shirt in place of a nightgown.

"You were right. They lost. It was a rout."

"Huh?"

"The Indians. They lost to the Yankees just as you predicted."

"Oh."

She handed me a mug. Hot coffee. Bless the woman. I cradled it in my hands. Steam gently rose from the cup and warmed my face.

"Shay? I barely remember talking to you about the Yankees and the Indians last night. I was so out of it when I got home I just remember you sashaying out of here to watch Fuji play. Did I predict the win?"

She took a swig from her own mug and glared at me.

"Yes. You said the Yankees would slaughter Cleveland. They did."

"I'm sorry. Well, I'm not sorry the Yankees won, 'cause they're my favorite team, but I'm sorry Fuji's team lost."

Shay's expression brightened.

"It wasn't all bad. The Indians had their regular pitcher in for the first six innings and that's when the Yanks were getting all the hits. Then, when all seemed lost, their bozo manager put Fuji in and that ended the scoring from New

York. Plus he hit a home run himself in the ninth inning. It was orgasmic."

I had taken my cup and was staring out the living room window. I hadn't heard a word she'd said.

"Am I boring you? I thought at least the word orgasmic might spark some interest."

I came back and sat down on the sofa.

"I'm sorry. I'm distracted. My focus is nowhere near anything like reality. That damn white limo that belongs to Miss Terresota Tracy Tasteless Toblaroni is still parked down the street. I did get the home-run story, though, and I'm glad Fuji performed up to his usual brilliance. It's time he got a break."

"He did so well the Yankees are talking to his agent about bringing him over next season. He hates Cleveland. He's thrilled. And are you ready for this? He wants to go out with me, as in dating. He doesn't need citizenship by marriage anymore, but he said he wouldn't have minded getting married to me anyway because he's always had a crush on me. At least, I think that's what he said. His English has improved but sometimes he gets confused. Maybe he said he thought the manager was a lush?"

"That's nice. I'm happy for you."

I stood up again and paced back to the window. Shay stood up and grabbed me by the shoulders.

"Abby. It doesn't do any good to keep looking out there. The stinking car has been there all night. It doesn't look like it's going anywhere, and whether it does or doesn't, what does it matter?"

I slumped back down in our only comfortable chair after dumping one of Cherry's more lurid costume pieces to the floor. A smattering of gold sequins showered and glittered in the morning light.

"I should be glad the damn thing is still parked. At least that means that hulk of a driver isn't somewhere chasing

Johnny for some unknown reason. What the hell do these comedians want with him anyway? Or me? Why on earth are they tailing me? Why can't they go shoot up a garage or something? Isn't that what mobsters do? Isn't there something in Contract Killing 101 that suggests these things?"

Shay tried, unsuccessfully, to hide a smirk.

"They tried that in Chicago about eighty years ago on St. Valentine's Day if I recall my history. Pretty successfully, too. I guess they need new horizons and felonies to delve into. Actors, lawyers, theatre."

"That's another thing. I'd love to know what's behind all this. The subtext, if you will. On the surface it seems that Johnny is being blamed for a stupid affair that his libidinous sire was engaged in. Okay. Then it turns out the affair-ee is the wife of a mob boss. Which the affair-er, Kieran Gerard, must have known. The man is many things, but none of them are stupid."

"Affair-ee? Affair-er? Where do you come up with these words?"

I ignored the interruption.

"Where was I? Ah, yes. Kieran. Tracy. Nicholas, the spouse with the chocolate last name. It all seems very simple. Then we throw in Johnny as the scapegoat, which draws in the Noteblooms as possible money-laundering partners. Okay. There's some connection with an immigrant paralegal run down in the street. My bet is on the sexy chauffeur who to-night followed me out of Cherry's club, but was stopped by Guido the Magnificent, who has a crush on Cherry by the way, and a bizarre, wonked-out phone call from one of Kieran's staff at the D.A.'s office and the fact that Kieran's office was trashed and it all adds up to?"

"Muffins!"

I blinked. Shay blinked.

Cherry gleefully kicked the front door to open it and sailed in carrying a bagful of breakfast goodies. Vito and Guido, each of whom was balancing two cups of coffee apiece, closely followed her.

"I got muffins! Want some?"

The answer was a rousing yes from both Shay and me. Scandals and affairs and mob activity may come and go, but when hot lemon or chocolate muffins are offered, one accepts without hesitation.

Twenty minutes of silent munching later, the five of us were sated and happy. Well, four people were happy. I was remembering why I'd been upset all morning. I waved part of my third chocolate muffin at Guido.

"Did y'all find out anything about the Toblaronis and what's going on?"

Guido wiped a crumb off his chin and nodded.

"Tracy's chauffeur was a bust. Says he don't know nothin' and wasn't followin' you. I know he's lyin' but without less subtle methods of interrogation I also know he's not givin' anything up. Hey, ya know the guy's a fairy? Yeah. I swear he had the nerve to come on to me. I woulda bloodied his nose, but he was still in the white limo and I didn' wanna mess it up."

I had to get him back on the topic of whatever information they'd managed to gather concerning Johnny and Kieran and the Toblaronis. The fact that Tracy's chauffeur may or may not be gay wasn't really relevant, except perhaps to Tracy's chauffeur.

"Guido? Vito? What happened after your chat with Mr. White-Limo-Driver? Whose name is Siegfried, by the way, in case you see him again and want to get his attention."

Guido growled. "That kinda attention I don't need."

Vito chugged down a swig of coffee, then mumbled with a mouth still full, "We spent most a da night down in Little Italy talkin' to some guys we know. And eatin' ravioli and clams and salamis at Mario's."

"Vito! Don' forget the cannolis! Mario makes great cannolis. What's that spice he puts in the fillin'?"

"Uh, I don' know. It's almost like nutmeg, but it isn't, ya know?"

I was either going to scream, shove the brothers Mariccino out the window, or jump myself. I'd been cursed with friends and amateur detectives who found it impossible to stay on topic. Admittedly, I myself have been known to stray off a given subject, but today I wanted answers. Not the recipe for the Italian dessert pastry, no matter how scrumptious it sounded. I did file Mario's cannolis in the back of my mind for taste testing should I survive the current crisis.

I stood.

"Vito? Guido? Yo. Did you find out anything? At Marios? About the Gerards?"

Vito looked surprised.

"Didn' we tell ya'? There was a lot a talk about the fact that everybody in town knows that Tracy wasn't being *schtupped* by Gregory Noble. Only person too stupid to think it is that stupid reporter, Crackhead."

"Cracknell," Shay mumbled.

The brothers stared at her.

"His name is 'Cracknell,' not 'Crackhead.' Not that it matters."

The brothers continued to stare.

"Sorry. Go on."

They jumped right back on track.

"Oh yeah, there was sumpin' about Tracy seems to be playin' both ends of the fiddle. Sumpin' like that."

Shay covered a sudden laugh with her napkin and quickly changed the sound to a cough. I stared at the twins.

"Both ends of the fiddle?"

Cherry threw her wadded up napkin at Vito.

"You two can't get anything straight! Jeez. Abby, he means that Tracy broad is playing both ends against the side of the middle. I think. Talk like a normal person, you stupid moron."

Guido crammed a muffin into Cherry's mouth to silence her. She didn't seem to take offense. I got up and started a frantic pace around the living room.

"Wait a second. What does that mean, Tracy is playing both ends against the middle? Middle of what? I've passed confused and gone into baffled. I feel like some game is being played without all the players knowing they're even in it, like Johnny, and some of the players aren't signing up even though they run the game."

Amazingly Vito, Guido and Cherry nodded vigorously in assent to this ridiculous statement as though I'd solved a mystery that has stumped Hercule Poirot, Sherlock Holmes and Nero Wolfe for years.

Shay lifted her chin in a thoughtful pose.

"Abby, in your incredible coffee-deprived, rambling manner, you may have come up with something. There's a lot more to this than a simple sex scandal that one politician isn't owning up to."

"I agree. But what?"

"I haven't a clue."

We smiled at each other.

Guido was eyeing me with some concern.

"Hey. Abby? Where's Johnny? After we ate and tried getting info from the guys, we went over to the address you gave us that's Johnny's apartment. But he ain't there. We, uh, we even managed to, uh, sneak into his place, but he ain't there."

I wasn't about to quibble over this spot of breaking and entering. Johnny wasn't at his apartment. I had hoped when I hadn't been able to reach him earlier that he was simply not answering the phone, preferring not to talk to persistent reporters, but if Vito and Guido hadn't seen him there—he wasn't there. These guys had nightglow vision.

"Hey, Guido, remember, we did see him *once* last night. He was outside of the building around three or so."

I stared at them.

"The building. This building? He was?"

"Yep, he stood there for sumpin' like fifteen minutes. Then he took off towards the subway."

Vito puffed out his chest. "We followed him to Penn Station."

Cherry sniffed. "Then they lost him. Stupid dumb morons."

"At Penn Station?"

"Yep, he just like disappeared into nothin'."

The total illogic of it was somehow making me sharper. That and my third cup of coffee in ten minutes.

"Did he go anywhere in Penn before he vanished?"

Vito squinted, trying to remember.

"Yeah, come to think of it, he went to that big drugstore by the 7th Avenue stairs."

I grinned.

"Guys, you didn't lose Johnny. He lost you. Well, not you particularly. Anybody who was following him. I'll bet he bought glasses and a cap and maybe even make-up to change his appearance. He thinks he's that damn soap character and he's going to go out and prove his innocence about this deal with the mob somehow. What an idiot. I'm in love with a man with no brains. Plenty of guts, but no brains."

Shay, Cherry, Vito and Guido were all staring at me like I was the one who'd lost their mind. I stared back. Vito reached across the coffee table and patted my hand.

"Hey. It's okay. He can do it! I'm tellin' ya. Greg Noble is sumpin' else. He tracked down three murderers by himself last year. No help from NYPD at all. And that was the same time he was skiing in the Olympics and winning the gold medal."

Shay fell off the sofa. I shot her an extremely piercing

look. It in no way deterred her. She tried to sit up, but she was laughing too hard.

"Johnny was an Olympic skier? I mean Greg Noble."

"Yeah! It was tremendous. He caught Devlin Corwin, a dirty cop who'd set up another cop and got him killed, and he did it just before he goes slamming down the Alps. He was being shot at the whole way down the slopes but he keeps on skiing and hits the ribbon at the finish line, then turns around and starts doing like karate-kick things with his skis. Hit Devlin's guys in the legs. They was wailin' and squoochin' around in the snow and Greg just handcuffed 'em. Even stuck a ski-pole thing in one guy's jacket cause he was trying to get away."

This was too much. The writers for *Endless Time* had the poor man catching criminals, winning medals in the slalom, figure skating, disco dancing in a coma, crashing while sky-diving with a busted parachute courtesy of an evil wife, and all the while being fought over by divas playing nurses and murderers. I would have been laughing right along with Shay if I hadn't been so worried about Johnny's whereabouts. And planning how I was going to exonerate his name.

Where was Gregory Noble when you needed him?

TWENTY-FOUR

I WASN'T SURE WHAT was the dress code for a bar named Habeas Corpus, but I *was* sure I didn't care. Chase would be neatly clad in a business suit (my guess was charcoal) that would have cost more than the combined incomes of the three occupants of Apartment Seven-D. That thought alone was enough to make me pull out my oldest jeans and rattiest sweatshirt. I stared at myself in the mirror for at least five minutes before deciding I needed extra pizzazz if I was to survive this date, rendezvous, interrogation, or whatever the heck it was. I pulled out the summer-weight cream-colored cashmere sweater Minette had given me at Christmas. It was soft and it looked and felt expensive. My faded jeans made me feel comfortable, the sweater made me feel sexy and confident, the red cowboy boots under the jeans made me feel tough. I added an extra layer of mascara to my lashes. I was ready. Bring 'em on. Lawyers, politicians and shady mobsters. Abby'd level 'em all.

The Mariccino brothers had taken a noisy and cheerful leave. Shay had gone off to the health club, and Cherry had crashed in her bedroom. I'd calmly started studying every piece of my music for *Boundaries,* making sure I knew every note, every nuance and every word. Perhaps it was a false sense of bravado or hope but by rehearsing the songs for the show I felt as though it would have no choice but to open. All would be well.

I took a break sometime around four in the afternoon and baked two dozen oatmeal cookies. With chocolate chips, coconut and walnuts. Very healthy. Oatmeal wipes out the cholesterol and walnuts are full of Omega three's. Or sixes. And of course, chocolate is good for kicking one's serotonin levels on high. I needed serotonin today.

Cherry woke up around 4:30 p.m. and joined me in a binge, devouring over half of the "healthy" cookies. Then she wrapped herself in a towel and grabbed the phone for her daily chat with Guido and Vito. I truly hoped Guido would get the courage to ask her out—solo. I just couldn't see a romance blossoming for the pair if this strange *ménage à trois* continued as it was. I was in hopes that *someone's* love life in Seven-D would work out.

I took a nap around six after the sugar high from the cookies turned into a severe crash. I needed my strength for an evening I knew could easily turn into a fencing match with Chase Jaffert.

He'd said to meet him after nine. I waved goodbye to Cherry who was on the phone again—had she ever been off?—and dashed out the door. No white limo was parked down the street. For some reason, this did not reassure me. I'd gotten used to its presence.

Habeas Corpus turned out to be an unassuming little bar filled with large, assuming attorneys. The thought flashed through my mind that I wished I owned stock in Brooks Brothers. There wasn't a pair of jeans in the crowd. I looked, and felt, extremely out of place.

Chase was already seated near the back of the bar. He saw me as I entered and politely rose to accompany me to an elegant, leather-upholstered booth. He was wearing, not surprisingly, a tailored three-piece suit. I'd nailed it. Charcoal.

"Abby! I'm so glad you could make it. I have been looking forward to this all day. You look lovely. What a beautiful sweater. It brings out your eyes and your hair."

Aha. So. It was to be *that* kind of evening. Flattery and insincerity from the get-go.

I plunked down in the booth. A glass of white wine had been ordered for me. I took a sip. Dry. I hate dry. I smiled sweetly at Chase and signaled to the waiter.

"I'm so sorry, but I think I'd just like a beer. Whatever you have on tap will be fine."

I hate beer.

The waiter removed the wine and brought me something dark and cold in a tall glass. I ignored it for the moment.

"So, Chase. Can you enlighten me as to what's going on in the Deputy District Attorney's life?"

Chase blanched. That's the only word for it. He took a large swallow of his martini and smiled at me.

"You're direct, aren't you?"

"Yep. It's that Texas thing. You're from Texas, right? You understand."

"Where in Texas did you grow up? You don't have much of an accent."

Now we were going to play "dodge the question." Fine. I took a huge gulp of the beer (which wasn't half-bad) and responded, "El Paso."

"Oh. Gorgeous out there, isn't it? I used to go skiing in Ruidoso and often stopped in El Paso to visit friends. Do you ski?"

"No."

I knew I wasn't being cooperative. I knew Chase probably felt like a talk-show host with an unresponsive and stubborn guest. But I didn't want to be here. I didn't want to make idle first-date conversation. Chase seemed determined to turn this into a dialogue.

"Where did you go to college?"

"University of Texas. Austin."

"You're kidding! That was my undergraduate alma mater. Then, of course, I went to law school at Harvard. I guess I must have graduated some time before you did. From University of Texas, that is. Not Harvard."

He quickly added, "What was your major?"

Dear heaven.

"Double major. Dance and theatre."

Chase laughed. Three women in tailored suits turned around from their perches at the bar and stared. I could see lust in their eyes when they looked at him and envy and astonishment when they turned their gaze to me.

Chase was speaking.

"I'm sorry. That wasn't directed at you. I was laughing at myself. What an inane question. Of course it was dance. Aren't you in that show, the new one that's got everyone in New York buzzing?"

Was he serious? *Yeah, Chase, I'm in that show. The show that is now languishing in purgatory waiting to see if it will be allowed to ascend to heaven. The show that stars Johnny Gerard, son of Kieran Gerard, the man we're supposed to be discussing. The show that could transport Johnny out of daytime drama and me out of low-paying Off-Off-Broadway productions. That show.*

"Yes, Chase. I am. Look. Not to interrupt the flow of this conversation about the good old days in Texas, but can we talk about what's been happening with Johnny and Kieran Gerard? You told me on the phone last night that you knew a little something about this situation."

Chase waved at the waiter.

"Let's order some dinner first, shall we? What would you like? The burgers here are excellent. They have a wonderful soup-and-salad combo. The fish and chips are also quite good. Very fresh."

I stopped him before he could go through the entire menu. I considered asking what the most expensive item was and ordering it, but just went with the deluxe cheeseburger and fries. It seemed the most appropriate meal that would go with my beer and my mood.

Chase gave our order to the waiter (he chose a London

broil with veggies and baked potato) then diverted the topic of discussion to the law.

"How familiar are you with the district attorney's office?"

"How exactly do you mean?"

"Well, do you know how everything works here at Centre Street?"

Did I *look* stupid? Was it because I'm a dancer and dancers are supposed to be oblivious to anything in the world that doesn't involve a toe shoe and sweat? Did this man think before he spoke? I hoped his cross-examination technique was better than his direct. If not, his lawyering skills bordered on malpractice by reason of simplemindedness. I lifted my chin a bit.

"Chase, I'm very informed about the entire judicial system. I understand that prosecutors attempt to convict alleged perpetrators of crimes and defense attorneys attempt to make sure those alleged criminals are given fair trials and judges sit on high and attempt to keep the attorneys from tearing out each other's throats in court before those same attorneys adjourn to this bar and drink together. Does that pretty much sum up the Centre Street scenario?"

I'd silenced him with that long-winded, run-on, but essentially succinct statement. Color drained from his perfect cheekbones.

"I'm sorry, Abby. Was I being patronizing?"

I decided to cut him a break. After all, antagonizing the man wasn't going to get me the information I needed. Assuming he had any to give.

I smiled.

"Patronizing? Just a tad. But then, I'm sure I was rather rude in my answer. I grew up with a mother who constantly hosted fund-raisers and parties for politicians. She adores politics and politicians. Many of whom one time or another were lawyers. So I've been hearing about cases and courts and criminals from the time I was first allowed to be the peanuts-and-cheese distributor at her parties. Which was when I turned four and could balance the little platter while the guests helped themselves."

Our food arrived just as it seemed Chase was about to ask me another question. We spent the next minute or so salting, peppering, buttering and mustarding our respective dinners. I took a huge bite of my cheeseburger. Chase was right. It was excellent.

Eating a meal is not conducive to serious talk. So in the thirty minutes it took us to finish, we relaxed and discussed non-argumentative issues. Would the Yankees win next fall's World Series? I told him about Fuji, which seemed to amuse him. Would the stock market rise or fall? Would the Jets beat the Cowboys next season? On that we finally found common ground. Although we loved our adopted city of New York we'd both been Cowboy fans since birth. Who would run for mayor in New York in the next election? That brought us back to politics. The perfect opening.

"Chase. Why on earth did Kieran Gerard take up with Tracy Toblaroni in an election year? Is he nuts? Or did he just figure that if he blamed Johnny for the affair no one would bother to look further?"

Chase shook his head.

"I was going to ask you the same thing. It's beyond my comprehension."

"Look. I don't know Kieran Gerard at all. I know Johnny. You work with the man. You play racquetball with him. What's going on? Is this thing with Tracy just a smokescreen for mob connections?"

Chase didn't answer. His attention had been drawn to the front of the bar. Johnny Gerard was striding from that direction to our table with eyes blazing and mouth set.

"What the hell are you doing here with him?"

Johnny yanked me out of the booth with both hands. It was not a good way to attract my attention. I pushed him away.

"Who do you think you are barging in here like some Western hero into the saloon with guns drawn? Gregory Noble, Supercop?"

Chase stifled a chuckle. Both of us glared at him. He rose and exited the booth with calm haste.

"If you two will excuse me, I'll go take care of the check."

We barely heard him. We were too busy breathing equal parts of fire and ice at each other. I was so relieved to see he was alive after a day and night of no word at all that it *almost* doused my anger that he hadn't bothered to give me that word. I didn't appreciate his macho greeting either. He cast his eyes down to the table.

"I'm sorry, Abby. I called your apartment and Cherry told me you had a date with this Jaffert jerk. I hauled it down here, and when I saw you cozily engaging in conversation I just lost it for a second. Guess I was jealous."

His apology made me mad all over again.

"What? Johnny Gerard jealous? I see. It's okay for you to go traipsing all over New York with Mrs. Toblaroni in her white limo for Lord only knows what reasons, but *I* can't have dinner with a man?"

"Do you like this guy? This pompous jerk?"

"He's not a jerk. He's very nice." I thought over those last statements. I'd sent them into the air just to be argumentative. "Okay. That's not true. He is a pompous jerk, and he's not all that nice. Although he's trying hard to pretend he is."

"Why did you agree to have dinner with him?"

We were back to that.

"I just told you. It's my right to go out with whomever I choose. Even if the guy's a jerk. Just like it's your right to make an idiot of yourself with whatever greasy dame your wandering eye happens to fall on. A right you've obviously taken advantage of the whole damn time we've been seeing each other."

Johnny looked stricken. The look quickly turned to exasperation.

"Will you please listen to me? I have *never* had a sexual encounter with Tracy Toblaroni. May I turn into a tenor if I'm lying."

I closed my eyes. I could see Tracy's hand crawling up Johnny's sleeve back at O'Malley's pub months before. I could hear Cherry's voice telling Johnny that "some broad named Tracy" was on the phone and then watching Johnny leave as though the Angel Gabriel had summoned him. I could see Tracy enter the warehouse during the disco taping as though she was sure she'd be quite welcome there. I could see that white limousine parked in the alley behind the theatre and hear Tracy's voice imperiously calling Johnny over.

"Why the hell is it then, if you two haven't been engaged in an affair, why the dickens you've jumped whenever she's called? Why you've felt compelled to keep me in the dark even though you say you love me?"

Johnny gestured for me to sit back down in the booth. Neither of us noticed that Chase hadn't come back. I sunk into the soft leather. Johnny took Chase's place across from me and sighed. "Enough. I'm sick of covering for my father. He doesn't deserve it. Here it is. Kieran has a thing for women. Well, you know that already. All women, but mainly very young, not terribly bright, women. Tracy certainly fits that bill.

"Kieran wanted his little affair with Tracy kept secret. Obviously it would not do to have the future District Attorney playing around with anyone who was married, much less the wife of someone whom we now all know is some big crime boss. Enter Johnny, idiot son. Johnny is naïve, even though Johnny has worked on the sleaziest soap on the air for the last few years. Well, let's amend that. Johnny is naïve when it comes to his father and believing him. The scumbag SOB. Skip that. I'm not going there now." He took a breath. "Okay. Johnny is single. Johnny is a lowly actor, not a politician. So it is not a problem if Johnny is seen in public for a few minutes with Tracy before depositing her at Kieran's place. And stupid Johnny doesn't even know the girl is married. Or that she has close ties to organized crime.

"Kieran set it up so Tracy would call me, and then we'd go to Kieran's apartment together making it look like I'm bringing *my* date to my father's for lunch or dinner or whatever. Needless to say, I felt more and more compromised and hemmed in. When I met you, I immediately told Kieran he'd have to make other arrangements. I was out of it."

My eyes were wide at this confession of Johnny's and his apparent lack of judgment. All of this to try and get closer to the man who sired him, then disappeared from his life until he found a reason to reclaim the blood ties.

"And did he? Make other arrangements?"

"Yes and no. He did call once or twice and I caved. And for all her bimbo traits, Tracy does have a kind heart at times. She's been horribly upset over this whole business with Cookie even though she only met him once. Which is another reason I'm sure Siegfried had nothing to do with his accident or poisoning. Although since this broke about Tracy being married to Nick Toblaroni, I've been wondering if maybe Siegfried is working more for his *male* boss than for Tracy. Anyway. Back to Kieran. You pegged him, Abby. He's a toad. I tried for a year to get to know him, to understand him, to put my father into my life. Mistake."

"Wow. I wished I'd known all this the first time I saw you with her at O'Malley's back in October."

"I can't believe you're not over that. Is it because Tracy called you and Shay bar chippies?"

I smiled sweetly.

"I never told you this, but I was having an internal debate

as to whether or not to douse Miss Expensive Furs with a nice glass of very red Merlot. I thought it might serve to attract your non-existent attention."

Johnny smiled for the first time since entering Habeas Corpus.

"I think I'd have paid a month's salary to have seen you give in to that impulse. Heck! I'd have bought another round or even a bottle and cheered from the sidelines."

I was back to the immediate problem.

"Johnny. Why has Tracy been following you around? And why did her chauffeur follow me? And what the heck did Vito and Guido mean when they said she was playing both ends against the middle?"

"What? Abby, you just wandered into uncharted territory. What are you talking about?"

"Oh, sorry. You haven't been in communication with the Vito/Guido connection. Or with me, but that's another story. I sent the twins out to play amateur detective and ask some of their buddies who might just possibly have less-than-stellar backgrounds. They came back with what I've just told you. Makes no sense. Except that there's more to this than just any of the Gerards being caught *in flagranto* with a married woman."

He shook his head as his expression again grew dark.

"Haven't a clue. About any of it. The day Tracy came to the theatre where you were waiting to audition for *Boundaries,* all she said was she needed to tell me to be careful. That everything was about to blow. As you know, that was six weeks ago. And of course, she was right. Things blew. They just blew in my direction."

We both grew silent.

He reached for my hands across the table.

"Please tell me you believe that my relationship with this woman was nothing more than escort service and trained stooge for my father."

Every brain cell in my head said "don't trust him." He's been hedging about this since you met him. And think of all the girls who throw themselves at him. Why shouldn't he have taken more than one up on tempting offers?

Every beat of my heart said: "I love Johnny Gerard."

I had no choice. Heart won, hands down.

"I believe you."

He reached across the table and kissed me, getting ketchup all over the green shirt that matched his eyes. We drew apart slowly and Johnny sat back down.

"Johnny? I have a question."

His response sounded a bit tense. "Yes?"

"Where the hell were you last night and today?"

He looked surprised.

"I went to the charity baseball game last night. Yanks versus Indians. Great game! Shay's buddy, Fuji, pitched one hell of an inning. Guy's phenomenal."

"You're kidding."

"No, he was terrific."

I interrupted him before he could continue the assessment of Fuji's talent on the baseball diamond.

"I didn't mean kidding about Fuji's abilities. I meant about going to the game. With all this mess going on?"

"I needed to get away from all of it. Not you. I tried to call you about twenty times once I got the tickets but your phone stayed busy forever."

I explained about the calls.

"So, where did you go after the game?"

He seemed a bit sheepish.

"I hung out at the stadium for awhile talking to some of the players. Soap celebrity has its privileges. Then I went by your apartment building. All your lights were out. I was thinking about buzzing and seeing if you might be awake but I spotted a couple of characters watching me from way down the block. I figured I'll pull a Greg Noble and try and shake them in case they might be friends of Tracy's or worse—reporters. I took the train to Penn Station, found an all-night drugstore, bought a few things to alter my appearance and snuck out. I ended up going to a hotel for the rest of the night. I didn't wake up until about three hours ago. I called your place and Cherry told me you'd come down to Habeas Corpus."

He grinned. "Which, incidentally she called Baby Burps Coping. I gather she wasn't listening too clearly when you told her where you were off to. But at least she had the address. So now I'm just wondering who was tailing me."

I grinned back at him.

"I hate to upset you, Greg Noble, undercover cop *par excellence,* but the only people you lost last night were your devoted fans that I asked to protect you as well as find out any info on Daddy's girlfriend."

He moaned.

"Oh, terrific. I outsmarted the Mariccino brothers. If I weren't in enough trouble with *Endless Time,* I'd probably get demoted from their police force for this."

TWENTY-FIVE

WE STOOD OUTSIDE OF Habeas Corpus and stared at each other. Johnny finally spoke first.

"I've got to find out just who's doing what to whom in this little farce. Including figuring out what this business of Tracy playing that double-sided fiddle is, as your Mariccino buddies put it. Now. Will you do me a favor? Go home, curl up under a warm quilt and let me handle it from here?"

I started to protest, then choked off the words. Johnny had become remote, removed from me and everything around him. There seemed little point in asking what he intended to do. I assumed that he'd probably try and track down Kieran and ask his father to at least reconsider his flippant comments to the press concerning Johnny's sex life. I assumed right.

"I'm going to see if Kieran's at his penthouse. He told me he had some political event he had to attend, and then he said he'd go home. It's what? Ten-thirty now? He should be there. He said he badly needed some rest." Johnny's voice grew bitter.

"Apparently the stress of all this is just too hard on his fragile heart. That's a shocker. I didn't know he possessed one. Damn. I know you can't choose your parents, but whoever drew Kieran's name out of the pile must have been either raging drunk or plain stupid. When it comes to fathering, Kieran Gerard does not get the award for best father of the year."

Johnny looked around and whistled for a cab. He then drew

me close and kissed me hard. We both tasted of beer mixed with apprehension.

"Go home, Abby. If there *is* any danger from Kieran's involvement with Tracy, I don't want you anywhere near it."

That put me right back to being ticked off at the man.

"Well, excuse me for thinking you might consider me a partner in this slimy investigation, Johnny Gerard. What is this? Women and children into the lifeboats first? I hate to tell you, but it's a new millennium and we can row with the best of 'em."

"I know you're capable of stopping steel bullets with one foot, but I still don't want you going up against some whacko stray member of any crime syndicate. Now quit arguing with me and go home. If you want to help, call Vito and Guido and see if they've learned anything else in their travels through Little Italy."

He grinned. "And pick up some cannolis. Okay?"

I nodded. He grabbed my hands and held them, then reached into his pocket.

"Abby. Wait. I was going to give you this as a 'good show' present, but since we may never get to do that show I want you to have it now. I've been carrying it around since yesterday. I guess you know it means more than just an opening night present anyway. I love you."

He gently pushed my hair off of the back of my neck and secured the clasp of a silver necklace around it.

I looked down at my throat. A small moonstone glowed in the dark.

"Johnny. I love you, too. Thank you for this. And our show will open. I'm sure of it. We'll beat this."

He kissed me once more and pushed me almost headfirst into the back of a waiting taxi. He patted my butt, rather like one love-taps a toddler, which got me angry again. Then he was gone.

Three blocks down the street my stubborn streak took over. I tapped the cabdriver on his shoulder.

"I'm sorry. I need to make a phone call. Could you stop at that booth on the corner and then wait for me? I'll pay the meter time."

He nodded. No sweat off his back. He'd get paid to sit while I hunted for quarters.

I found several at the bottom of my dance bag. I hadn't taken a purse to meet Chase. I don't own a purse. Only dance bags. It's an issue of comfort and security with dancers, I guess. We figure if we're ever in a tough situation we can whip out the tap shoes and start a routine. Shay did just that when she was accosted by a would-be but highly inept mugger. Of course, she didn't start tapping. She started bopping the guy over the head. He ran.

I smiled, remembering Shay's courage under fire, while I listened to a long succession of rings at my apartment before Shay's voice answered "hello." I promptly launched into my frustration with men in general and Johnny Gerard in particular, giving her a three-minute monologue concerning both of the men I'd talked to in the last two hours.

"Johnny doesn't believe I can help him. Why do men pretend to be such independent little cusses when in reality they need us as much as we need them?"

"Uh-oh. She's talking gender psychology here. Not a good sign. Abby. Calm down. Try and relax. If the man said he wanted to deal with his own father on his own terms then let him. You hate confrontations anyway, right? Why the hell do you even *want* to dive headfirst into a huge fight between parent and child?"

Shay was probably right. Did I want to be in the room when Johnny wrung the truth out of Kieran? Well, if I was honest, yes. I wanted to be wherever Johnny was, no matter the costs to life, liberty and my own limbs.

I said as much to my roommate.

"Look, I'm going to try and get a hold of Cherry and see if either Vito or Guido has come up with anything else."

"Wait. Wait. You were so busy with your discourse on the male of the species I didn't get a chance to tell you. Guido called. He said to tell you to meet them down at Mario's Trattoria on Mulberry Street. I gather Mario's is on the order of women gossiping over clotheslines in the backyard. Guido said there's a group of guys at a huge table trying to figure out who's doing what to whom in this sordid mess. Of course he mentioned all those guys have downed three bottles of Chianti by now, and not one of the bunch sounds younger than ninety, but Guido seemed fairly sober, so maybe the booze makes them all think better."

"Thanks, Shay. I'm off. If I don't come back I bequeath both Mischa and Ringo to you and tell Cherry she can have my black jacket. I know she's been lusting after it."

I gave the cabby my new destination (which was only about five minutes away), sat back and tried not to think about anything until I met with the Italian twins at the Trattoria.

Mario's was cute, clean and clichéd. Little café tables were set up outside. They were in danger of blowing away in the wind that had picked up considerably since I left Habeas Corpus. Red-checkered tablecloths and candles made up the décor inside. I expected Al Capone to walk through the door and order a pizza any moment.

"Abby! Hey! How ya doin'?"

I was hugged by both Mariccino brothers coming at me from opposite sides. I was absurdly comforted by their affection and support. I hugged them back, nearly decapitating Vito with the strap of my dance bag that had managed to wrap itself around his neck. Guido took me aside for a moment as Vito headed back to their table.

"I ast her."

"What?"

"What you said. About me gettin' Cherry alone. I ast her could we go out sumtime widout Vito."

I sent up a silent prayer to Saint Aphrodite that my match-making efforts would not be disastrous.

"So, what did she say?"

Guido turned red. "She said, and this is direct from Cherry herself, 'Why the friggin' hell didn' ya ask me a year ago, ya big dope?'" He grinned. "She likes me."

I hugged him again. Mario approached and ushered us both towards the back of the restaurant before I could inquire as to where and when this momentous first date would occur. I had a feeling I'd get the full story from Cherry, assuming I lived through the night.

We were escorted to a table that was filled with men who looked as though they spent their days in a village far removed from New York City. From what I could see, not one of them stood taller than 5'4". This assumed that any were capable of standing at all. I counted no less than twenty bottles of wine on the table. All appeared empty. Shay was right. The median age must have been eighty-five. Vito and Guido were the only men there under thirty. Even Mario looked as though he'd come through Ellis Island sometime in the late 1900's.

Every one of them was staring at me with nothing but concern etched on wrinkled faces. As I sat down, a glass of wine was immediately placed in front of me, followed by a plate of antipasto and a huge basket of garlic bread. I'd had a cheeseburger and fries at the lawyer's bar no less than an hour before. I was starving. I dove right into the sun-dried tomatoes on top of portabella mushroom slices and fresh moz-zarella cheese. If this crisis with Johnny and his dad didn't get resolved soon, I'd have to start looking for a job outside of dance. No costume would ever fit again.

The men chattered about local politics and food and wine and whose wedding would be held next. They studiously avoided any mention of a Gerard or Toblaroni until they saw I'd downed my glass of wine. Once I figured that out, I chugged the Chianti in two swallows. They were lovely, they were entertaining, but I was a girl on a mission. It was now eleven-fifteen and I had the urgent feeling I had to get to Johnny before midnight.

Vito was first to speak on topic.

"Frankie. Tell the lady what you heard from Tony over on 12th Street."

Frankie wiped an errant strand of linguini off his chin and smiled at me.

"Word is that a hit's been ordered."

I blinked.

"Excuse me? Did you say 'hit'? As in man with silencer sneaking into empty buildings and pointing and *boom?* As in quick one-way cruises down the East River wearing cement galoshes?"

Every one of my new buddies nodded. I apparently had a good grasp of the local terminology and what it represented.

I quit trying to be funny. It appeared that Frankie's statement was serious. Deadly serious. I was having trouble finding my voice.

"Just who is this hit against?"

Frankie spoke up again.

"All Tony said was he heard Gerard is gonna get whacked. Thass it."

I downed another glass of wine trying to decide what I needed to do. Gerard could mean Kieran, it could mean Johnny or it could mean both.

"Does he know who the hit man is? I mean, is this some contract hired killer? Is it someone involved with the Toblaronis? Is it someone else?"

A huge debate ensued over the possible candidates for the honor. A man who must have been over a hundred years old was sure it was Nick "Candy Man" Toblaroni himself who would do his own killing. Frankie's favorite was Tracy. Two gentlemen who were devouring huge plates of Fettuccini Alfredo were laying bets that the executioner was "Joey Carrota from Jersey." I felt as though I'd stumbled into a *Godfather* movie and was sitting with bored extras.

Vito and Guido's first choice in the contest was the guy they were calling "that fairy chauffeur in the white limo." As much as that might be plausible, I think their ingrained homophobia was coloring their outlook on the situation.

It didn't matter anyway. I had to get out and find Johnny and Kieran and warn them of the danger. These might be nothing more than rumors designed to perk up the pulses of the boys at the café, but it might also be advance warning of a very deadly threat. I asked Mario to show me to a pay phone. I left the gentlemen opening four more bottles of wine and ordering a dozen cannolis.

I spent a frantic ten minutes trying to call Kieran's penthouse number, Johnny's apartment, the theatre (okay, that was a long shot) and the Centre Street information line. I had no luck on any front. No one answered. Anywhere.

I was sure Johnny had gone back to Centre Street. He probably couldn't find Kieran at his apartment and logically figured his father would be hiding out in his office. I didn't know which member of the Toblaroni family was gunning for Kieran. I just didn't want Johnny caught in the crossfire. Oh hell, if truth be told, I didn't want Kieran shot either. He might be acting like a cowardly scumbag but he was Johnny's father and didn't deserve a death sentence from the mob because his hormones had gone into overdrive once too often.

I returned to the table. A cannoli was thrust into my hand. I love cannolis. The pastries are not too sweet, they crunch and are filled with spicy creams. Just what I needed before charging down to Kieran's office to rescue all involved.

I thanked the gentlemen for the food and the information. Mario refused to let me pay for anything.

"Come back with your sweetheart, no? On the house. We love *Endless Time* here. The boys and I watch it daily."

I hugged him and promised him we'd do just that if we lived through the night and we'd give him two tickets to *Boundaries* if it ever opened. He seemed truly pleased.

I shrugged back into my jacket. The last words from the group at the table came from Frankie.

"Tell Gregory Noble we're pullin' for him. Tell 'im he's the best. Oh yeah, don' led him marry Letitia. I don' like Letitia."

"Hey! She's bettah for 'im than Carla. Carla was the one what unplugged his parachute. Least Letitia hasn't tried to murder him."

If I saved Johnny's life, I *had* to get him off that show. The schizophrenia exhibited by his fans continued to be a source of irritation mixed with amusement for me. Admittedly, I was grateful that this evening the gentlemen didn't seem to comprehend the difference between the character and the actor. Either way, it appeared they were on our side. I waved at Mario as he opened a new bottle of wine for the group. Then I dodged through tables of well-wishers patting my back and headed for the street.

The door to Mario's Trattoria closed behind me. I shivered. Icy bits of rain stung my face. My jeans and sweater were soaked. Between the rain and the darkness, visibility was reduced to about four feet.

I whistled, and jumped up and down to attract the attention of any taxi driver willing to stop in this storm. The patches on my clothing that had managed to remain dry were splashed by at least three cabs hell-bent on finding shelter. I fell off a curb trying to flag a fourth and decided to keep my eyes on the street while continuing to wave my arms wildly over my head.

"Centre Street."

I looked up. Neon-pink turban over Raggedy Ann hairdo.

Orange-and-black fringed tunic. Madam Euphoria. She smiled and repeated, "Centre Street."

It wasn't a question.

I nodded. By now I figured the woman probably knew my birth date, shoe size and the name of the dog I had when I was ten. I wasn't about to argue if fate was now in the hands of my palm-reading, séance-holding psychic friend from West Harlem.

We stayed silent for the ride uptown. When we reached Centre Street she was again able to maneuver the taxi into a space meant for a tricycle. Gotta love New York cabbies. Even part-timers who commune with dead tribal chiefs. They have a talent for parking no one else in the universe possesses.

I handed over the fare. She patted my hand, held it as she had during the ride yesterday, and smiled.

"Abby, girl. You just keep remembering this. Fight for what you believe to be right. Which you will. You have a good soul. I promise this will all turn out fine. We'll have a beer and some barbeque up at Leroy's Soul Café on 138th Street when it's over. Leroy makes the best ribs this side of Memphis."

She grew serious again.

"Abby, you listen to me, though. The choice is yours. Are you more afraid of dying in that little room? Or of your own future after his death?"

I stared at her.

"What does that mean? Is this coming from Chief Black Hawk? Can you tell me anything else?"

"Nope."

"You are one exasperating woman, you know that?"

"Yep."

I sighed. I started to leave. Then I motioned for her to roll down her window.

"I forgot to ask you the last time you brought me here. And at Yolanda's party. What's your real name? If you don't mind telling me? I can't see your cab license from here."

She nodded.

"Wouldn't help if you could. This is my brother Jimmy's cab. Jimmy Doe. My name's Jane."

"You've got to be kidding!"

"Nope. I don't check into hotels with it, though, 'cause nobody ever believes me. I go by my professional name. Hotels love having mediums stay at their places. Makes the clientele think the hotel's haunted and they can up the price."

She smiled, waved and drove off, high beams flashing goodbye in the storm.

I sighed. I then began an argument with the wind as I headed for the doors to the attorneys' offices. I wanted to stay upright. It wanted me flat on my face. I wondered if I was about to see a witch and a small dog go flying down the street. Actually, Kansas sounded good right now.

A blast from the horn of a delivery van brought me back to my surroundings in a rush. I'd managed to step off the curb and nearly get run over. Great. I could join Cookie in the next bed over. I was blocking the loading zone and the delivery trucks were getting restless. I quickly moved out of the way and ran towards the Centre Street offices.

It took me more than forty-five seconds to push open the doors leading into the building. Centre Street was quiet. I made my way down corridors of silence. I saw no one. Not even Chase Jaffert came out to advise me on what a fool I was for believing in and backing up Johnny Gerard.

The contrast between the silence inside and the storm raging outside was almost comic. If I'd been writing a melodramatic movie I couldn't have chosen a better location. I could hear the wind angrily trying to blow through the windows in the hall. Those sounds were replaced by voices growing louder the closer I got to Kieran's office. I could make out the different pitches of three men. Johnny, Kieran and a male voice I didn't recognize.

The lights went out. I felt for the wall nearest me for

support. Then I lost any sense of balance. I was on a roller coaster going entirely too fast. I clutched the moonstone around my neck and had a vision that was no mere flash, or even a small scene. Great-Granny Dumas had never had this in mind when she passed down those genes. I was deep into what was fast becoming an Academy Award–winning hallucination into the future.

TWENTY-SIX

AN ELDERLY MAN, whose white hair was peppered with streaks of red, sat nearly unmoving on one of the benches outside of Kieran Gerard's office. He raised his head and stared at me.

"Who are you?"

"I'm Abby, Mr. Gerard. Abby Fouchet. Johnny's girl. Don't you remember me?"

He placed his hand on the arm of the bench and forced himself to stand.

"You can't be Johnny's girl. Johnny's dead. Died years ago right here. I went on trial for killing his murderer."

I gasped.

"What are you telling me?"

He handed me a newspaper he'd been holding in his left hand. It was yellowed with age, but intact. I took it and glanced at the headlines.

Soap Actor Murdered! Nick Toblaroni Shot Dead!
Johnny Gerard's Dad Arrested!

The date was July 11th.

I sank down in the middle of the floor in front of the bench. Kieran Gerard looked at me with more than a trace of concern. I had to ask.

"What day is this?"

"July 11th. The anniversary, God help me."

"What year?"

"It's nearly thirty years since my boy was murdered. It's thirty years that I've been making this pilgrimage to this damn courthouse wishing I could make it all go away. Thirty years living with the guilt that I should have been able to stop it somehow."

He extended a shaky, veined hand to help me up. We both sat back down on the bench in silence.

"Mr. Gerard? What exactly happened that night?"

He sighed. It was the cry of a terminally wounded soul.

"I don't really even know. There'd been a huge blowup in the New York papers about Johnny having an affair with the wife of a mob boss. It wasn't true. I knew it wasn't true. It was all my fault."

He stopped for a second and pulled out a pack of cigarettes. I was about to remind him that New York is non-smoking in buildings but I figured if some security guard cared to tangle with the man that would be that guard's bad luck.

He lit the cigarette and politely blew the first puff away from me.

"I'd been to a fund-raiser that evening. I was running for District Attorney. Imagine that."

He smiled ruefully.

"I haven't practiced law since that night."

He continued. "Then I went off to my penthouse. Got back to the office after midnight. The whole damn place was too quiet. I clicked on the light in my office. And I knew. Even before I saw him, I knew. Johnny was lying on the floor. No color in him. I knew. He was gone. I fell to my knees. I landed on another body. Nicholas Toblaroni."

He glanced up, pulled once again on the cigarette and stared into my eyes.

"Both of them. Shot. There was a gun still lying by Nick. I just stared at it. I remember thinking it looked staged, and I thought that was ironic given Johnny's profession."

He smiled sadly.

"He was an actor, you know. Quite good, I've been told. Funny. I never saw his television show. And never saw him on stage. Yet when I saw him lying there I kept thinking, 'It's a scene. He's going to pop up in a second and ask if he can do it again because he doesn't like the way he's fallen.'"

Tears were streaming down my face. The elderly Kieran pulled a clean handkerchief from his vest pocket and handed it to me.

"You seem like a nice girl. Who did you say you are?"

"My name is Abby. Abby Fouchet."

He squinted at me.

"Wait. I know you, don't I? You were a disco dancer? I met you. Once at my penthouse. Once at my office. They'd trashed it, you know. I should have known then. It wasn't Johnny. I blamed him but it wasn't Johnny."

I took his hand and held it for a moment.

"Mr. Gerard? Do you mind telling me what happened after Johnny died? I know you were arrested? But then?"

"The only smart thing I did that night was not touch that gun. Nick's fingerprints were the only ones on it. It seemed apparent he'd shot Johnny, but no one could prove I'd shot Nicholas. A young lawyer on my staff, Chase Jaffert, quit the D.A.'s office. He became the lead defense for my case. Got me acquitted, bless him. Just enough reasonable doubt."

"I see. And you never went back to the law?"

"I couldn't. The District Attorney didn't want me after that. I'd been in jail throughout the election I was supposed to be running in and I didn't want to run again anyway. Tell you the truth, I could have cared less about any of it. Hell. My job was the reason Johnny was murdered. After all, he was only seeing Tracy because of me. It was my fault. All of it."

THE LIGHTS SUDDENLY came up again. The wind seemed to have stopped from what I could tell when I peered out the window. Zero movement from anything in the street. Not even a paper cup rattled by.

I touched the moonstone pendant Johnny had given me a few hours earlier. Reality. I was back. From wherever.

I didn't stop to dwell on the insanity of this strange and certainly overly long vision of a lifetime. I had seen a future where a broken Kieran Gerard still mourned the loss of his only son. A loss that had happened in that man's past. Which was my present. I wondered where the ghost of Christmas Future was when he was needed. I wanted to ask whether I'd just seen a time thirty years from now that was unchanging, or whether I had the ability to rewrite history tonight.

There was no sense to it and certainly no sense in what I was about to do. But the headline about Johnny Gerard's death and the regret in the voice of a devastated parent pushed me forward. Without even considering I might become a bonus to the hit list of the executioner, I flung open the doors and made my dramatic entrance into Kieran's office.

TWENTY-SEVEN

FATHER AND SON STOOD and stared at each other. Neither was speaking. Neither looked happy. But this was good. They were both alive. Already the vision had been changed. Another man leaned on the corner of the desk closest to the door. He could have been cast as a science professor at an Ivy League school in an episode of *Endless Time*. Gold-framed glasses hid watery gray eyes. He was taller than Johnny, but probably weighed at least forty pounds less. I had the fleeting thought that he could use a good meal at Mario's. Mouse-colored, wavy hair curled lightly over the collar of an expensive charcoal-colored three-piece suit. I immediately dismissed the colorless man, because the action between Johnny and Kieran began heating up just after I spotted him.

Johnny and his father began spitting words at one another.

"Why did you let me become the scapegoat for your little fling with Tracy? Didn't you know my career would be ruined?"

"I'm sorry about that, Johnny. I know you don't believe me, but I had no intention of blaming you for anything that happened with Tracy. Someone on my staff saw you with Tracy, that is, Terresota, last year when you took her to the fundraiser for the mayoral candidate. They didn't think anything of it until this leak to the papers that Tracy was involved with you."

"And did you bother to try and change his mind when Jayce Cracknell began asking questions?"

There was a moment of silence.

"No. It just seemed better to let them believe you were involved. I couldn't let it be known that I even knew the woman. You're an actor. Actors are notorious for wild living and bad company."

I couldn't stand this. In my best quiet imitation of Georgia-born Minette, I interrupted. "Pardon me, Mr. Gerard. I'm just a dancer and actress, so I guess I get the same label as Johnny as far as our so-called wild lives. But you, sir, are quite a coward, aren't you? Hiding behind your own son? What a thoroughly despicable man you are. What is it that makes you do this? Is Johnny less worthy than you because he makes people happy and you put people behind bars? Are you more entitled to lie and destroy lives because you're a big name in politics?"

I looked hard at him. For a second I glimpsed that older, sadder Kieran from my vision of the future. I shook my head lest I suddenly sympathize with that father figure instead of the real man standing in front of me. A real man with fear in his eyes.

I almost spat out my next words.

"My God. You're scared, aren't you? You've jumped into the deep end with some very dangerous characters and you're afraid of them once they realize you've—what? Been messing with the boss's wife? '*Schtupping?*' as you so delicately phrased that activity to me at your party? So, you're taking the sissy's way out by siccing them on Johnny. You are so low, sir, that cockroaches would have to jump to cross over you."

Johnny hid a grin at that one. Kieran stared at me.

"Quite a talker, aren't you, Miss Fouchet. And with such a soft Southern attitude to go along with such stinging words."

He paused, then said with the first note of sincerity I'd heard him use, "You'd have made a good attorney. Pity."

Kieran sat down in his office chair so heavily the springs groaned. "Enough. It's time to tell you what's really going on here. I should have let Johnny know months ago. I'm sorry. Now with Cracknell's story in the papers, this has gotten too confusing and too out of control. Johnny. Miss Fouchet. This is so much more than some supposed affair gone public. This encompasses the entire District Attorney's office. And yes, Abby, there is great danger here."

We stared at him. On some level neither Johnny nor I were surprised. We'd seen it coming. The subtext.

Kieran continued.

"My office has been conducting a sting operation. Rooting out the source of acts of corruption here at Centre Street. Bribery, jury tampering, case fixing and murder. Much of it surrounding a messy little scheme to defraud immigrants seeking green cards. To no one's surprise, the people about to be exposed for criminal wrongdoing don't care to have that happen. In point of fact, they *will* kill to protect their identities. Have done so on more than one occasion, I'm afraid. Mrs. Toblaroni has been working on this investigation as an aid to me. No one knew that, obviously. It's been dicey as to whom to trust. And the so-called affair worked fine when I was Deputy D.A. here. But when I decided to run for office, things changed. I couldn't afford to be seen with her. For any reason. That's when you entered the picture, Johnny. We desperately needed a go-between."

Johnny stared at him.

After a year dealing with the mixed emotions his errant father had aroused in him, he blew.

"You double-dealing copper-headed oily Irish snake! Sting operation? I'll say. Only I'm the one who got stung. How could you set me up like this? Didn't it occur to you I'd be the one they'd go after? Didn't you even think to at least tell me what this whole thing was about? The truth? What a concept, huh?

And, hey! Stupid me. I was worried about you. Innocence dies hard, doesn't it?"

Kieran held his hand out as though asking for Johnny's forgiveness. "I'm truly sorry. I never meant for any of this to happen. I never meant for you to be involved like this. I'd go back and change it if I could. But it's too late."

It could have been a television show. The dialogue suddenly seemed trite. I could only think of Yolanda Barrett getting the word from a producer that someone was to be canned, trying to find a way to explain the unexpected departure of that character, then hastily crafting a script hours before taping.

This particular daytime drama was set amongst the desks and chairs and file cabinets of the District Attorney's office. It seemed absurdly tidy. Not a stack of paper or a yellow legal pad disturbed the wooden desk. Khaki-colored walls in shades lighter than the taupe carpet apparently had been installed to calm any manic attorneys in the midst of deals. But the effect was antiseptic, even cold. In clear opposition were the emotions in the room that were chaotic, hot and out of control.

All the actors were now in place for the climax of a scene that had been written months ago. Unfortunately, no one had told either Johnny Gerard or Abby Fouchet the new roles they had been assigned to play. No one had relayed the information that they were the ones who were about to be cut from this madhouse of a show due to the whim of an anonymous producer.

Kieran's face now registered more than a trace of shame. He took a deep breath, but before he spoke again, another voice was heard. Mine.

Even to myself I sounded as though I was some distance away, in another place, another time. But my words were said with a calm that falsely hid the panic permeating my entire body.

Everyone involved in this little scene turned as I delivered my lines. "Oh, Sweet Saints Alive! Um. Hey! Johnny? Kieran? This is not good, y'all! He's got a gun! And I think he's fixin' to shoot."

The men stared at me as if I'd lost my mind. Then their eyes were drawn to the doorway where another actor had just made a dramatic and unexpected entrance. This character was holding a .38-caliber revolver in his right hand, while using his left to motion to me to join Johnny, Kieran and the anonymous third man. The blonde and gorgeous Mr. Chase Jaffert stood smiling at us all.

Kieran looked perplexed.

"Chase? What's with the hardware? We're not in imminent danger here."

Chase continued to smile.

"Oh, but you are. Abby, I'm very sorry you stumbled into all this. But in good conscience I can't let you walk out again. I'd truly have liked to have gotten to know you better. I always did think you were a pretty little thing. And talented. Sorry."

He seemed genuine about that last remark.

Kieran stayed silent, obviously stunned to discover one of the major players in the game he'd been trying to win was one of his own. I was almost calm. I knew the guy was a pompous arrogant ass. I figured it was an easy jump to assassin. I screamed at him.

"You slimy double-sided prancing peroxided python! What did you think? You'd shoot Johnny and Kieran, then date me when it was over as long as I wasn't aware of what you'd done?"

He shook his head with an air of sadness.

"But you wouldn't have been aware, Abby. Believe me. I have this entire scene planned. And I'm very creative. You weren't originally part of it, but now that you're here..." He shrugged. "Sorry."

Johnny reached out, grabbed me and pulled me close to

him. We held each other as he quietly asked, "Abby. Why the hell did you come down here? I thank you so very, very much for standing by me and trying to help, but I told you there was danger. God, I love you so much. Why didn't you stay at home?"

"I came to warn you that Nicholas Toblaroni had a hit on you! You and Kieran. Vito and Guido told me. But I thought the hit man would be Siegfried sent by Nick Toblaroni. Or at least Joey Carrota from Jersey!"

Johnny's eyebrows soared into his red hair.

"Joey who?"

"Never mind."

The third gentleman, who'd been silent up to now, suddenly spoke.

"Your story is a bit twisted, Ms. Fouchet. It's time to set you straight."

I stayed in the security of Johnny's arms enfolded around my waist, but turned to face this wraith of a man who could have been cast as Marley's ghost in *A Christmas Carol*. The man in the corner.

"Who the hell are you?"

He smiled.

"Nicholas Toblaroni. Or, if you prefer—Candy Nick."

TWENTY-EIGHT

CANDY NICK. LIVE AND IN COLOR. The color happened to be gray, but still, there he was. I stood with my mouth hanging open. I couldn't have closed it if I'd tried. Nicholas Toblaroni smiled at me.

"Miss Fouchet. I'd like to say I'm glad to make your acquaintance. Only not under these particular circumstances."

"But you? You? I thought you were the Godfather, the guy contracting out the hit man. Who was supposed to be Siggie or Joey, but now turns out to be Chase?"

I wasn't being entirely coherent, but the man understood me.

He shook his head.

"No. Kieran gave you the basics. There has indeed been a sting operation, thanks to Mr. Gerard. What he didn't get around to telling you is that I was the one who first came to him. I own several large factories in the tri-state area and employ a great number of people, many of whom are here from other countries. Three of my workers informed me that they were being forced to pay for green cards. If they didn't pay, they'd be deported. If they told anyone, they'd be shot."

He swallowed hard. "Their spokesman, a good man named Juan Hernandez, was discovered in an alley with a bullet in his chest. It looked like a mugging."

He closed his eyes, but not before I'd seen very real pain over the loss of an employee who obviously had been a friend.

I remembered the news stories about the Dominican men who'd been killed. I remembered Kieran's eyes blazing over the injustice and the waste, and Chase Jaffert flirting with the female reporter from "News at Noon."

Kieran took up the story.

"Added to that, Nick had been arrested two years ago on a very trumped-up charge. He was totally innocent. I read his file and smelled the proverbial rat. Shortly after his arrest, several members of the judicial system began falling over themselves offering to spring him. Nick told me the offers came with a steep price. He's not hurting financially, but the whole thing infuriated him."

Nick jumped in again.

"I knew Key from years ago. We were at Yale together as undergrads. I contacted him with what little I knew. Turned out a young paralegal on his staff, Carlos Gutierrez, had also been hassled with this green card extortion scheme."

Johnny coughed as his eyes opened wide.

"Cookie? Cookie was being squeezed?"

Kieran nodded.

"Cookie offered to go along to see if he could uncover a few more bits of this puzzle. But Nick and I needed a way to communicate information that would seem natural, even amusing in a snide way, to anyone at the D.A.'s office. We constructed this little piece of theatre, making it appear that Tracy and I were having affair."

Nick interrupted.

"Tracy was our go-between. I couldn't be seen with Kieran without arousing suspicion. Tracy was as angry as I about all of this. Not only because of my own arrest, but because of our workers. She's originally from the Dominican Republic herself, you know. Anyway, she didn't want these men losing their life-savings. Or their lives. Johnny then got put in the picture when Kieran became worried that people in his office were catching on that he and Tracy weren't really having an affair."

Nick smiled at me.

"Miss Fouchet. Abby. There has *never* been an affair between my wife and either of the Gerards. Believe me. Tracy has wanted to be able to tell you, but the time just hasn't been right. And it's been too dangerous for everyone involved."

"So you're not the villain? And Tracy's not the...?"

I stopped before the word "bitch" crossed my lips.

Nick Toblaroni smiled at Johnny and me as though there were no gun pointed at any of us.

"I think you've seen just how 'facts' in a news story can get skewed."

A huge sigh followed his words. "Enough! I can't believe the lot of you are gabbing like you're at a cocktail party. For supposedly intelligent people, you're all behaving quite idiotically."

Chase waved the gun at Nicholas and motioned to him to take his place among our soon-to-be demised trio standing next to Kieran's desk.

"This has been charming, perhaps even informative, but we don't have time for any more discussion, Mr. Toblaroni. I don't want to be here if some enterprising young security guard decides to check offices after hours."

Chase took another step inside the office as he directed his next remarks to me.

"Abby, your presence here does indeed make the story I intended to present a bit difficult, but not completely unimaginable. The original plan was for Nicholas to have shot Johnny on the assumption that the brilliant actor was sleeping with his wife. Kieran was to have shot Nicholas in retaliation."

Kieran made a movement as though to lunge at the young lawyer. Chase casually aimed the gun in his direction.

"Back off, Key. And don't even think about your gun in that second drawer down. I will be using it to dispose of Candy

Nick here, but I'd prefer placing *your* prints on it after I've shot you and your son."

I was amazed that Chase continued to ramble. Maybe the thought of murdering three people in cold blood was too much to handle. Fixing cases, bribery, jury manipulation and extortion are felonies, but they aren't violent crimes. Maybe he wasn't ready to graduate to the next level.

It was as if he read my mind. He looked at me and grimaced slightly.

"If you're wondering why I haven't started shooting just yet it's because I'm still deciding where to put you in this equation."

So much for graduation day. But at least he was talking. Chase Jaffert had an enormous ego and he obviously enjoyed hearing himself blather. The classic murderer's mistake. As long as words are spewing, bullets weren't.

"So, Chase, were you the one taking potshots at Johnny and me back in December? In Central Park?"

He laughed.

"Yes, but that wasn't at *you,* Abby. Just Johnny. After all, I didn't know you then, did I? I'd seen Tracy with Kieran one day, then with Johnny. The pieces didn't fit for some sort of father/son trade-off with the woman. I knew she was Nick's wife. I knew Kieran had set up a sting. But I thought I'd scare Johnny off from meeting Tracy again in case they started sharing information about the dealings at the office of the District Attorney. Then, of course, there was Carlos. Another spy and Johnny's roommate as well. Cookie. How sweet. A rice-and-bean eater who was far too inquisitive and who'd discovered far too much information."

Johnny turned white.

"You stinkin' bastard! You ran over and then poisoned a good man. A decent guy who has never harmed another living soul."

Chase yawned.

"He bothered me. And he made such an easy target. Manhattan dwellers are notoriously confident about crossing the street in full traffic. Cookie was no exception. As to the poison? As Key might recall, I pulled a muscle during one of our racquetball sessions and was prescribed Diazepam as a muscle relaxant. It didn't agree with me. But I kept the doses that were left and simply injected the drug into a few apples. Cookie is a food hound. I knew he couldn't resist snacking on everything on a tray. And he was talking. Remember your outburst at the disco taping, Johnny? All about Cookie's ramblings concerning men in black, judges and cases? He knew too much. Including who'd run him down. So. A simple gift of fruit mixed with a generous helping of something to help him sleep. For a long time."

Johnny started to lunge for Chase's throat but stopped when the gun cocked inches from his nose. Johnny bravely, if not exactly smartly, spat at the man.

"You're an idiot, Jaffert. Neither Cookie nor Tracy ever told me anything that they knew about the D.A.'s office. I didn't even know there was a sting. All you did was make me wonder why the hell Tracy's chauffeur might be shooting at me, curse the police for not being able to identify a hit-and-run driver, and fume at Kieran for not doing anything to stop all this deception. I was madder at him than anyone else. I didn't even know you existed."

Chase smiled and motioned for Johnny to step to Kieran's side.

"I *needed* you angry at Kieran. I needed you as the bait. And you snapped it up. By the way, the hospital called Kieran's office an hour ago. I took the message. Your fat little friend is again awake and talking. In Spanish, fortunately, but it looks like I'll need to silence him again when I'm finished here. I have a long night ahead."

Johnny looked elated for the two seconds before he realized he might die before Chase ever managed to get to Cookie.

Chase sighed.

"Now. Be quiet. All of you. I'm going to place you where you need to be for this delightfully droll piece of theatre. What is it they call them at that inane soap opera? Marks? Well, time to take your marks on my set and let the action begin."

He began to roam around the room like a caged panther sizing up his prey. Neat, no wasted steps, ultimately deadly.

"Abby. Please move next to Johnny. Thank you. Your interference throughout this night has wrecked my original scenario. But perhaps I can suggest that *you* were the reason Johnny was here in the first place. He knew you'd been trying to convince Kieran to own up to that alleged affair with Tracy. Yes, that's good. Johnny came to find you, Nicholas shot both of you; Kieran shot him. Then Kieran shot himself. Nice. I believe I can make that work."

He smiled once more and raised the gun. I prayed to all the saints in heaven plus Sisters d'Agostino and Errol Flynn while I was at it. I could use all the help I could get.

I'd be damned though if I'd just shut my eyes and wait for a bullet to pierce my gorgeous new cream-colored sweater. Johnny tensed beside me. And with wordless communication we moved together.

I executed a perfect hitch-kick and knocked the gun out of Chase's hand with my right foot, encased in a pointed-toed red cowboy boot. Simultaneously, Johnny karate-chopped Chase's neck in true Gregory Noble fashion, then pulled the man's left arm up and behind him. I heard a snap. It sounded the same way my ankle had when I'd popped those ligaments that day of rehearsal for *Superstar*. I winced. Screams, howls of pain and curses no well-brought-up daughter of Minette Dumas Fouchet should ever hear, issued from the mouth of Mr. Jaffert.

We'd managed to dent, but not destroy. Chase charged at Johnny with his good hand swinging. He connected with Johnny's chin. Johnny reeled and crashed against Kieran's desk, hitting a rib. Then he let out a few choice words of his own.

Chase turned to me and did what no gentleman should be allowed to do. He socked me. Right in the jaw. I sank.

I'd managed to send the gun flying to the other side of the office during my little hitch-kick routine. Chase now ran to retrieve it. A silent, furious Kieran Gerard calmly stuck his leg out and Chase tumbled to the floor.

Even that didn't stop the intrepid blonde attorney. Like a slasher in a horror flick, he got to his feet, aimed a karate-style kick right into Kieran's stomach and then headed once again for his gun.

As he leaned over to pick it up, Nick Toblaroni lifted his own foot and kicked Chase in the back. Again, dented, but not demolished. Chase quickly scooped up the weapon with his right hand and with the athletic ability he'd boasted about, immediately whirled around to wave the gun at Johnny again. All movement stopped.

Chase held the gun in front of him and backed up near the door of the office.

I saw movement. My eyes involuntarily flickered to what was behind Chase in the doorway. Two men.

Chase smiled.

"Good try, but I'm not falling for it, Abby. Old, tired, used, 'look behind the bad guy' routine. I expected better. And you know all that you and your misguided heroes have done is delay the inevitable. Sorry, Johnny. You're first. But I did want to tell you I enjoyed watching you on the show the few times I tuned in."

I was too far to kick, turn or leap into the air. Johnny was hanging on to Kieran's desk, clutching his side, still dazed from the punch Chase had delivered and the subsequent cracked ribs.

Chase took aim. At the same time the shadow of a cylindrical object rose up behind him. The object hit him squarely in the back of the head. Chase finally went down and stayed down.

I politely stepped over his unconscious body to reach Johnny's side.

"Pardon me. But did you earlier label your father as a double-dealing copper-headed oily Irish snake?"

He grinned broadly.

"Seems to me I heard that phrase from a little Texas Terror who was throwing lamps one evening in Philadelphia. Very descriptive when one aims it at a Gerard. Gets our undivided attention."

I nodded, then turned to the two men who were now standing guard above the prone figure of the murderous attorney. One of them leaned over and retrieved the blunt instrument he'd used to bop Chase on the head. Then he smiled at me.

"Hey, Abby! Greg! How ya doin'?"

Johnny and I looked at each other.

In unison we proclaimed, "How *you* doin'?"

Wearing identical huge grins and identical blue baseball caps, Vito and Guido Mariccino waved and proudly held up their weapon of choice. A frozen salami whose packaging cover claimed it was from Mario's Trattoria.

The Mariccino twins, Johnny and I engaged in an enthusiastic group hug. Johnny was the first to speak.

"Gentlemen. You have just earned lifetime backstage passes to *Endless Time*. Hey, I'll even introduce you to Carla and Letitia."

Just when it looked as if all the players in this scene had been accounted for, two more actors appeared. Tracy Toblaroni raced inside the office and hurled herself on her husband's neck the way my old Labrador retriever used to when I got home after school. And in the doorway stood Siegfried. His immaculate, handsome bulk effectively blocked the door as a means of exit for anyone in the room.

Tracy quit depositing tiny lipstick-filled kisses on Nick's

face and turned around to face Johnny and me. She held out her hand tentatively, as if afraid it might be slapped down.

"Abby?"

I was still wary of Mrs. Toblaroni. "Yes?"

"I just want to tell you how sorry we've been to have put you through this whole charade. Both of you. You have no idea how grateful we are."

She fluttered her eyelashes at Johnny who naturally melted before the poignant gaze. He heaved a huge sigh.

"So, is this whole sting operation whatchamacallit over with? Can I finally tell the world I'm not sleeping with a married woman and that the only woman I love is little Miss Dancer here?"

I grinned. I liked the sound of that.

Kieran tapped Johnny lightly on the back of his shoulder.

"I think we've got all we need now to wrap this whole nasty affair up for good. I'm sure Mr. Jaffert will be more than happy to provide this office with those few names we lacked in exchange for lessening the charges against him just a bit. He's on the low rung of the ladder of corruption and I'd like him to provide the evidence on those above."

Johnny didn't look happy about Chase getting any kind of deal out of this. I didn't feel great about it myself, but it wasn't really our choice to make. Kieran saw we weren't thrilled and hurriedly continued with this little speech.

"I will also call a press conference and let the world know that Johnny was in no way involved in an affair with Mrs. Toblaroni and that there was no money-laundering scheme using the Notebooms and their theatres. I will make it clear no one in this office has anything to do with organized crime."

He winked.

"Including Nicholas Toblaroni."

I was again confused.

"I do understand that you weren't involved in this whole

mess with the D.A.'s office and the immigration stuff. But—no offense, Mr. Toblaroni—aren't you the heir apparent to a big crime family?"

For only the second time that night, Nick spoke. First he smiled at me and I nearly fell out of love with Johnny. Nondescript and skinny he might be, but Candy Nick had the warmest, most charming smile I'd ever seen. No wonder Tracy had risked her reputation and possibly her life to help her husband.

"My great-grandfather was, in a word, a gangster. He oversaw bootleg operations and gambling and all the other ventures that went with that title back in the 1920's and '30's. My grandfather did not care to follow in those footsteps. He moved to South Dakota…only came back to New York a few years ago. My father and mother raised me in the Northwest. My mother and I came back to New York and moved in with Grandpa after my dad died. But I inherited the Toblaroni name and with it the notoriety. I'm honestly nothing more than a very honest businessman."

He winked.

"An honest, *wealthy* businessman."

Kieran nodded.

"The fact that Nick is who he is made all the difference. The gentlemen we were after had no idea that Nick is legit. They fell right into the trap."

I was fascinated.

"With all the talk about mobsters, I don't think I ever heard anyone mention just what wealthy business you're in, Mr. Toblaroni."

He smiled broadly.

"I have factories all over the tri-state area. We make pastries. Muffins, éclairs, pies, cookies, the works. You may have heard of us. In honor of my wife they're called 'Tracy's Tarts.' Her brother suggested the idea."

"Brother?"

Tracy blushed.

"That's the one other thing we never told anybody. Except Kieran. Cookie Gutierrez is my brother."

Johnny almost bit through his lip on that remark. I didn't know if it was from thinking about "Tracy's Tarts" or the fact that nearly everyone in this room had ended up not being who they appeared to be. Make that *out* of this room as well, since Cookie was still in the hospital. Before I had a chance to ask Tracy if she'd heard anything more about his recovery, Siegfried appeared in the doorway.

He smiled, waved and opened his mouth to say in pure Brooklynese, "Hey! How ya' doin'?"

Johnny was shaking with suppressed laughter. So was I.

"We're doin' okay? You?"

Siggie shrugged cheerfully.

"Yeah, okay."

The handsome chauffeur moved aside to let us pass into the hallway. I turned back to him.

"Siegfried? Why have you been following me? And Johnny?"

He was a man of few words.

"Mister T ast me ta make sure youse both was safe."

Johnny and I both nodded. There was nothing else to say.

I looked at Johnny.

"My mouth is completely dry. I need a soda. Maybe several. Got any change? Lots of change. I want a pound of candy bars, too. So. Is this really over, Johnny? Think we can get back to a boring life without people following or shooting at us?"

"I'll risk it if you will."

He pulled out a handful of coins as we left the office and walked towards the vending machines.

"How about a bribe, Abby? Since we're in the halls of justice discussing extortion. One soda for one kiss?"

I didn't have a chance to answer. He leaned down to kiss me, backing me up against the soda machine. What should have been a passionate kiss ended up in pain as both of us winced from the bruising blows Chase had delivered moments before. We drew apart and just smiled at each other. We were alive. Kissing and other pleasurable activities would have to wait.

A cell phone rang from somewhere down the hall. It appeared to be Vito's.

"Yo! Abby!"

"Yeah?"

"It's Cherry. Says to call this number, pronto."

I raised an eyebrow at Johnny, then quickly jotted down the number Vito provided. Johnny gave me a quick kiss.

"Abby. I'll leave you some privacy for your phone call. I'm going to go talk to Vito and Guido about putting together some kind of celebration. For everyone who's been through hell tonight. And see if Kieran has aspirin in his desk. My ribs are killing me."

"Hey, Johnny? Add Madam Euphoria to the invitation list. She needs to be there. Although she'll probably know already. Oh yeah, I'd suggest Mario's as the place. Great cannolis. And you'll love his customers. All serious *Endless Time* fans."

He kissed me again, nodded and trotted off to chat with the Mariccino brothers.

Five minutes later, I was back standing by the vending machine. I couldn't move. Vito and Guido waved goodbye in my direction and I managed to wave a limp arm in the air. Johnny hurried over.

"What's the matter? You look stunned. What's up? Are you okay?"

I stared at him.

"I have just been on the phone speaking with George. Remember George, the stage manager for your soap? *Endless Time?* Yep. The one and only. Okay. They've been holding auditions now for a month or so, but hadn't found the right actress, so Yolanda Barrett brought my name up. It's a go."

"What are you talking about?"

I grinned.

"*Endless Time* has just offered me a recurring role. It won't interfere with *Boundaries* or any other nighttime gig. Pay is great."

He closed his eyes and exhaled.

"I'm afraid to ask. Just what is this part?"

I avoided his eyes.

"I'm playing a new character. Carla's long-lost illegitimate daughter. Vanessa."

The two of us slid down the wall to the floor. After we wiped the tears from our eyes and quit coughing, Johnny toasted my soda can with his.

"Aren't you a bit close to Carla's age for even a soap?"

"Uh, Yolanda did mention something about cloning."

Johnny was in the middle of swigging his soda. Mistake. I handed him a tissue. When he was almost composed, he inclined his head to me.

"Well, then. Welcome to the show, Vanessa. You realize this makes you my long-lost illegitimate stepdaughter, since Carla is my wife. At least until Letitia bumps her out of the picture or she lands in jail for attempted murder. I can just imagine the plotlines Yolanda is dreaming up in her evil brain. By the way, how are they introducing Vanessa?"

I fixed my eyes on the wrapper of the chocolate bar I'd gotten from the vending machine moments earlier, silently and carefully studying the nutritional content.

Johnny nudged me.

"Yes?"

"From what George told me, she's a Jane Doe who was discovered in a wheelchair on the beach in the same spot

where a certain parachute landed. Apparently, she was hot-air
ballooning and the balloon kind of sank to the earth. Now
Vanessa's in the hospital in the bed next to Gregory Noble.
She's in a coma."

REQUEST YOUR FREE BOOKS!

2 FREE NOVELS
PLUS 2 FREE GIFTS!

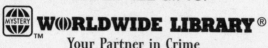

W**O**RLDWIDE LIBRARY ®
Your Partner in Crime

WWL10